# THE ELEVENTH GRAVE

## A DETECTIVE MARK TURPIN CRIME THRILLER

## RACHEL AMPHLETT

SAXON
PUBLISHING

# CHAPTER ONE

It was a perfect Sunday morning.

A fine mist clung to the banks of the River Thames, hugging the reeds and long grass that swallowed the footpath winding its way out of Sutton Courtenay and on towards Abingdon. It curled into the air as the sun's warmth gradually seeped into the day and created a hazy softness to the landscape that blurred the edges of the horizon.

In the distance, the village church bells rang out across Culham, casting a melody that carried over the undulating landscape. Somewhere, beyond the riverbank, a tractor bumbled back and forth in a field, its engine thrumming amidst the rattle of a seed drill.

A group of four ducks paddled downstream, followed at a distance by a pair of swans that dipped graceful necks into the water, their pace languid while they kept a watchful eye on their surroundings.

Then there was a split-second flash of turquoise and orange to the left-hand side of the river before a soft *plop* preceded a series of ripples as a kingfisher darted beneath the surface. It reappeared moments later, exploding from the water with a small fish in its beak before disappearing into a small hole burrowed into the muddy bank.

A magpie chuckled its approval from the upper boughs of a blossoming tree, and then launched itself across the river, the emerging sunshine catching the purple-blue hue of its wings.

Helen Maddison rested her paddle on her lap and tilted her chin upwards with a faint smile on her lips, letting the sunlight warm her face while the kayak coasted under the propulsion of her last stroke.

Jason, her husband of eight years, kept a steady pace in front of her. The dip and splash of his paddle broke the water at even intervals, and she could hear him humming under his breath.

And then he laughed.

'If you keep doing that, you're going to be moaning you can't keep up with me again.'

She opened her eyes to see him looking over his shoulder at her, and grinned. 'I can't help it. It's the first time this year it's been warm enough to do this without having to wear loads of layers.'

'You'll be complaining about having to top up your sunscreen next.'

'Very funny. The Easter weekend is meant to be rubbish, even if it is late this year.'

He paused and rolled the paddle shaft from his wrist to his elbows before lobbing it into the air and catching it. A contented sigh escaped his lips as he caught it. 'This is perfect. I was worried there'd be more people out this morning.'

'Me too.' She dug her paddle into the water and brought her kayak alongside his as the river widened. 'There was only one other car in the car park though, and it looked like it had fishing stuff in it.'

'Depends what else is on this morning, I suppose.'

'There's a craft market in Abingdon today, isn't there?'

He wrinkled his nose. 'That means the pub'll be busy. I knew I should've booked a table for lunch.'

'We can always sit outside if it's too crowded inside.' She squinted against the light. 'It's meant to be like this all day.'

She turned at the sound of a dog bark to see a couple with a Golden Retriever walking along the footpath towards them, the animal bounding left and right as it sought out sounds and smells. A squirrel flashed up a towering oak tree, the mammal's outline silhouetted amongst the fledgling leaves, and the dog's eyes followed it with interest as it passed underneath.

'Morning,' Helen called.

The man held up a hand in reply, his other around his partner's waist while she smiled at the passing kayakers. The dog paused to watch them with curiosity before the man called to him and it went tearing off after the couple.

'I thought he was going to jump in then,' said Jason.

'I was wondering that.' Helen grinned. 'I don't think they would've thanked us – did you see the mud up his paws already?'

After a few more paddle strokes they were passing gaps in the hedgerows where thin beech and alder saplings had been planted the previous spring. Beyond these, Helen could see freshly tilled arable soil with its grey texture common to the South Oxfordshire landscape, while the sound of gulls now accompanied the tractor in the distance.

Rooks circled overhead, keeping a wary eye on the world below, their caws accompanying lazy spirals as they drifted up and down on the air.

'There's that fisherman.'

Jason's voice turned her attention back to the river ahead, and she squinted. 'Where?'

'He's crouched next to the water, just before the bridge – see him? Must've lost a line or something. You'd better go in front of me and keep close to this bank, otherwise he might moan that we're scaring the fish away.'

'Right-o.' She watched as the man rose to his feet and eyed their approach before turning his back.

As they drew alongside, she noticed he wore a thick navy sweatshirt over muddied jeans. He kept his back turned, his head lowered, and she realised he was looking at his phone.

'Morning,' she said.

He glanced up, his features rugged as if he spent a lot of his time outside, then looked away without replying and moved towards the bridge.

Jason caught her bemused eye-roll and grinned before they passed beneath the bridge. 'Friendly.'

'Shhh,' she said, smiling, her voice echoing off the wood and metal structure. She shivered as the shadows claimed her, then breathed a sigh of relief when they emerged the other side, sunlight bathing her shoulders once more. 'So... what do you think? Paddle up to the weir at Abingdon, then turn back and find a spot for lunch?'

'Yeah, I reckon that's our best bet. What time do we have to pick up the kids from your mum's?'

'Seven thirty. She said she'll feed them before we get there. I suppose if we—'

A strangled cry pierced the air, followed by a splash from behind.

Heart racing, Helen twisted in the cockpit of the kayak to see small waves breaking the surface of the water below the bridge.

Jason stabbed his paddle in the river, spinning around to face the other way. 'What the…?'

Then a hand broke the surface, fingers clawing desperately before a man's head appeared.

'It's that fisherman,' Helen said. She started paddling back towards him. 'He'll never be able to swim to the bank in this current.'

The man's eyes widened in panic as the cold water started to drag him down, his mouth opening in an "o" of shock while his arms thrashed.

Then he was under the water again, leaving behind concentric ripples that spread out until they lapped at the roots of bullrushes and long grass on either side of the waterway.

Helen gritted her teeth, dug the paddle blade in faster, and slewed the kayak around as she drew level with the man's last position.

Tightening the sash of her life vest, she leaned out with the paddle as the drowning man resurfaced. 'Grab this!'

He gasped, swallowed a mouthful of water, and then spat it

out, eyes widening in realisation. He thrashed his arms in an attempt to swim closer, burdened by his clothing and weakening by the second in the frigid river.

She swore under her breath as her kayak began to drift away from him in the current, unwilling to take her gaze away and lose sight of him.

Then there was a soft *thud* on the opposite side of her kayak, and she glanced over her shoulder to see that Jason was using his paddle to push her gently towards the man, his jaw set in concentration.

Turning back, she leaned out farther.

'Come on,' she urged. 'Just grab hold of the paddle and we'll tow you back to the bank.'

The man tried again, but his hand slipped down the aluminium shaft. He cried out, spluttered as he took in more water, and then started to slide beneath the river's surface once more.

'No…' Helen ignored the hard edge of the kayak's cockpit sticking into her hip and stretched the paddle out as far as she could. 'Try again. You can do it.'

The man attempted a feeble breast stroke, then cried out in frustration as his sweatshirt billowed around his shoulders, thwarting his efforts.

Helen glanced at her clothing, then the water. 'I'm going in. It'll be easier for me to swim ashore with him.'

'No – the water's too cold and he could pull you under with him,' said Jason. He nudged the kayaks closer, and the man snatched at air before his fingers found Helen's outstretched paddle.

This time, he didn't let go.

'Got him,' she gasped and started dragging him towards her kayak, her shoulders and arm muscles protesting against his weight.

'Hold onto the bow,' she called out, keeping her voice calm. 'Hang on, and we'll paddle back to the bank with you.'

The man gave a weak nod, his sodden hair clinging to his forehead trailing traces of weed that lent a green sheen to his pale skin.

When she got him alongside, he reached out with one hand to touch the pointed prow of the kayak, then with one final spurt of energy he wrapped his arms around the bow.

She pulled in the paddle and started to turn her kayak.

'Hang on, mate,' said Jason, waiting while she twisted in her seat and grabbed onto the sides of his kayak. 'Helen will keep an eye on you while I paddle us to the bank. It's not far, but it's deep here. We've got dry clothes for you, and we'll get onto emergency services.'

Helen could hear the man's breath coming in shallow gasps, a wracking cough seizing him as his lungs ejected the water he'd inhaled. He groaned, a deep agonising sound that sent a shiver across her shoulders despite the warm light that now bathed the stretch of water as the sun reached its zenith.

Turning away from him for a moment, she saw that Jason had almost managed to get them to the bank.

Just another two metres and they could get the man out of his wet clothes and phone for an ambulance…

The hull of her kayak bumped against mud and a soft judder passed through the vessel as they reached land.

'Here, hold them steady while I help him out.' Jason didn't wait for an answer, and tossed both of their paddles onto the bank before hurrying to where the man was trying to crawl out of the water.

He placed his hands under the man's armpits and staggered backwards, dragging him away from the swirling depths and through the long grass and rushes to the path.

Helen watched while Jason lay him on his side, crouching beside him while keeping his voice calm, reassuring him before he started pulling the man's sodden clothing off. Rubbing at the man's limbs to get the circulation going, he peered over his shoulder at her. 'There are dry clothes in my bag. I reckon they'll fit him.'

Rolling over, she stumbled over to the kayaks and dragged them to the far side of the path. She popped open the front hatch on Jason's and pulled out his dry bag. Rummaging through the contents, her fingers found the thick fleece he had packed in case the weather turned foul and a pair of shorts left over from the summer that had somehow never made it to the washing machine.

She tossed them over to him, then turned her attention to her own kayak and pulled her mobile phone from her dry bag.

Once she was certain the emergency responders had the correct GPS location for them, she ended the call and pulled off her own fleece.

'Here, we'll use this over your legs,' she said to the man. She wrapped the top across his legs, tucking it in. 'I'm Helen, by the way. And this is my husband, Jason.'

The man opened his mouth to speak, his teeth chattering. 'B-B-Barry.'

'Nice to meet you,' Jason said. 'Shame about the circumstances though.'

That raised a small smile. 'No kidding.'

'Where's all your fishing gear?' said Helen. 'Do you want us to fetch it for you?'

The smile changed to confusion. 'What?'

'I thought I saw you fishing. Before we went under the bridge.'

Barry shook his head. 'No. No fishing gear.'

'Oh. Okay.' She noticed his hands were still icy cold and started massaging the skin while Jason did the same to the man's feet and ankles. 'Is there anyone we can call for you? To let them know what's happened?'

'No. Don't worry.' His body trembled, and he emitted a loud sigh. 'Thank you.'

'Don't go to sleep,' Jason commanded, his voice a notch louder. 'The ambulance will be here soon.'

'With lots of warm blankets,' added Helen. She peered over her shoulder at voices to see the dog walkers returning, their faces full of concern.

'We saw a commotion up here,' said the woman when they drew closer. 'Is everything all right?'

'It is now. Thank you.'

'Can we call an ambulance for you?'

'Already done, but if you've got some spare clothing we could use to keep him warm, that'd be good.'

The couple called their dog to heel, clipped on his lead and promptly shrugged off coats and sweatshirts, passing them over to Jason, who draped them over the man.

'I'll wait on the bridge to spot the ambulance,' said the woman. 'They'll probably use the track leading to the hydro place to get here.'

'Thanks.'

Helen could hear the sirens in the distance now, and sent a silent prayer of thanks for an ambulance being in the vicinity.

Five minutes later, two paramedics were hurrying across the bridge towards them, and then she and Jason were gently pushed aside while Barry became their central focus.

She watched as they kept up a steady stream of conversation with Barry, constantly reassuring him while checking his vital signs and manoeuvring him onto the stretcher. Blankets were wrapped around him, swaddling him into warmth, and then they were ready.

'Let me have your details,' said the younger paramedic, taking out his phone. 'Just in case the police want to talk to you.'

'The police?' Helen's heart lurched. 'Why would the police want to talk to us?'

He shrugged. 'It's only a formality, in case there's an enquiry about how he fell off the bridge.'

'Insurance companies,' Jason said, the scorn in his voice tangible. 'Always the case, right?'

The paramedic gave a polite smile. 'Phone numbers will be enough.'

That done, the emergency responders began packing away their kit and preparing to leave with their patient, praising the Maddisons for their quick thinking.

Helen blushed under the scrutiny of the dog walkers as Barry reached out to shake her hand, his grip weak.

'Thank you,' he said.

'Good job these two knew what to do to get you out of the water.' The older paramedic smiled and patted him on the shoulder before taking his share of the stretcher weight. 'You're a lucky one, mate.'

Barry coughed, then shuddered, his voice a mere rasp. 'This time.'

# CHAPTER TWO

*Two days later*

There was a palpable frost to the air in the incident room by eleven o'clock that morning.

Despite the bright early April sunshine splintering the window blinds and casting zigzags across the threadbare carpet, the air conditioning had broken over the weekend. The vents in the ceiling were now discharging an icy breath across the necks of a dozen or so officers who huddled at their desks, some still wearing their outer garments over their uniforms or shirts.

Two whiteboards took up the far right-hand wall, one bare – for now – and the other criss-crossed with different-coloured text that was being erased with an old tea towel by a junior constable. A steady squeak accompanied her work while the smell of an alcohol-based solution wafted across the frigid air, mixing with the tangible odour of stale coffee beans.

A steady hum of conversation filled the room, desk phones shrilled across the open plan space, and the whirr and spit of two large printers against the far wall carried over to where a group of detectives of varying rank congregated around a man in his mid-thirties, their faces a mixture of concern and bemusement.

Detective Sergeant Mark Turpin sat with his right hand cradling a steaming mug of coffee while his left held an ice pack to a bruised eye socket that was an angry shade of red.

He cursed under his breath, the welt obscuring his vision on one side.

'I told you I thought she might take a swing at you.' Detective Constable January West looked at him over her computer screen, her green eyes narrowing. 'And you said—'

'—that she wouldn't be so stupid. I know.'

She sighed, adjusted the ponytail holding her light brown hair back from her face and huffed her fringe from her forehead. 'Well maybe you'll listen to me next time, Sarge. Might save me doing all this paperwork for a start.'

Mark aimed a mock snarl her way, then looked at DC Caroline Roberts. 'Any news from the court?'

'The woman has been taken into custody, and her husband's been returned to HMP Bullingdon.' The DC cocked an eyebrow. 'And that looks painful, Sarge. Maybe we need to get you some martial arts training or something.'

'Very funny.'

'I'm serious,' she said. 'At least you'd learn how to duck.'

'Get out.'

She grinned and held up a small white plastic bubble pack. 'I found some painkillers in Alex's desk. Want them?'

'Please.' He popped two into his mouth and swigged the coffee as Alex McClellan wandered over. The younger DC's eyes were wide.

'Woah. I heard the missus was arrested,' he said. 'What did you do?'

'Nothing,' Mark protested, pushing the empty coffee mug away. 'She walked past with her husband's lawyer, calm as anything. Next thing I knew, she'd lashed out. I didn't have time to react.'

'Did she say anything?'

'It's not repeatable.'

'Martial arts,' said Caroline, wagging her forefinger at him.

'Like I have time. Besides, it's not as if I could—'

'I need you two to head over to the morgue in Oxford.'

Mark turned at the sound of the voice to see Detective Inspector Ewan Kennedy advancing towards them, a flimsy manila file in his hand and his face one of determination. 'What's up, guv?'

'I just got off the phone with Gillian Appleworth.'

West frowned. 'We're not expecting any post mortem results this week, are we?'

The DI sidled past Alex and leaned against the younger detective's desk before opening the file. 'We aren't, but she's done one this morning that's causing her some consternation, and she's asked us to make some enquiries. I've assigned it a new reference number in HOLMES2 and I want you two to lead the investigation.'

Mark raised his eyebrows, then winced as a fresh jolt of pain tore across his face. Blinking to offset the effect, he tried to refocus. 'What're the circumstances?'

'A bloke by the name of Barry Windlesham fell into the Thames at Culham on Sunday morning. He was pulled out by a couple of kayakers and ambulance'd to the John Radcliffe. Everyone was saying how lucky he was given the water temperature's still bloody cold, but he died a few hours later.'

'What from?' said West, pulling her notebook closer and turning to a fresh page.

'Delayed drowning,' said Kennedy. 'Gillian says she found traces of water-induced inflammation to his lungs when she opened him up this morning. According to the hospital records, he developed breathing difficulties at around two in the morning yesterday, and deteriorated pretty quickly after that.'

Mark put the makeshift icepack beside his keyboard and pocketed the remaining painkillers. 'How did he fall in?'

'That's unknown. The kayakers told the ambulance crew that they only heard him cry out when he hit the water before they turned around and rescued him.'

'What did he tell the hospital staff?'

Kennedy's mouth downturned. 'Nothing at all.'

'What do you mean?'

'According to them, he refused to talk about the incident at all, other than to say he fell off the bridge.'

West frowned. 'I know the bridge – Scott and I have often walked along that stretch of the river with the boys. It's got guardrails so it'd take some doing to fall in.'

The DI leaned forward and tapped the file against her arm. 'So why are you both still sitting there?'

'On our way.' Mark took the file and pushed back his chair, shoved his mobile phone into his pocket and waited while West swung her bag over her shoulder. 'You okay to drive? I'll make some phone calls and see if there are some contact details for the kayakers on the way.'

He saw her cast a sideways glance at Alex before she swept a set of keys from the younger detective's desk.

'No problem,' she said.

'Give me a call once you've spoken with her and the kayakers,' said Kennedy. 'We'll make a decision then whether to open a new case for this one, or whether it can be passed over to the coroner's office for a ruling.'

'Understood, guv.' Mark hurried after West, then held open the incident room door for her.

'First a punch-up, then the morgue,' she said as they headed for the stairs. 'You're on a roll today, Sarge.'

# CHAPTER THREE

A cool breeze feathered against the bruise on Mark's eye socket when he pushed open the exit door at the rear of the police station.

The wind carried with it the honk and rumble of traffic on the other side of the building and that from the A34 to the west of the town, a distinct white noise that accompanied the incessant drilling from a sewage works crew on the industrial estate across the street.

There was blossom on the brambles that tangled through the wire mesh fence on the right-hand side of the car park, and the pink and white petals were a welcome splash of colour after weeks of grey skies and drizzling rain.

He had noticed the subtle changes along the tow path where he and his girlfriend, Lucy O'Brien, moored their narrowboat as well. There was less frost in the mornings, making for a pleasant dog walk to start the working day, and catkins had made way for the first tentative buds on oak trees and alder. Wild garlic filled the tow path with a heady scent accompanied by the sweeter aroma from an early sprinkling of bluebells, while in the town centre there were refreshed hanging baskets outside many of the pubs and boutique shops in anticipation of warmer weather.

Clouds scuttled here and there across an otherwise azure sky, the sun warming his back as he followed West past the parking bays assigned to senior officers and visiting VIPs.

Mark flicked through the scant contents of the manila file while he walked. 'Looks like Kennedy did us a favour – he's done a quick online search about Barry Windlesham at least.'

'Oh? What do the notes say?'

'Apparently he was the director of a medium-sized construction company. His driving licence has an address on it out near Chalgrove.' Mark turned the single page in the folder and sighed before closing it. 'And that's it.'

'Okay, well I'm sure Alex and Caroline will make a start on doing a wider social media search while we're talking to Gillian.'

As they rounded the corner of the red bricked building, a trail of blue smoke emanated from a recess beside a fire exit moments before the telltale whiff of nicotine-laden air filled Mark's nostrils and tickled his throat. A pair of administrative assistants paused in their conversation with three men he recognised from Force Control, the small group eyeing him warily as he passed.

West jangled the keys in her hand, then turned and led the way towards a pool car parked off to the far left of the staff parking area.

It was an unassuming silver hatchback, only five years old but with a higher than average mileage and a spectacular dent in the front wing that was showing signs of rust around the creased edges.

Its one saving grace was a 1.8 litre engine that belied the car's worn exterior, offered exceptional handling, and often caused consternation within the Thames Valley accounting team once they caught sight of the petrol receipts.

It was the last of its kind from a time when the perception of speed overrode any budgetary common sense, such that each week the tight-knit group of Abingdon detectives fought for the prize of who would get the keys, leaving the others to drive newer vehicles with smaller engines.

Mark glanced across and saw West wearing a smug smile as she started the car. He fastened his seatbelt then frowned and peered across the surrounding bays. 'Hang on. I thought we were assigned the poky little car over there this week.'

'We were, until this morning.'

'Who did you bribe to get this then?'

'I didn't bribe anyone. Alex lost a bet.'

'A bet? How come I didn't hear about an office sweepstake? What was that about?'

She didn't answer, and instead concentrated on the barrier across the exit while it lifted before she accelerated into the traffic approaching the roundabout on Marcham Road.

'Jan?'

'It was just a bit of fun, all right, Sarge? I didn't expect to win or anything.'

'So, what was the bet?'

West waited until they were on the A34 heading north to Oxford, then sighed and risked a sideways glance his way. 'I bet him that given half a chance, that bloke's wife would try to have a go at you outside court.'

His jaw dropped. 'Seriously?'

'We didn't think she'd actually do it, Sarge.' She had the decency to blush. 'It's just that she's got a bit of a reputation as a hothead, and you kept going on about how you thought she would dob in her husband for all the other stolen goods we think he's selling via their mobile phone shop. They've been married since they were eighteen. She's too loyal to him.'

Mark brushed his fingertips against his face and winced. 'You could've warned me.'

'I tried, remember? I said this morning that I reckoned we wouldn't see the back of that pair once he was sentenced.' She accelerated past a German-registered truck laden with two twenty-foot shipping containers, unable to conceal her smile as the car's engine purred. 'Besides, we get this for a week now.'

'Oh, that makes it all worthwhile then.'

# CHAPTER FOUR

Twenty minutes later, West pushed open one of the double doors that led into the mortuary building, the sound of an ambulance siren becoming muffled as it swished shut behind them.

The reception area was gloomy compared with the fresh spring morning outside, and a distinct smell of bleach hung in the air.

There were stock photographs of various landscapes hanging from three of the walls, and Mark noted the familiar hues of a Scottish loch displayed above a metal rack containing various brochures about funeral arrangements and bereavement counselling.

The floor tiles were chipped in places, the polished surface reflecting the strip lighting in the ceiling that gave the whole room a harshness. A bunch of lilies thrust into a white ceramic vase on the wooden desk in the corner did little to lift the sombre atmosphere.

A reception desk was in one corner of the room, behind which a tall slim man in his early thirties watched them with sombre eyes, his mouth downturned.

'Morning, Clive,' said Mark. 'Busy?'

'Always.' The man pushed across a visitor register then picked at something between his uneven teeth while they signed in. 'Mind you, it helps we've had nothing from you these past few weeks.'

'Be grateful for small mercies,' West murmured, handing him back his pen. 'Gives us a chance to catch up with all the other cases on our desks.'

Mark turned at the sound of a door opening on creaky hinges to see a woman bundled head to toe in blood-spattered protective overalls looking at them.

'I heard there was an altercation outside the court house this morning. I might've known you'd be involved.' Gillian Appleworth's cool grey eyes peered over her mask before she lowered it, her mouth quirked into a sympathetic smile. 'I hope it was worth it.'

'Almost. Although whether his wife assaulting a police officer on his behalf will make any difference to his sentencing next month remains to be seen, given the list of offences he's going down for. I wouldn't mind, but I think she was planning it all along. Certainly felt like it.'

'I'll bet.' Gillan gestured to her overalls. 'Get yourselves a coffee while I'm changing out of these and have a shower – I'll be about twenty minutes given how long the hot water's taking to warm up this week.'

'The system's on the blink,' Clive explained after she had

disappeared back through the door and Mark and West had armed themselves with coffee from the vending machine. His eyes wore a baleful expression as he shuffled a sheaf of paperwork into an already overstuffed envelope and sealed it shut with a flourish of sticky tape. 'We called a plumber yesterday but he was bloody useless. Kept saying it's on a different supply to the rest of the hospital, so now we're waiting for someone else to get in touch.'

'Could be worse. It might've happened in the winter,' said West cheerfully before taking a sip of her drink.

Clive visibly shuddered. 'Perish the thought. Can you imagine what she'd have been like if it had gone wrong then?'

'Absolutely,' said Mark. 'You forget, I used to be married to her sister.'

West choked on her coffee and patted her chest before glaring at him. 'You really need to warn me before making comments like that.'

'Sorry.' He grinned, then led the way upstairs.

Gillian's office was tucked at the end of a corridor that overlooked the car park. Sunlight cut through the grime on the windows and bathed the thin carpet tiles lining the passageway, lending a warmth that soon disappeared the moment he opened the door for West.

The office consisted of a wide mahogany desk that was hidden beneath stacks of manila folders of varying thickness on one side and a large computer screen on the other. A three-tier black plastic tray behind the folders was pushed precariously close to the edge of the desk and West gave it a gentle nudge to safety as she sank into one of the visitor's chairs.

Mark shrugged off his jacket and placed it on the back of the remaining chair before sitting, while West cradled her coffee cup to her chest, closing her eyes for a moment.

'Late night?' he said.

'The boys had their karate grading and did really well so we ended up getting pizza to celebrate, and then watched a film. Then I forgot they didn't have any clean trousers for school this morning because we were at Scott's mum's over the weekend so…' She shrugged, then blinked. 'I was ironing at midnight.'

'Ouch.'

'I know. I live such a rock 'n' roll life don't I, Sarge?'

Mark looked up at the sound of footsteps in the corridor, before the pathologist swept into the room accompanied by the faint scent of a jasmine-based perfume, and eased into the leather chair behind her desk.

'Right, I've got a colleague from Bicester conducting the next two PMs,' she said, 'so let's take a look at Mr Windlesham while he's doing that, shall we?'

Without waiting for them to answer, she reached out for a manila folder on the top of the pile, flipped it open and unclipped a series of photographs from a typed report.

'Kennedy mentioned delayed drowning,' said Mark, taking a slurp of coffee. 'How did it happen?'

'According to the hospital records he was brought in by ambulance late Sunday morning after being pulled from the Thames,' Gillian said, shuffling the photographs into an order she favoured. 'Two kayakers heard him fall in and luckily for him – well, at the time anyway – managed to paddle back and get him to the riverbank before calling triple nine. They kept him warm until the first responders got there. When he was admitted into Accident and Emergency he was showing the usual signs we'd expect to see for someone who'd been in cold water for a length of time but he stabilised quickly.'

'So, what went wrong?' said West. She looked around for a space to put down her empty mug then gave up and slid it under her chair. 'Did he have a heart attack or something?'

'Well, eventually but only because he developed breathing difficulties first.' Gillian slid across the photographs. 'These are copies of the X-rays I took of his lungs before the post mortem. As you can see here, there's a lot of activity here, and here. That's indicative of water inflammation, the sort I'd expect to see from a case like this. When I opened him up, that was easily confirmed by the traces of weed he'd ingested – both in his lungs and in his intestinal tract.'

Mark frowned. 'But is that inflammation enough to cause a drowning death?'

'Absolutely, yes.'

'And a heart attack?'

'In my opinion, yes.' Gillian tapped the report. 'You can take this with you, and I'll email you a copy of course but during the PM I also checked for any indication Mr Windlesham might have suffered from any heart disease or other conditions I'd normally find in a heart attack victim. There wasn't anything.'

'Have next of kin been informed?' said Jan.

'There's a sister in Cardiff who was contacted when his health deteriorated, but she and her husband were unable to get here in time. I believe they're travelling over here on Friday – the contact details are in the file. Clive's been in touch with the appointed funeral director to explain that there'll now need to be a coroner's enquiry.' Gillian handed over the folder and waited while Mark added the photographs. 'Hence why you're here. Do you know the stretch of river by the hydro station?'

'Not very well – we haven't had a chance to take the boat that way yet, and I usually walk Hamish through Abbey Meadows or out towards Nuneham Courtenay.'

'Jan?'

'Not for years,' said West. 'If we take the boys there, it's usually so they can swim in the shallower waters beyond the weirs. I know the bridge, though – but I remember that it had railings.'

'Okay.' Gillian clasped her hands together. 'So, here's what's troubling me. From what the kayakers told the first responders, they saw Mr Windlesham at the water's edge a few minutes before he fell in. After they heard him enter the water, they assumed that he'd fallen from the bridge connecting two footpaths to the riverbank. I know that walk – Alistair and I were last there over the summer. There's no way someone could have fallen from the bridge by accident. The guard rail's simply too high.'

West nudged Mark's arm, and held out her hand for the folder before she started flicking through it. 'It says here that he told his doctor he was familiar with that stretch of river, and according to his GP he had no medical history of depression or anxiety or anything else that might suggest he was suicidal.'

'Exactly,' said Gillian. 'So, why did he end up in the water?'

# CHAPTER FIVE

Jan unclipped the photographs, running her thumbs over the smooth surfaces as she flicked through them.

The ceiling lights cast a reflection across each, and she turned them this way and that to better see the details. Any qualms about looking at a dead man's image were swept aside by an intrigue that nibbled away at her thoughts.

There was still a faint smell of disinfectant mixed with printer toner emanating from the photographs, and as she worked her way through the sequence, she could see how Clive had started taking them at a distance before homing in on any specific details that Gillian had identified.

She slowed, taking her time as she passed through the motley collection once more.

To the left of her, on the wall, a clock ticked past the seconds, a silence stretching out between the pathologist and her colleague while they watched her.

Glancing up, she saw Gillian eyeing her keenly. 'Was there anything to suggest he slipped or fell?'

'No, only what his rescuers – the kayakers – told the emergency services. That they saw him standing on the bank to their left as they paddled past, and then that they heard a splash after they'd gone some way past the bridge.'

'What about this wound on his right hip that's been stitched up?' Jan turned the photograph and held it out to Turpin. 'What might've caused that?'

'His clothes were sent over at my request before I conducted the post mortem,' said Gillian. 'There was blood on the inside of his shorts that matches the position of that wound, but no tears to the material. I've sent the clothes over to the lab for testing, but I'm sure we'll find that it's Mr Windlesham's blood.'

'Shorts? In this weather?'

'Maybe he was out for a run – the nursing staff said he wasn't very talkative, so who knows what he was doing.'

'Were there any bruises that might've suggested a struggle?'

'There weren't, no.'

'Anything in this wound when they patched him up?'

'Only some mud from where he was landed on the riverbank after being pulled out.'

'So he might've knocked against something on his way into the water.' Turpin frowned. 'Maybe he bumped into something sticking out from the bridge, or caught himself on something under the water?'

'Could be.' Gillian gestured to the copied hospital records in the open folder. 'The treating team noted it as a fresh injury, quite deep. It appeared to pass from the front of his hip to the back – it's about three centimetres in length.'

'Any sign of infection?'

'Not in his notes, no. In fact, I believe if Mr Windlesham hadn't died as a result of the inflammation in his lungs caused by delayed drowning, he would've healed up quite nicely.'

'Was he drunk?' said Turpin.

'He tested negative for alcohol and drug testing when he was admitted on Sunday lunchtime.'

'When did his breathing difficulties start, Gillian?' said Jan. 'It says here he died at two in the morning yesterday.'

'At about ten o'clock on Sunday night, so approximately eleven or twelve hours after he was rescued. He'd been heard clearing his throat on and off once he was transferred to a ward, but according to the nursing staff, he assured them he felt okay. That throat clearing escalated quickly such that by ten they had him on oxygen and were keeping an eye on his vitals.' Gillian shook her head. 'Unfortunately once that inflammation took hold it proved impossible to reverse the damage to his lungs and he slipped in and out of consciousness for the next few hours, until he died.'

'Poor bastard,' Turpin murmured. 'To go through all that, to think he was safe…'

'Sadly, although it's unusual in adults, it's very common in infant drownings,' said Gillian. 'More often than I'd like to acknowledge.'

Jan gathered together the photographs and closed the folder before turning her attention to Turpin. 'How do you want to approach this, Sarge?'

He scratched his chin for a moment, then straightened. 'Gill, I presume you've requested some additional toxicology tests to rule out anything beyond the usual drug and alcohol ones?'

'I have. I put a rush order on them too so hopefully we'll get those back in the morning – Thursday latest.'

'Okay, thanks. I think, then, that we need to take a look at the place where he fell in while it's still light enough to get a feel for the situation. After that, we'll see if we can speak to the kayakers this evening and get a formal statement from them – the coroner's going to want that anyway.'

Jan nodded, pulled out her notebook and started a list. 'What about his next of kin? That sister who lives in Cardiff. We could arrange for someone to speak with her tomorrow over the phone perhaps?'

'Sounds good.'

'I'll also ask Caroline and Alex to include his construction business in their search parameters and start organising interviews once we track down employees, neighbours and the like.'

'Do that. Also, let's see about any CCTV cameras around the area, just to confirm when he might've arrived at the river – we're assuming he drove at the moment, aren't we?'

Jan nodded. 'I think so. What about house-to-house enquiries in the village?'

'Let's wait until we know about the vehicle situation, otherwise Kennedy'll have my nuts for spending too much of his budget chasing our tail. At the moment, this is still a drowning incident, nothing more.' Turpin rose and waited while she tucked away her notebook and shoved the manila folder in her bag. 'I'll drive, and then you can try to get a hold of the kayakers to see if they're available later.'

Gillian chuckled. 'Didn't I see you pooled the racing car this week?'

'We hadn't,' he said. 'Until Jan decided to start a sweepstake about whether I'd get into a fight this morning or not.'

'Hence why he wants to drive,' said Jan, pouting.

Turpin grinned as she tossed the keys to him. 'You owe me.'

# CHAPTER SIX

Mark shielded his eyes against the low sun bathing the river, and stood to one side as a pair of mountain bikers zipped across the bridge, the two riders speeding away as soon as their tyres found the lumpy chalk track leading towards the village.

The water was calmer here, away from the churning roar of the weirs nearer Sutton Courtenay, but due to heavy rainfall over the preceding months, its level was still swollen by the run-off from the neighbouring fields and roadside ditches.

The current was strong, swirling in eddies as it passed beneath him.

He cast his gaze over the steel railings, ran his hand along the pitted surface, then leaned over and looked at the dark water below.

A pervading stench of rotting vegetation wafted up to where he stood, and he leaned over the guardrail to see sodden tangled

THE ELEVENTH GRAVE   33

clumps of weed drifting in the current from where it had become tangled around the bridge's concrete pillars.

Mud clung to his trouser hems, and he was sure his left boot had sprung a leak during the walk from the car park, given the damp seeping between his toes.

He could see where the two kayakers had rescued Barry Windlesham from the water two days ago.

The long grass and reeds a few metres upstream from the bridge were flattened with the telltale outline of two kayaks carving a path through the bullrushes. The surrounding earth had been churned into mud, trampled by the man's rescuers and the emergency services who had attended, and yet within a few weeks all evidence of his existence would be erased as nature took over and spring turned to summer.

A shiver crossed his shoulders, and he tweaked his coat collar as the breeze turned cool before he glanced up at the sound of footsteps.

'Well, I can't see anything to show he slipped in where he was seen standing on the bank,' West said, shoving her hands in her pockets as she walked towards him. 'There're a few footprints there and some trampled-down grass, but nothing to indicate a struggle, so I don't think he fell in there.'

Mark frowned, and took a step back to see through the railings down to where she had been standing a moment before. 'What about the brick ledge that goes under the bridge? Isn't it slippery?'

'It is, and there's moss covering it.' She wrinkled her nose as she followed his gaze. 'I suppose that's a possibility.'

Mark paced the length of the bridge away from her before

turning back. 'The railings are lower at each end, and only waist height in the middle section. He could've tumbled from one end or the other if he was leaning too far over.'

West walked back to the far end and rested her hand on one of the rails. 'It's below my hip, so given Windlesham's height, I suppose he could've gone over like that.'

Dropping to a crouch, Mark surveyed the rough surface of the painted steel before crossing to the other side and doing the same there. 'I can't see any torn clothing on here like the photos of his shorts at this end, can you?'

'Hang on.'

He rose to his feet and cast his gaze towards the forked chalk track leading away from the river, one route cutting though two ploughed fields before disappearing between a clutch of houses on the fringes of Culham village, and the other snaking back towards the car park near the lock.

There was nobody about, and he realised with a start that the light was starting to fade, the remnant sun catching the windows of a farmhouse on the fringes of the fields and bathing the tops of the trees lining the river in a pale gold that lacked any warmth.

'Sarge?'

He turned to see West staring at the wooden railings on her left, the farthest side from where the kayakers had pulled Windlesham from the water. 'What is it?'

'I think you ought to take a look at this.' She waited until he'd hurried over, then pointed. 'What do you make of that?'

Mark looked, then moved closer, his mouth turning. Pulling out his mobile phone, he aimed the light at a small round scar that cut through the wooden structure. 'Did you touch this?'

'No. I called you over as soon as I saw it.'

'Good.' He straightened, and faced her. 'Well spotted.'

'Is it what I think it is?'

'Yes. It's a bullet hole.'

'Do you think that's what caused that wound on Windlesham's hip?'

'Could be. Small calibre given the size of this, and if he ducked out of the way, it might've grazed him on the way past.'

'Well that'd explain how he ended up in the water.' She peered over the railing. 'I'd have bloody jumped if someone was shooting at me.'

Mark flicked through his contacts until he found the number for the lead crime scene investigator. 'We'd best get on with securing this as a crime scene before it gets dark.'

West turned back to him. 'Hang on, where's the bullet?'

'I presume it's in the water somewhere.'

'Oh.' She grimaced. 'Jasper's going to hate me.'

'Not as much as Kennedy will when I tell him we're going to need a dive team as well.'

# CHAPTER SEVEN

A fine mist clung to the Abingdon stretch of the River Thames just after six o'clock the next morning.

The sun was barely cresting the horizon amongst the scurrying grey clouds, and a few street lights along Bridge Street were still shining an artificial orange hue across pavements that had been dowsed by a late-night rain shower.

An occasional car crossed the bridge, and the distant swish of tyres splashing through puddles cut through the monotonous tone of diesel engines as commercial vans and trucks of varying sizes made their way to supermarkets and shops in the town, ready to begin another day's trading.

The alarm burst into Mark's subconscious a split second after a pair of ducks began quacking outside the cabin window.

He woke with a start, then grimaced when pins and needles shot through his right arm.

A mound of curls tickled his nose and chin, and after hitting the snooze button on his phone with his free hand, he gently slid his arm out from under Lucy's shoulder and rolled onto his back.

The ceiling was a natural white oak finish that changed depending on the time of day. In the summer, sunlight flashed off the surrounding water and illuminated the finish, whereas on duller days like this, the tone of the wood seemed moody.

The narrowboat rocked gently on the water lapping against its hull, and a weak sunlight dappled the walls of the cabin with the reflection of swirling eddies.

On the other side of the river, beyond the Abbey Meadows, the crash and tinkle of glass shattering tore through the suburban housing development as recycling bins were emptied one by one.

'I thought you said you and Jan were meeting Jasper at seven,' Lucy murmured, her voice muffled by sleep.

'I am.'

'You're going to be late at this rate. She won't thank you if she has to walk over the field after last night's rain. It was bucketing down.'

He smiled, then leaned over and kissed her shoulder. 'Do you want the bathroom heater left on?'

'Please.' She groaned and rolled over to face him. 'Otherwise I'll miss the light I need to finish that watercolour this morning.'

Mark raised his head at the sound of scratching at the door, then a whine.

'Would you mind walking Hamish this morning?'

'No, that's okay. I need to pick up some more eggs from the farm along the tow path anyway.'

'Thanks.'

A hurried shower and shave later, Mark looped his

waterproof jacket over his arm, ruffled the scruffy schnauzer-sized mongrel between the ears, and stepped over the gunwale onto the riverbank.

It was flat here, a wide-open expanse that formed part of the Thames Path. To his left was the lock and weir that helped to control the water flow along this stretch of the river, and to his right was the medieval bridge leading into Abingdon. A row of cottages framed the meadow on that side and, beside a metal five-bar gate that barred vehicle access into the field, a lone figure stood waiting.

He raised his hand and hurried over, the wet grass swooshing against his trouser legs.

West held up a takeout cup of coffee when he reached the gate. 'Thought you might need this.'

'You're an angel.'

'That's what I keep telling Scott and the boys. Haven't convinced them yet though.'

Five minutes later, she parked beside a grey panel van and plucked two remaining takeout cups from the car's middle console. She jerked her chin towards the faint outline of a patrol car that was parked at the end of the track near the bridge. 'According to Control, Nathan Willis and Marie Collins have the current shift. They've been on since two o'clock this morning.'

'They'll be needing that coffee, then.'

The CSI team had used the cordoned-off track leading to the river as its base, and when Mark sidled between another patrol car and a second panel van, he was acutely aware of the number of residential dwellings surrounding them.

He glanced over his shoulder to see a net curtain fall back

into place over one downstairs window, and an elderly man eyed them keenly while his Jack Russell terrier pissed against a lamp post.

'The sooner Kennedy gets that media release signed off, the better,' he muttered, falling into step beside West. 'We're probably already all over social media.'

'More than likely,' she said.

They scuffed along the chalk and stone-littered path in silence until Mark spotted a CSI technician clad head to toe in protective coveralls heading towards them.

'Where do we need to suit up?'

The technician jerked a thumb over his shoulder. 'Not until you reach the bridge. We got here at sunrise and just finished taking a look at the path this side of the river. Check with Jasper when you get down there though.'

'Will do.'

Turning up his collar, Mark fell back into step beside Jan and inhaled a deep breath of air to focus his mind.

Ruing the fact that he had chosen to set the alarm for a later time instead of rising early and taking Hamish for his usual pre-work walk, he ran his gaze over the purple and yellow spring flowers that bobbed and swayed amongst the long grass on either side of the track. Crows swooped and cawed as they grouped together in a corner of the field to his right, their calls interrupted by the squeal of excited gulls that searched for worms and grubs amongst the freshly seeded soil, while a pervading stench of freshly spread silage emanated from the opposite field.

A single black panel van had been parked in front of Nathan and Marie's patrol car. The loading door on its side was wide open, and he could see scuba tanks and an assortment of diving gear inside.

Jasper Smith saw them approaching from his position beside two of his colleagues on the bridge, and raised a hand in greeting before wandering over to meet them.

His bulky build filled his protective suit, and he lowered the hood before running a hand over closely cropped dark brown hair. 'I swear blind they've made this latest batch of suits even hotter than the last.'

'Thanks for getting set up so quickly,' said Mark. He kept his hands in his pockets rather than offer to shake the CSI technician's gloved hand.

'You're lucky. You caught us having a relatively quiet week. Plus there're two more teams available to cover the Oxford area this morning.' Jasper turned to West. 'I heard you found the bullet hole?'

'Yeah. I was lucky though,' she said. 'It's only because we were looking for where Barry Windlesham fell in, and Mark was trying to find anything like scraps of clothing that might've snagged on one of the guard rails.'

'Still.' Jasper shrugged. 'It was a good spot.'

'Was I right?'

'Absolutely. We've just finished taking swabs to confirm the scarring but I'm sure we'll find traces of gunpowder. Failing which, we've got photographs to show the tooling from the round that passed through the timber.'

'Now we just have to find the bullet – and the gun,' said Mark. 'Have the dive team made a start?'

'They've completed their first sweep – you're in time to watch the next one.'

'Where do we suit up?'

Jasper pulled spare gloves and bootees from his coveralls. 'You'll only need these if you stay on the demarcated path I've set up. Usual rules apply.'

'No problem.'

Mark waited while West walked over to where Nathan and Marie were standing next to their patrol car, handing over the coffees with a smile before wandering back to him.

'What're the chances of them finding anything?' she said, leaning against him while she tugged on the bootees and then put on the matching gloves. 'A needle in a haystack springs to mind. That river's going to be full of silt and other crap after the winter, isn't it?'

'They'll have the metal detectors out. That'll give them a head start.' Mark led the way over to where Jasper waited beside the riverbank, and watched while one of the divers emerged from the frigid waters.

Jasper reached out a hand to help them negotiate the mud, and then the diver pulled off her mask and lowered the protective neoprene hood, exposing short ash-blonde hair. A faint red welt mark circled her eyes and nose where her mask had pressed into her fair skin, and when she removed her gloves, her fingers were wrinkled from the cold.

'You do pick some difficult ones, Jan,' she said by way of greeting.

Alison Forbishaw was helped up the bank by one of her team

members, and paused to kick dark green weed from her protective neoprene bootees before joining them.

'Ali, this is DS Mark Turpin,' said West.

'Good to meet you,' said Alison. 'You're both leading this investigation, then?'

'It started out yesterday as a delayed drowning,' said West. 'Until we found the bullet hole.'

'And you think it's related to the victim's drowning?'

'He had a deep graze to his hip when he was admitted to A and E on Sunday,' said Mark. 'He didn't say anything about being shot.'

'So the bullet hole could be historical?'

'Maybe.'

'Okay, well it's going to be a long day. The river's deep here, and with the rainfall last night there's even more run-off from the fields to contend with – they're still waterlogged from the winter.' Alison turned and gestured to where a second diver was working his way along on the western side of the bridge. 'Carl's concentrating on the side where the victim was pulled out of the water while I'm taking the side the bullet may have travelled through. Jasper's confirmed your findings that there's nothing in the structure of the bridge on this side to indicate the bullet lodged itself in there, so like you, we're assuming it went in the water for now.'

'The couple that rescued him reckoned they saw him fishing on this side of the bridge as they went past,' said Mark. 'And yet he wasn't wearing typical clothing for a fishing trip, and there's been no equipment left lying around here that can be attributed to him.'

Alison frowned. 'Okay, well if we find anything, I'll let you know. Where will you be?'

'Arranging an interview with Mr and Mrs Maddison, the kayakers,' said West. 'Hopefully they can remember something that'll help us.'

# CHAPTER EIGHT

Jan switched off the engine and eyed the pretty end of terrace cottage beyond a low privet hedgerow.

The red brick Victorian building had been modernised over the years, and either the previous owners or the Maddisons had extended it upwards into the roof, evidenced by a pair of dormer windows that protruded from the dark grey slate tiles.

A chimney on the left-hand side of the building housed a stainless steel cowling that caught the sun's rays as it spun lazily in the wind, and a pale wisteria trunk twisted up the stonework on each side of the front door, its branches laden with new buds.

When she led Turpin up three stone steps and through a wooden gate, she noticed that the tiny front garden had been turned to pavers and decorative gravel. Flower pots of various sizes were dotted under the front bay window with bright red geraniums and colourful pansies in full bloom while two large terracotta pots beside the front door were home to different-coloured tulips that left petals scattered over the coir doormat.

She pressed a digital bell with a darkened lens that eyed her with empty interest, and heard a soft chime beyond the frosted square glass pane set high into the wooden surface of the door.

'What time did Caroline say they got home from work?' said Turpin under his breath.

'Helen's got a day off from her job at the hospital, and Jason was working from home today,' she said. 'She reckoned she'd give them an hour before we interrupt their evening, so she made this appointment for six. Do you want to lead it?'

'Sounds good. Interrupt me if I overlook anything.'

'Will do.' She took a step back as the door opened, and Helen Maddison peered out.

The woman was in her forties with dark hair tied back in a stubby ponytail. She looked comfortable in leggings and an oversized thin sweatshirt, and eyed them with keen green eyes.

'Are you the detectives?'

'DC Jan West, and my colleague, DS Mark Turpin,' said Jan, holding out her warrant card. 'I believe my colleague, Caroline Roberts, spoke to you earlier today.'

'She did. Come on in.' With that, Helen stood to one side and waved them to a door off to the right a short way along the hall. 'Go through to the living room – Jason's in there already.'

'Thanks.'

Jan ran her gaze over a collection of photographs on the hallway wall as she walked past.

The Maddisons appeared to lead an active life, with plenty of travel thrown in if the locations were anything to go by. A mixture of snow-capped mountains, rainforest and desert peppered the images with the couple smiling in each as they kayaked, skied or trekked their way around.

When she walked into the living room, Jason Maddison rose from a two-seater sofa under the bay window and held out his hand.

He was about the same height as Turpin with a mop of sandy-coloured hair and cornflower blue eyes. He wore a shirt over scruffy jeans paired with laced-up work boots and gave her a bashful smile as she introduced herself.

'Thanks for being on time,' he said. 'I'm meant to nip out to a client's house at seven to do a quote and I've already had to change the appointment once.'

'No problem,' said Jan cheerily. She positioned herself in an armchair nearest the door, leaving the other for Turpin while Helen sat beside her husband. 'What do you do?'

'I'm an architect, although most of the time I end up managing some of the construction projects I design,' he said. 'It's mostly extensions to domestic houses, but every now and again I get something different turn up. This evening's project is for an indoor swimming pool.'

'Very nice,' said Turpin. 'And you, Helen?'

'I'm a financial administrator for one of the private hospitals.' The woman shrugged. 'Although I think I'll be looking for something different to do this year.'

'She's too good for them, and getting bored,' said Jason, the pride evident in his voice. He reached across and squeezed his wife's hand. 'I'm trying to persuade her to finish her CPA studies and set up her own accountancy or bookkeeping business.'

Helen huffed her fringe from her eyes. 'Yes, well. I don't know if two of us being self-employed is wise.'

'I'm sure you'll work it out,' said Turpin kindly. He eased back in his seat. 'Well, we'll try not to keep you from that appointment, Jason. Mind if we ask you a few questions about Sunday morning, when you fished Barry Windlesham out of the river?'

'Of course.' The smile faded from Jason's face. 'We were sorry to hear from Detective Roberts that he died. He seemed okay when the paramedics were checking him over.'

'There were complications with his recovery,' Turpin said. 'So, at the moment our involvement is to ascertain what happened prior to his falling in the water. Could you take us through your movements that day in your own words?'

'Sure.' Jason glanced at his wife, who indicated that he should continue, then turned back to him. 'Well, we parked at Culham Lock at about ten o'clock. It's the first time we'd been out on the river since the winter and we fancied a lazy paddle up to Abingdon. We figured we'd have lunch at a pub on the river there before coming back. We hadn't been in the water long before we came across the man who fell in.'

'Did you see anyone else prior to spotting him?'

'A couple, walking their dog. That was a few minutes before Helen spotted him fishing.'

'He was fishing?'

'I think so,' said Helen. 'He was crouched next to the water by the bridge and I assumed he'd lost a line or something.'

'Which side of the bridge?'

'The side nearest the car park, before we went under the bridge.'

'There was a car with fishing gear in that Helen spotted while we were unloading the kayaks,' Jason added. 'We assumed it was his.'

'What gave you the impression he was fishing?' said Turpin. 'Did he have any gear with him, or any bags?'

'Not that I saw, no,' said Helen. 'It was only that he was right next to the water that I thought he was eyeing up somewhere to fish.'

'Did you hear or see anything before he fell in?'

'No, I only realised he'd fallen in when I heard him call out.'

'What about other noises around you?'

The woman frowned. 'Like what?'

'Anything that sounded out of the ordinary?'

'No. We were busy talking though, so I don't know if we'd hear it.'

'The church bells at Culham were ringing. I remember that,' said Jason. 'And there was a tractor working somewhere.'

Turpin nodded, then glanced over his shoulder and raised an eyebrow.

Finishing her note-taking, Jan turned her attention to Helen. 'When you saw Mr Windlesham, did he appear to be injured in any way, or having trouble walking?'

'He was crouching beside the water so I couldn't say,' said the woman. 'He didn't appear to be in any distress. When I said good morning, he just stared at us and then moved back to the path.'

'Did he seem surprised by your being there?'

Helen paused for a moment, then gave a shrug. 'Not surprised, no, but perhaps a little annoyed.'

'What makes you think that?'

'He sort of scowled at us. Like we'd interrupted something. I just assumed he was cross we might've scared the fish away. We get that with anglers sometimes, even when we give them plenty of room.'

'How long was it from first seeing him to when you heard him call out?'

'Only a few minutes. We weren't far from the bridge.'

'What did you do then?'

'Paddled back and got him out of the water as quickly as we could,' said Jason. 'It was freezing cold, despite the sun being out, and we were worried he'd get hypothermia.'

'Did he say anything to you?'

'Only to acknowledge the commands we were giving him about hanging onto the paddle, that sort of thing.'

'There was something. Afterwards I mean,' said Helen. 'When the paramedics were getting him comfortable and chatting with him, one of them told him how lucky he was, and he said "this time". I wondered whether perhaps he might've attempted to take his own life or something.'

'Did he say anything else?'

'Only to thank us. He was very weak by then though. They whisked him away pretty quickly after that.' Helen sniffed. 'It's so sad that he died.'

'You did well to rescue him,' said Turpin. 'How did you know how to do that? It must've been tricky from two kayaks.'

Jason leaned forward, resting his elbows on his knees. 'We

did a few courses with the local canoe club when we first started, including a first aid course that had a water rescue element to it. That's how we knew how to use the paddle to fish him out and get him back to shore. As soon as we managed that, Helen phoned triple nine while I helped him get out of his wet clothes and into spares we always carry in our dry bags.'

Turpin scooted forward in his seat. 'You changed his clothes?'

'Yes. We were worried he wouldn't warm up otherwise.'

'What was he wearing when you pulled him out of the water?'

'Now that I think about it, his clothing wasn't really cut out for fishing,' said Jason. 'The jeans, for a start. I mean, he'd be wearing waterproofs wouldn't he? And the sweatshirt – it was thick, but I wouldn't have thought it warm enough in this weather. He was wearing work boots, rather than wellingtons too – it's probably why he was struggling to stay afloat.'

'What happened to his wet clothes?'

'I put them in the empty dry bag that Jason's clothing had been in and gave it to the paramedics along with the boots,' said Helen. 'They said they'd get the hospital to return Jason's clothes at some point and asked me to write my phone number on the outside of the bag. I just figured they'd give me a call when they were ready for us to collect.'

'And has the hospital phoned you?'

'No, not yet. I was wondering, after your colleague called, whether I should phone them to see what happens next.'

Turpin was already on his feet. 'Don't worry, Helen. We'll do that for you. Right now.'

# CHAPTER NINE

Weak sunlight was glinting off the windows of the John Radcliffe hospital by the time Mark drove through the main entrance.

He had turned up the car heater on the way from the Maddisons', ruing the fact that he hadn't brought the thick padded jacket currently hanging off the back of his chair in the incident room.

A fine condensation kept threatening to form on the side windows. He used the sleeve of his suit jacket to wipe it away to better see the door mirror and turned his attention to the automatic white and red-striped barrier that began to rise in front of them.

Driving around the car park for a spare space, he batted down the visor to offset the fading pale gold rays streaming between grey clouds and eyed the stiffening breeze that riffled through the budding branches of alder, oak and lime trees surrounding the hospital buildings.

'That rain better hold off until Jasper's lot have finished,' he muttered. 'Otherwise we'll be even more unpopular.'

West lowered her phone. 'According to Alex and Caroline, the car with the fishing gear in it was traced to a local who lives in Sutton Courtenay. His alibi for Sunday morning checks out so they're now in touch with the DVLA trying to trace the vehicle registered to Windlesham. And Jasper hasn't found anything yet. But then…'

'It's like looking for the proverbial needle in a haystack. I know. Ah—' He broke off as a small red hatchback reversed from a space at the end of the row, and parked before peering across at her phone screen. 'What's the weather forecast like?'

'Says it won't rain until five.'

He checked his watch. 'Four hours.'

'Caroline says Kennedy wants us back at the incident room after this for a briefing at two thirty.'

'Okay. Well, let's get a move on then.'

Locking the car, he led the way across to the larger of the concrete and glass buildings that towered over the surrounding residential area and through a set of double glass doors.

'Where are we meant to pick up these clothes from?' he said, heading over to a bank of elevators.

'The Legal Services department.'

A steady stream of outpatients and visitors passed by, and they stood to one side to let others pass before slipping into an empty car.

Mark waited until the doors closed behind him. 'Have Alex or Caroline managed to speak to any family members?'

'They're working on it. Caroline said something about it being politically sensitive so Kennedy's involved, and so is the DCI at Kidlington.'

He frowned. 'Really?'

'Apparently.' West shrugged. 'I guess we'll find out more at the briefing.'

The doors swished open then, revealing a busy corridor that was awash with the bitter stench of antiseptic floor cleaner and stress.

A woman in a smart navy suit and pale blue blouse stepped inside, gave them a curt nod and stabbed her forefinger on the button for the next floor. She turned her back on Mark before glancing at her phone.

'Bugger,' she murmured, then edged past the opening doors as soon as a dull chime pinged above their heads and scurried away.

West suppressed a smile. 'Someone's having a bad day by the sound of it.'

Pausing to read a signboard listing the various departments on level four, they took a left along a narrow corridor painted bright white that would have been startling if it weren't for the grey chequered carpet tiles lining the floor.

A wilting fern peered over a blue plastic tub filled with moss-covered earth beside a closed door halfway along, and Mark spotted a brushed aluminium plaque with the department name embossed onto it, although some of the black lettering was missing.

'This is us,' he said, rapping his knuckles against the door before holding it open for West.

'Oh.'

She stopped in her tracks, and he almost collided with her before peering over her shoulder.

The woman from the lift was standing beside a beech-coloured desk that was strewn with paperwork, her eyes widening.

'You're early,' she managed.

Mark checked his watch. 'Only by about five minutes. Is this a bad time?'

She huffed a stray strand of hair from her face in reply, then gestured hopelessly at a towering pile of lever arch folders stacked beside her computer screen. 'It's always a bad time.'

She attempted a light laugh, but it came out slightly hysterical.

'DS Mark Turpin,' he said, holding out his warrant card. 'And my colleague, DC Jan West. I believe you spoke to DC Alex McClellan earlier today. We're here to collect some clothing that was handed in when one of your patients – Barry Windlesham – was admitted to A and E on Sunday.'

'Hilary Cottishall.' She glanced at the warrant card, then walked around the desk and sank into a battered and torn cloth-backed chair with a sigh. 'I'm the liaison officer assigned to Mr Windlesham's case.'

'What is it you do here, apart from looking after the deceased's belongings?' said West, a wary look in her eyes as she ran her gaze over the bulging archive boxes littering the floor of the small office.

'Apart from herding cats?' Hilary shot them a sardonic smile. 'Like the role title suggests, I provide a liaison service between the hospital and families when a patient passes away within our care, no matter the circumstances.'

Mark eyed the precariously stacked folders. 'Every single person?'

'Yes.' Hilary edged forward in her seat, which gave an ominous squeak at the sudden movement. She folded her arms on the desk and followed his gaze. 'Every single person. For our partner hospitals as well, not just this one.'

He was unable to stop the soft whistle that passed his lips. He cleared his throat. 'So… Mr Windlesham's belongings…'

'Are causing problems.' Hilary directed her attention to an open manila file on her desk. 'As you know – and as confirmed by your colleague on the phone – the clothing Mr Windlesham was wearing at the time he was admitted was passed on to the morgue after his death.'

'We're after his original clothing,' Mark said. 'The clothing he was wearing when the paramedics dropped him off at A and E belonged to his rescuers. Apparently they removed his wet clothing, put it in a bag, and gave it to the paramedics. They were assured they would be able to retrieve that clothing from the hospital.'

Hilary thumbed through the papers in the file, her brow creasing further with every page. 'That's strange. There's a note here about a waterproof bag being handed in, but it wasn't with Mr Windlesham at the time of his death.'

'What do you mean?' Mark tried to ignore the sudden twitch

in his chest as his heart skipped a beat. 'Was he moved from the main ward before he died?'

'No, sadly we don't have enough private rooms to allow for that.' She flicked the page around to face them. 'What I meant was, there was no sign of the bag when one of the nurses cleared out the cabinet beside Mr Windlesham's bed. Only the clothing that's been provided to the morgue.'

'You mean, the bag's been removed without your knowledge,' said West.

Hilary blushed. 'Or it's simply been misplaced.'

Mark saw West raise an eyebrow in response, then turned back to the liaison officer. 'Did he have any visitors after being admitted?'

'None that are listed here, no. I understand his next of kin is a sister, but she lives too far away to see him before he died.'

'In that case, Ms Cottishall, we're going to need the ANPR and CCTV footage for the car parks.' Mark rose and held out his hand for the manila file. 'And a list of every single staff member or contractor working that night.'

# CHAPTER TEN

Mark glanced at his watch before glaring at the small screen above the lift door.

The red digital display counted down the floor levels while a red arrow pointed the way, and he willed it to go faster while trying not to clench his jaw.

The thought of how much additional work had now been created by the disappearance of Barry Windlesham's clothing was almost overwhelming, and he bit back a groan as he wondered what DI Kennedy's reaction would be to the increased man-hours required to process all the enquiries that would follow.

And that was before the camera footage was obtained and every single vehicle movement was accounted for.

Beside him, West balanced the manila folder in one hand while she scrolled through her phone, checking emails from the team at the incident room, and muttering under her breath.

She nudged his arm, pulling him from his reverie. 'Here we go. It says here that the person who treated Barry Windlesham on Sunday when he was admitted to A and E was Doctor Kendric Duncan.'

'Is he working today?'

'Yes – according to Caroline, he should be on duty.' She tucked her phone into her bag. 'And hopefully, they're not too busy downstairs so he can talk to us.'

'Fingers crossed.'

West glanced over her shoulder to watch as an ambulance roared into the A and E parking bay and two paramedics jumped out before hurrying to the rear doors and wrenching them open. 'So much for a quiet afternoon here.'

'Let's go and find Dr Duncan before he gets busy.' Mark set off towards a corridor off to the right. 'Did you have a chance to find out anything about him?'

'Only that he's been based here for the past five years. He was in Manchester before that, and qualified fifteen years ago. Married with a wife and two daughters according to the professional biography I found online for him.'

'Okay, thanks.'

After checking with a harried-looking porter, they found Kendric Duncan leaning against a plasterwork wall beside a vending machine just outside the A and E department, his face haggard.

The hiss emanating from the machine cut through the various automated and ad hoc messages spouting through the speakers set amongst the ceiling tiles, and steam rose into the air while hot liquid spat into a plastic cup.

THE ELEVENTH GRAVE   59

'Dr Duncan?' Mark flipped open his warrant card as he approached. 'DS Mark Turpin, and DC Jan West. We wondered if we could have a quick word please?'

The hissing stopped with an impromptu cough, and Duncan picked up the coffee cup before grimacing. 'Shit, it's out of milk again.'

He turned and eyed the pair of them, his height requiring him to look down his nose at Jan with an imperious gaze. 'This is the first break I've had in six hours,' he said, exhaustion clouding his words. 'And I've just had to tell the parents of a six-year-old boy that their son's going to need his leg amputated after he was hit by a bus while cycling home from school yesterday. Can't this wait?'

'I'm sorry,' said Mark. He stood to one side at the sound of rattling wheels as the two paramedics he had seen outside hurried past with a woman swaddled in blankets on a stretcher. She moaned as one of them adjusted the oxygen mask covering her nose and mouth before the paramedics swung the stretcher to the left and disappeared behind a plastic curtain. 'Is there somewhere a bit quieter we could talk? Perhaps somewhere you can sit down while we have a chat?'

Duncan took a sip of the coffee, then nodded to a colleague who disappeared behind the curtain before he could be heard talking to the newest arrival. 'Okay, but no longer than ten minutes. We're understaffed this week. Come this way.'

He called over to a passing nurse, telling her to dial his pager if another emergency case arrived, then led the way across the wide corridor and into an anteroom no bigger than a broom cupboard.

The walls were filled with locked glass-fronted cabinets and shelves laden with various medical supplies, and Mark shifted sideways to negotiate a dilapidated folded wheelchair with one missing front wheel to let West pass through the door.

Duncan closed it, put down his cup on the laminated counter that ran beneath the shelves and folded his arms, biting back a yawn. 'What can I help you with?'

'We're investigating the death of Barry Windlesham,' Mark said. 'He was admitted here on Sunday after falling into the Thames at Culham. We understand you were his treating doctor.'

'That's right.' Duncan rubbed his hand over the stubble forming on his chin. 'He was pulled out by a couple of kayakers, wasn't he? Such a shame, the way things turned out though. Of course, we do all we can to prevent infection but when a person's body has been through that much trauma...'

'We were wondering if you knew what happened to the waterproof bag that was brought in with him? According to his rescuers, it's bright orange and contains Mr Windlesham's original clothing.'

The doctor frowned. 'I can't say I do. But then, my focus was on Mr Windlesham, not his belongings. You'd be better off asking patient services about that.'

'We did, and they don't have a record of the bag being transferred over to the ward or to the morgue after his death.'

'Have you checked with the ward staff?'

'They're next on our list. When Windlesham came in, what did you notice about the wound on his hip? Was it you that stitched him up?'

'Yes. Once my team got his clothes off him and got him

comfortable, I was able to give him a thorough examination. That graze was deep, so it was a case of giving him a local anaesthetic and cleaning him up before putting in some stitches.' Duncan took another sip. 'He would've been left with a scar though.'

Mark waited while Jan caught up with her note-taking. 'In confidence, we believe Mr Windlesham may have been the victim of attempted murder, and that the wound you saw was caused by a bullet grazing his hip before going into the water.'

Duncan's eyebrows shot upwards. 'Bloody hell.'

'Hence the confidentiality please. His original clothing may provide us with that crucial evidence, as would any information about the state of his hip. Did you notice any powder in the wound while you were cleaning him up? Anything that might suggest a gunshot wound?'

'I can't say I did, no. Obviously with him falling into the water, anything like that would've been washed away.'

Mark sighed. 'That's what I was afraid of.'

'Shooting someone is pretty drastic.' Duncan drained his coffee before checking his watch. 'And Mr Windlesham didn't say anything about being attacked.'

'What did he say?'

'Nothing much, to be honest. Once we'd got him comfortable I did ask him how he came to fall into the water, and all I could get out of him was that he said he slipped. I assumed it was an unfortunate accident – until you showed up.'

'We've asked the liaison officer in patient services to provide us with a list of staff working that day, as well as trying to obtain a note of any visitors to Mr Windlesham's ward.' West handed over her business card. 'Would you mind texting or emailing me with a note of your team's names from Sunday afternoon? We'd like to interview each of them, in case anyone saw what happened to that bag.'

'No problem.' Duncan glanced down as his pager trilled. 'I've got to go.'

Mark followed him out the door, hurrying to catch up. 'One last question – how busy was it on Sunday?'

'Very.' The doctor glanced along the corridor as another paramedic team appeared with a bloodied man on a stretcher they rolled into the emergency department. 'And if that wasn't enough, someone decided to try and start a fight in here too.'

'Sorry to hear that.'

'Well, it happens all too often, sadly.' Duncan held up his hands. 'And now I really have to go.'

'Thanks for your time.'

West tucked her notebook away as the doctor disappeared into a throng of nursing staff and checked her watch. 'We've got an hour until the briefing. What do you want to do next?'

'Let's go and find the ward Windlesham was moved to after they'd treated him down here,' said Mark. 'Surely somebody has to know what happened to that bag of clothes.'

His phone began to ring as the lift doors swept open, and he hurried over to a corner out of the way. 'Turpin.'

'Mark, it's Jasper. We've got a couple of things that might interest you, starting with a mobile phone that was submerged in the water near the bridge.'

'Really?'

'It was placed in a plastic sandwich bag and dangled under

the surface by a piece of string. Whoever put it there had lodged it into place using a stainless steel screw pushed between a crack in the mortar of the concrete pier.'

'Does it work?'

'No, but then it might just have run flat. I'm having it couriered over to the lab for analysis. Even if the phone doesn't work, we might be able to do something with the SIM card.'

'The Middletons – the kayakers who rescued Windlesham – said they saw him crouching by the riverbank as they got close to him on Sunday. It makes sense the phone might belong to him.'

'Hasn't the hospital got his phone?'

'Not to my knowledge.' Mark checked his watch. 'I'm going to have to go. Jan and I are going to head up to the ward he was on to see who we might be able to talk to.'

'Before you do, there's something else. We found the bullet.'

'You did?' He lowered the phone for a moment and beckoned to West, lowering his voice. 'They found the bullet. And a mobile phone.'

Her eyebrows shot upwards. 'Really? Bloody hell.'

He returned her fist bump before angling the phone to his ear once more. 'Jasper? Whereabouts was the bullet?'

'Buried in the bank about fifteen metres from the bridge.' The forensic specialist emitted a relieved sigh. 'We were lucky – the velocity must've slowed after going through the bridge rail, and the banks around here are soft thanks to all the rain we've been having lately. If it had gone in the water, I don't think we'd have been so lucky, not with the current and depth here. As it was, the metal detector picked it up. I've had it taken over to the lab for processing as a matter of urgency.'

'I don't suppose there's any chance you've found the weapon?'

'Not yet. I'd say we've got another two to three hours of decent light available to us today so we'll keep looking. How are you getting on?'

'Trying to find the clothing Windlesham was wearing when he went into the water. If we can find it, we can get it tested for any remnant traces from that bullet grazing him to tie the two together.'

'Were they not kept with his belongings?'

'It's all gone missing.'

'Shit.'

'Let us know the minute you find anything else, will you?'

'No problem.'

Ending the call, Mark blew out his cheeks. 'That's something, at least.'

'Only if the weapon was used in another crime on our database,' said West. 'But what the hell was Windlesham doing hiding his phone in the river?'

'There's something else we need to consider.'

'What's that?'

'It might not be his phone.'

# CHAPTER ELEVEN

As soon as Jan walked out of the lift and through a set of wooden doors into the busy ward on the fifth floor, she was swathed within an oasis of organised calm and efficiency.

The all-male ward comprised several beds, some with curtains drawn around them, others with patients reading books or engrossed in tablet computers or mobile phones.

There were windows at the far end of the ward, through which the skyline of Oxford City Centre could be seen, with different church spires pricking the gaps between the university colleges, museums and commercial buildings.

The low ceiling offset the acoustic brittleness of the polished tiles underfoot and softened conversations with a subdued resolve.

Visitors were scant – an elderly man in a bed nearest the windows was regaling a young couple, his hands expressive and a smile on his lips while a younger man halfway along the row of beds cuddled a young boy and spoke to a woman in hushed tones, his face ashen.

Two nurses were behind a desk to the left of the doors, one standing over the other while they contemplated a computer screen and spoke in murmurs.

The older of the two looked up as Jan and Turpin approached, a professional smile on her face. 'Can I help you, officers?'

'Are we that obvious?' Jan held out her warrant card and made the introductions. 'We wondered if we could speak to anyone who was on duty on Sunday through to the early hours of Monday morning?'

'I was.' The younger nurse's eyes widened. 'Is there a problem?'

'Hope not.' Jan read the name badge pinned to the woman's shirt – Emily Crake – and shot her a kindly smile. 'We were hoping to locate a bag of clothing that was brought in with an A and E case. Barry Windlesham. He passed away that night after falling into the river at Culham.'

'I remember him.'

Her colleague moved away from the desk. 'If you want to have a chat, I can monitor things here, Em.'

'That'd be great,' said Jan. 'Thanks. Is there somewhere we can talk in private?'

'There's a visitors' lounge down the hall,' said Emily, plucking a cardigan from the back of the chair. 'I don't think there's anyone in there at the moment. It's a bit quiet up here this afternoon – most visitors turn up after five.'

'Lead the way.'

Moments later, Jan and Turpin were shown into an airy space that was furnished with eight sagging armchairs upholstered in various faded fabrics and a pair of wooden occasional tables covered with gossip magazines.

There was a vending machine in the corner half filled with chocolate bars and soft drinks that Emily studiously ignored, instead walking over to a chair beside a frosted glass window.

'I had a phone call from Hilary Cottishall about twenty minutes ago,' she said. 'She was in a flap because two police officers were asking about a bag of clothes that went missing. To make it very clear, I didn't take it.'

'I wasn't going to suggest such a thing,' said Jan, taking the seat beside her while Turpin stood next to the door. 'But I would like to know what usually happens to any belongings that are brought in with a patient.'

'Oh. Okay.' Emily exhaled, her shoulders relaxing. She sank back into the worn chair. 'Normally, any valuables would be labelled with the patient's name and placed in the hospital safe.'

Jan looked up to see Turpin staring at her.

'The woman in Legal Services didn't mention any valuables,' he said.

The nurse shrugged. 'Maybe he didn't have any. I only mentioned it in case he was wearing a watch or something when he was brought in.'

Jan updated her notes. 'Would the bag with the clothing have been put in the safe?'

'Not if they were still wet, no. They'd have probably been put in the sluice room by the emergency staff. From there, the clothing should've been transferred up here with Mr Windlesham.'

Turpin was already out the door by the time Emily had finished speaking.

'What about visitors on the ward that day?' Jan continued. 'How does that normally work?'

'Well, we limit visitor numbers to two at a time, and they're only allowed in between eight in the morning and eight at night. We tend to try and restrict visitors during mealtimes to give everyone some peace and quiet, especially at weekends – you can imagine how busy that can get.'

'We understand that Mr Windlesham's next of kin, a sister, wasn't able to get here but did he have any other visitors?'

'Not that I'm aware of, no,' Emily said. 'But there was a steady stream of visitors from about five in the afternoon until eight and we were busy fitting those in around the evening meal.'

'Who was on shift with you?'

'Selina Gunnerston. She's off today.'

'Do you often work a shift with her?'

'Yes – we've both been on this ward for about eleven months now. I worked in the paediatric ward before that.'

'Did you notice anyone acting unusually on Sunday, prior to Mr Windlesham's death?'

'No, I can't say I did – but like I said, we were really busy.' Emily shrugged. 'Weekends are always like that, obviously – not everyone can get here during the week what with work or school commitments I suppose. We rarely get any trouble here, anyway – it's why most of the security guards work downstairs in A and E.'

'How do you keep a record of visitors' names?'

'We don't, not on this ward. We just monitor that the number of visitors doesn't exceed two at any time, and that conversation is kept at a reasonable level so as not to disturb any patients that might be resting.'

'What time did your shift start that day?'

'Seven thirty, in the evening. I finished at eight the next morning. I had yesterday off before switching shifts to the daytime this morning.'

'And when do visiting hours finish?'

'At eight.' Emily gave a rueful smile. 'Although often it takes half an hour to get everyone away.'

'How many people were visiting patients here on Sunday?'

'About a dozen I suppose – but then I wasn't always at the desk. There are welfare checks to do on patients, reports to email, other staff members turning up needing information, or new patients being admitted, like Mr Windlesham, phone calls… the time goes really quickly at weekends.'

'Who else was admitted to the ward on Sunday?'

'I can't give out names, not without some paperwork, but the elderly gentleman you probably saw on the ward just now came up from A and E before visitor hours were over.'

'Is he okay?'

'He will be. Thanks for asking.'

'Did anyone turn up to see Mr Windlesham?'

'Not during visiting hours, no.' Emily frowned. 'There was a bloke who came in at about nine o'clock asking to see him, but of course we had to turn him away.'

Jan bit back her excitement and instead kept her face passive. 'Oh? Did he leave a name?'

'No. He seemed a bit cross that he'd missed visiting hours though. Selina let him know to come back at eight the next morning, but of course Mr Windlesham died in the night...' Emily paused. 'I hope we didn't screw up by not letting him in.'

'Did he say if he was family?'

'He wasn't, no – we checked that, as sometimes we can make an exception of course. When Selina asked him, he said he was just a friend passing by who'd heard about the accident, so of course we had to ask him to leave.'

'What did he look like?'

'Um, average height I suppose. Navy sweatshirt, black jeans.' Emily's eyes narrowed. 'He had a scar across his top lip and jaw line.'

'A bit like a cleft palate scar?'

'No, it was ugly. Definitely not a surgical scar. It was more like he'd once been attacked with a knife.'

# CHAPTER TWELVE

Mark locked the car door and tossed the keys to West before they hurried across the police station car park towards the security door at the rear of the building.

There was less than an hour of daylight remaining, and as he glanced at his phone, he bit back the frustration that clouded his thoughts.

Jasper and his team would have packed away their equipment by now, leaving the crime scene to be managed by a small team of uniformed constables overnight before they returned in the morning to resume their search.

There was no news from anyone regarding the weapon used in the attempted murder of Barry Windlesham.

And there had been no sign of the bag of clothing in the emergency sluice room, either.

Swiping his card across the security panel and opening the door for West, he paused to take in the purple and yellow hues streaking the sky as the sun faded, and he watched as a chilly breeze ruffled the trees behind the farthest line of cars.

There was a thick smell of fat and carbs emanating from the fast-food restaurant on the other side of the police station, and a steady roar of traffic on the Marcham road in front of the building, both disappearing the moment he let the door fall back into place.

Stomach rumbling, he texted a message to Lucy to see if she wanted him to pick up a Chinese takeaway on the way home, then hurried up the staircase to catch up with West.

The incident room was still busy when they walked in, despite several of the administrative staff having already left for the day. Four uniformed officers were sitting, shirt sleeves rolled up, with phones to their ears at the far end of the room, and as he walked past he overheard some of the conversations.

It appeared that Kennedy had delayed the afternoon briefing to await Mark and West's return. In the meantime, he had tasked the small team with working their way through all the statements taken over the course of the day from the house-to-house enquiries that encompassed the immediate vicinity of the bridge and tracking down residents who had been at work.

The detective inspector emerged from his office as Mark reached his desk, and beckoned to him.

'Alex and Caroline have made a start with interviewing Windlesham's friends and work colleagues that they've managed to track down via social media,' he said. 'They're due back any minute so we'll start the briefing as soon as they get here. I want the team out of here by half seven so they're able to focus in the morning.'

'Sounds good, guv.' Mark looked around the room. 'You've managed to find some more officers.'

'I haven't, yet. That lot were brought over from another investigation I'm managing but it's waiting for the Crown Prosecution Service to review it, so they might as well help with this one in the meantime.'

'So we could lose them.'

'Indeed.' Kennedy peered over Mark's shoulder at the sound of the incident room door opening. 'So let's make the most of the situation and see where we're up to.'

Mark turned to see Alex and Caroline speaking with West, and waved them over. 'Okay to start the briefing straight away, or do you need five minutes?'

'We're ready,' said Caroline. 'We haven't got much yet, but it's a start.'

'Okay, find a seat and I'll gather up the rest of them.' Kennedy emitted a loud whistle and pointed towards the whiteboard. 'Everyone – briefing. Now. No exceptions please. There's a lot to cover before you head home.'

He led the way over to the far side of the room to a whiteboard that was already covered with handwritten notes and photographs.

Jasper had emailed through images of the bullet that had been found, its metal alloy casing dulled by mud, and the mobile phone.

The phone appeared in two of the photographs, the first one taken while it was still within the plastic bag it had been found in, and the second showing the phone once it had been unwrapped.

Above these, Kennedy had pinned a photograph of Barry Windlesham that appeared formal in nature.

He wore a white shirt with a blue patterned tie and a black jacket, and bore an expression of practised warmth that didn't quite reach his eyes.

Mark guessed that the photograph was a few years old – the man's face was tanned and he appeared to be carrying less weight than the images taken during Gillian's post mortem examination.

Taking a seat beside the other detectives, he nodded to the two uniformed sergeants that had been assigned to the investigation.

Peter Cosley had worked with Mark before, and was sitting with his notebook open while he twirled his glasses impatiently between his fingers.

Michael Stanton was standing by the photocopier, affecting a nonchalant air that was countered by his keen gaze at the whiteboard.

There were twelve uniformed constables gathered in the room as well, six of whom Mark recognised from previous cases and who he knew would be emphatic in their contributions to the caseload that was unfolding.

'Right,' Kennedy began. 'For those of you who've just joined us today, this investigation started out as a delayed drowning incident that has escalated to a homicide enquiry. You'll find the case summary and the reports to date lodged in HOLMES2. Caroline, could you give the team an overview of what you've found out about Barry Windlesham to get us started?'

'No problem, guv.' The detective constable moved to the

front of the group and cleared her throat. 'So, to confirm the basics, Windlesham was fifty-two, divorced these past eight years with no kids, and was the sole director of a construction company based near Chalgrove. Alex and I did a background check on the company, and its last filed accounts with Companies House was in October. The balance sheets look fine, with a decent profit margin that was pretty consistent with previous years. He's been trading under that company name for seven years.' She paused to flick through her notes. 'Prior to that, his ex-wife was a joint director, so it appears that he folded that company after the divorce and rebranded it before registering the new name a few months later. His registered office address belongs to that of his accountant, in Didcot.'

'What about his social life?' said Kennedy.

'That's me, guv.' Alex joined his colleague. 'Windlesham's social media accounts are locked to private but we could still see some of his followers and managed to draw up a list of forty people we want to speak to. They seem to be a mixture of friends, university alumni and work associates so we've concentrated on the friends today, taking statements from nine of them in person. Uniform have conducted the other interviews over the phone so we'll review those in the morning before moving on to the work colleagues and alumni. And one of his neighbours has a spare key to Barry's house.'

'Anything in the business or social media reviews to suggest he had any enemies?' said Mark.

'Not yet.' Caroline watched while Kennedy updated the notes on the whiteboard before continuing. 'I had a look at what current projects Windlesham's business might be involved with, and apart from the company appearing on three different council tendering lists in the past six months, the name also appears in relation to a new exclusive housing development that's been tabled for planning permission at Ravenswood, an old disused airfield.'

'Have there been any threats to his business or to him personally?' said Kennedy.

'There's nothing on our system about him at all, guv,' said Alex. 'Nothing by way of threats, and no speeding convictions or anything like that. He's clean in that respect.'

'We'll head over to the house and speak to his neighbours tomorrow,' said Mark. 'Just because there's nothing on the system, that doesn't mean he hasn't been threatened. He just might've chosen not to report it.'

'True. Well, at least the neighbour's got a key so that'll avoid getting a locksmith out. With regard to the mobile phone that the dive team found under the bridge, can you arrange to get it over to digital forensics in the morning for analysis?'

'Will do, guv.'

The DI added the task to the notes on the board. 'Has anyone been in contact with his sister today?'

'I spoke to her this morning to let her know we were investigating her brother's death,' said Caroline. 'She's understandably shocked, but couldn't offer any information about who might've attempted to kill him. She's given us permission to enter his house though, and I've given her my contact details until we get a family liaison officer assigned to them when they arrive on Friday.'

'Good work, thanks. Hopefully we'll have someone in place

by the time she and her husband get here.' Kennedy finished writing and faced the team. 'As most of you are aware, Jasper and his team somehow managed to find a bullet in amongst the mud alongside the river earlier this afternoon. He assures me that a ballistics report will be with us by the end of the week but in the meantime we still need to find a weapon. He's heading back to the river in the morning but if he finds nothing then we're going to have to keep a watchful eye on any reports coming in via CrimeStoppers or other means in case a member of the public finds it.'

'What about a media release?' said West. 'Are you going to tell people about it?'

'We are, but we're not mentioning attempted murder. We're simply going to say that we're looking for it in relation to a serious crime and that if anyone does find it, they're to call it in and not pick it up.'

'Did anything come out of the house-to-house enquiries?' said Mark. 'Did anyone hear a gunshot?'

'No, but then given that the two kayakers reckon they didn't hear anything either, I'm inclined to think his attacker used a small calibre weapon,' said Kennedy. 'And that's a worry.'

'Why?' said Alex, his eyes widening.

'Because,' said Mark, 'it means we're possibly dealing with someone who has access to illegal firearms.'

# CHAPTER THIRTEEN

The next morning, Mark shoved his hands into his pockets and stared up at the rendered walls of a two-storey glass and concrete building.

It looked more like an office than a home, all darkened privacy glazing and awkward angles. The off-white render was stark against the old ash and beech woodland that hugged the immaculate lawn, and the ornamental gravel driveway and front path was weed-free.

A border comprising different coloured clumps of grass formed a guard of honour towards the solid oak front door that was set under a shallow portico, and two tall square-shaped pots framed the entrance, both containing miniature fig trees.

West tugged on protective gloves, jangled a set of keys in her hand, then inserted a small brass one into a sturdy lock and gave it a twist.

The door opened on well-oiled hinges, exposing a marble tiled floor and a handful of leaflets amongst some post on a coir doormat that was encrusted with dried mud.

A pair of well-worn running shoes had been left to the right-hand side of the door, accompanied by a pair of polished brogues and an abandoned sandal.

Stepping over the threshold, Mark put on his own gloves and peered around the reception hall. Its plasterwork walls had been painted the same colour as the outside of the house, and the walls were left plain. There were no photographs, no artwork, and—

'No soul,' said West, screwing up her nose. 'Did he really live here?'

'The key fitted.'

'Very funny.' Her low heels clacked across the tiles, the sound echoing up the wide staircase to their right as she led the way into the first room off the hallway. 'Well, at least this is a bit better.'

Mark followed her into a living room that stretched the length of the house, a single window looking out over the driveway while the floor-to-ceiling arrangement at the end provided a sweeping view of the woodland beyond.

There were two sets of sofas – a pair of two-seaters arranged in an L shape nearest the door and a second one, a six-seater, placed in front of a large television hanging on the wall near the patio windows.

He ran his gaze over the glass and chrome coffee table beside him, taking in the magazines that had been left in a haphazard pile. There were two business-related ones, a popular car magazine and a local residents newsletter from two weeks ago that had a coffee cup stain on the front cover and a dog-eared page in the middle.

Mark flipped to it, and then held it up to West. 'There's a feature in here about that potential development at Ravenswood that Caroline was talking about. Looks like there's a planning meeting due to take place tomorrow at the local village hall.'

'We should probably go along to it,' she said, rummaging between the books, vinyl records and various knick-knacks that were displayed across two shelving units beside the television. 'It might help us get an idea of how Windlesham was perceived around here. Alex said he phoned his office yesterday and the woman he spoke to was a part-time temp that's been working there since early March.'

Mark frowned. 'Didn't she wonder where he'd been all this time?'

'She only works Wednesday afternoons, Thursdays, and Friday mornings so she just assumed he was out when she got there yesterday. Apparently, she's got her own key.'

'Okay. Best we pop over there when we're done here and have a word with her.' He moved across to the windows overlooking the woodland and ran his hand over a door leading out to a paved barbecue area that was shaded from the elements by a large trellis covered in ivy. 'Doesn't look like anyone's tried to break in, at least.'

'The place is immaculate.' West circled the rest of the living area with a look of wonder on her face. 'If my two were here, there'd be clothes strewn everywhere and leftover pizza smushed into the cushions.'

'I don't think this is going to take long. Do you want to finish down here while I tackle upstairs?'

'Go for it. I'll give you a shout if I find anything.'

'Same.'

Removing his shoes at the bottom of the carpeted staircase, Mark padded up to the next floor in his socks, eyeing a hole in the big toe of the right one with a rueful glance and vowing to order more online the moment he got a free moment – and remembered.

The first room off the landing at the top of the stairs turned out to be Windlesham's home office, a spartan affair comprising a glass and chrome desk similar to the coffee table downstairs, an adjustable leather chair, and an all-in-one-style computer screen and keyboard. The cables for the computer were tidied away with a single black wire and snaked down the wall behind the desk to a multi-socket extension cable. A small table beside the desk housed a printer that appeared to double as a scanner.

Mark lifted the lid, but there was no abandoned documentation on the glass document table.

The window would have overlooked the driveway, but the wooden Venetian blinds were pulled down, obscuring the view and – he guessed – preventing sunlight from reflecting on the computer screen while Windlesham worked.

There was a single oak bookcase against the wall opposite the window largely taken up by lever arch files. Each of these was labelled with the contents, and after having a quick flick through three or four, Mark concluded that they were simply copies of contracts, correspondence and invoices for the past seven years.

However modern Windlesham's house was, it appeared that he preferred a more traditional method for his record-keeping rather than relying on technology to save his work.

Walking across the landing, Mark entered a guest bedroom that was furnished with a functional pine bed, matching side cabinets and a chest of drawers. A built-in wardrobe stretched the length of one wall, and the same style of Venetian blinds covered the window to afford Windlesham's guests further privacy at night.

The second bedroom he found was the master, and included a sizeable en suite that resembled that of a five-star hotel. The overall effect was offset by a collection of supermarket brand toiletries that cluttered the shower tray and bath rim. The faucets and wall heater gleamed under the LED spotlights set into the ceiling, and two thick burgundy cotton towels adorned the hooks on the back of the door.

In the bedroom, a television was set amongst a built-in storage system of drawers, hanging space and dressing table. Three different bottles of aftershave were gathered in one corner of this, with a comb and a crumpled return train ticket to Paddington keeping them company.

Crossing to the built-in wardrobe, Mark opened the doors to be confronted by a row of matching suit jackets and trousers, all in dark grey. There was one black suit at the end with a black tie draped around the metal hanger hook. Below the jackets and trousers was a second rail, this time housing a collection of white or pale blue shirts.

The opposite door gave way to more casual attire – T-shirts, polo shirts, shorts and jeans.

There were shoes lined up along the carpeted floor.

And a safe.

'Bingo,' Mark murmured. Crouching on his haunches, he eyed the lock. Rather than a digital combination, it required a key and he rose to his feet once more while he ran his hand around the inside of the wardrobe door frame.

There was nothing there, so he crossed over to the bedside tables and rummaged through the drawers, brushing aside the detritus of a man's life on one side and eyeing the empty second cabinet with a brief glance.

'Where'd you hide it, then?' he muttered. Standing in the middle of the room, he looked up as West appeared at the door. 'Did you come across any keys downstairs?'

She smiled, and held out her hand. A pair of brass keys dangled from her forefinger. 'Like these? I found them amongst the tea bags.'

'Nice one. Let's see if they fit.'

Returning to the safe, he took the keys from her and inserted the first.

It fitted perfectly.

He opened the heavy door and pulled out a bundle of documents from the upper of two shelves. 'Birth certificate, Will, divorce certificate... lasting power of attorney...' He flicked it open. 'Names his sister.'

While he worked his way through the papers, West crouched beside him and shone her phone inside.

'Well, well, well,' she said.

He looked up. 'What've you got?'

She reached in, then twisted to face him, her prize clutched between her gloved fingers. 'Letters about the airfield development – and some of them are threatening him.'

# CHAPTER FOURTEEN

West spun the wheel, expertly slewing the car's tyres over a moss-covered cattle grid and straightening up as they met the uneven track at the fringes of the airfield.

In the far distance, a tumbledown assortment of dark red brick and concrete buildings huddled together as if trying to ward off the impending demolition.

Broken windows gaped out over the long grass covering much of the pothole-riddled taxiways, and there were piles of rotten timber and twisted steel girders and barbed wire littering the expanse.

'You're having way too much fun driving this,' Mark said, glancing up from his phone as the flat landscape shot past the window.

'No such thing,' she retorted. 'Besides, how else am I going to get this thing over seventy unless I'm on an abandoned runway?'

'Fine, but do me a favour and slow down before someone around here reports us to Kennedy – or you hit one of those potholes.'

She sighed, but did as he suggested, a faint smile crossing her lips.

Turning back to his emails, Mark flicked to a new one from the detective inspector. 'Kennedy says he'll get those letters processed by the same lab that's analysing the bullet that Jasper found.'

'Okay, but I think we'll be lucky to find any fingerprints on the letters.' West slowed further as the buildings at the northern end of the abandoned airfield drew closer, and pointed through the windscreen. 'I'm guessing it's those over on the far right that Barry was hoping to get demolished.'

'I don't know if I'd want to buy a house out here. It's pretty desolate, isn't it?'

'And open to the elements.' She corrected her course as a savage gust buffeted the car. 'Do you think the planning permission will still be granted?'

'It depends on what Windlesham put in place to wind up the company in the event of his death I suppose.'

West braked to a standstill beside a dark blue hatchback with worn tyres that was parked next to four corrugated steel containers to the left of the dilapidated buildings. She craned her neck to look up at the old concrete control tower that cast a shadow over the car. 'It'd be a shame to lose all this history.'

'I suppose, although it's not being used for anything. Not like some of the other old World War Two airfields around here. Where's the office?'

'In one of these containers apparently.'

He climbed out, following her around to the other side of the containers, and then narrowed his eyes against the stiff breeze that was channelled between them.

A white sign bearing the logo of Windlesham's company was nailed to the third one along, and a modern-looking set of double-glazed patio doors had been inserted into the side of the container. A reverse-cycle air conditioning unit on the outside was whirring gently, and a warmth enveloped him as he and West stepped inside.

The office layout was busier than Windlesham's home, with a six-seater conference table squashed into the area directly in front of the doors and a small refrigerator on the opposite wall doubling as a kitchen counter. A kettle, coffee jar and a box of teabags jostled for space amongst a motley collection of chipped and tannin-stained ceramic mugs.

'Are you the police?'

He turned to see a middle-aged woman getting up from behind a wooden desk at the other end of the container. She sidled between it and two metal filing cabinets, a flustered expression in her eyes.

'We are.' He held up his warrant card and introduced West. 'And you're…?'

'Belinda Masters.' She went to hold out her hand, then changed her mind, a faint blush crossing her cheeks. 'I'm only here part time so I didn't know about Barry until your lot phoned yesterday, and then I felt really bad because I didn't report him missing or anything and I just assumed he'd gone out to a site that had no signal because that sometimes happens, and…'

She paused, gulping for breath.

'It's okay.' Mark guided her over to one of the chairs at the conference table. 'Take your time.'

'Thanks.' She sat for a moment, staring sightlessly over his left shoulder, then blinked. 'I only started working here last month.'

'Did you know Barry before that?'

'No, the job was advertised through an agency. The hours work out well with when my kids aren't with me. They stay with my ex or his mum otherwise, you see – we have shared custody.'

'Where were you working before?'

'With my ex.' Belinda's features turned from defeated to defiance. 'We ran a legal practice together, so I made him buy me out of that, and the house. I didn't want anything to do with either after he screwed our paralegal last summer. Once the kids got used to the new arrangements, I felt like I needed a change of scenery before I get back into conveyancing work.'

Mark felt the woman's bitterness wash over him, and leaned back, taking a moment to look around the container once more. 'Bit of an unusual arrangement here, isn't it?'

'It works, and Barry reckoned it kept the costs down. I mean, he was only dealing with the contractors that were doing the preliminary project surveys before he was going to start the tendering process. That's what the other three containers are for – the contractors keep their equipment here.'

'Barry was confident that the planning permission is going to go through, then?'

Belinda smiled benevolently. 'He was confident about everything.'

'Any issues around here?'

'Like what?'

'Anything like a break-in, or vandalism?' Mark jerked his chin towards the patio doors. 'I noticed that some of the buildings aren't fenced off or boarded up. Doesn't that cause safety issues?'

'We've had a bit of a run-in with urban explorers, that sort of thing since I've been here, but nothing too bothersome.' The woman frowned. 'Although Barry did say the other week that he thought maybe someone had been hanging around.'

'What made him think that?'

'Most urban explorers don't leave a trace – they don't want us to know they've been, so they can come back or brag about it on social media and encourage others to try the same. Barry used to say that often, the first time he knew they'd been here was seeing the airfield tagged on social media when they uploaded their photographs.' Belinda shivered. 'This was different – he came back from doing one of his regular walks around the place and seemed quite shaken. When I asked him what was wrong, he said he thought someone had been in the old officers' mess building.'

'Did he have any idea who it might've been?'

'No, and then he said... I thought it sounded silly when he mentioned it, but now... He said he thought someone had been watching him from the woods over by the perimeter fence.'

'How long ago was this?'

'About two or three weeks ago.' She chewed her lip for a moment. 'Yes, it was two weeks ago, on the Thursday because I was in an hour late that day after a dentist appointment. He really did seem upset about it.'

'Angry?'

'No, more like he was... scared.'

# CHAPTER FIFTEEN

'Where do you want to start?' Jan shielded her eyes and squinted beyond the parked car to where a small flock of sheep ambled amongst the grass that covered the farthest reaches of the old airfield.

Crows circled in the sky, wheeling and diving between the crumbling landing strip and a cluster of enormous oak trees while a lone sparrow hawk rode the air currents, its graceful flight arcing above the flat landscape.

'Might as well check the fence over by the woodland first,' said Turpin. 'If what Belinda said is right, and Windlesham was convinced someone was here, I'm assuming they wouldn't risk driving through the main entrance like we did, so maybe they accessed the site through there.'

'It looks too high to climb over from here.' She glanced up at the corner of the converted shipping container, then at the red brick buildings either side of it. 'He put CCTV out here too, look.'

'Okay, before we leave we'll ask Belinda for copies of recordings. Hopefully, those cameras work at night too.' He started walking towards the woodland, his long legs setting a quick pace while he peered at his phone. 'Have you got any signal out here? Mine's struggling.'

'A bit.' She inhaled, savouring the fresh breeze that tugged at her hair. Tucking a strand behind her ear, she hurried to catch up with him. 'What do you think Windlesham was involved with, apart from trying to develop this site?'

'I'm not sure. I mean, we have a successful businessman with his own construction company, who seemed to have a good reputation in the industry given the reviews online. The team haven't found anything to suggest anyone was attacking him on social media, and yet there are threatening letters in his home safe, and his comment to the paramedics who took him to A and E suggests his life had been threatened before.' He slowed a little to match her pace. 'Hopefully his sister can shed some light when we speak to her in the morning.'

Jan gave him a gentle shove to the side. 'Mind the sheep shit.'

'Thanks. What about you? Any theories yet?'

'Not yet. He was obviously worried he was being watched, enough that Belinda noticed his change in behaviour.'

'And within the past four to six weeks – she'd only started working for him at the beginning of last month.'

'But who would want him dead? And why? I mean, Belinda didn't mention any threats in the post or anything here, did she?'

'Maybe uniform will turn up something during the house-to-house enquiries with his neighbours.'

'I bloody hope so.' She sighed. 'We've already lost time on this one, given Windlesham survived the initial attempt on his life on Sunday and everyone thought he'd died of natural causes. Until Gillian did the PM, anyway.'

'True.' Turpin paused and jerked his chin towards the diamond-patterned wire fencing that stretched around the airfield. 'And that's a start.'

She looked to where he stared, and blinked.

There was a zigzag-shaped scar sliced top to bottom, about half a metre in length. It had been roughly pushed back together, almost concealing the ragged cut.

'Blimey, that was well spotted, Sarge,' she said.

Turpin moved forward slowly, his eyes sweeping the ground. 'I can't see any footprints, but then it's been dry these past few days and windy out here so I'm guessing they've already faded. Keep an eye out though, just in case.'

'Will do.'

On closer inspection, she could see that the wires had been individually snipped apart, the sharp edges now curling away from the hole that had been cut.

There were still a few centimetres intact at the top and bottom of the fence.

'Whoever did this didn't want the sheep getting out,' she said.

'Makes sense – it would've alerted Windlesham to the break-in.' He walked a few metres to each side, then returned, shaking his head. 'I can't see any other cuts, but if necessary we'll get uniform to walk the perimeter. Let's go back and take a look at that officers' mess.'

She stared at the ground in front of her as they made their way back towards the abandoned buildings, her gaze sweeping the tufts of grass and bare earth in between where the sheep had been grazing.

As Turpin had surmised, there were no footprints to show where the intruder had been, and she reached the business end of the airfield with a growing sense of unease.

'It feels exposed out here, doesn't it?' she said. 'Whoever was watching him took a hell of a risk.'

'Yes, but why?'

She shrugged. 'Where do you want to start?'

'That one over there. I think that's what must've been the officers' mess.'

Moments later, Jan peered through the splintered crack in the thin wooden boarding covering one of the windows of the officers' mess and wrinkled her nose.

A thorny cluster of brambles and nettles at her feet were doing their best to thwart her attempts at protecting her legs with a thin plank of plywood she had found lying beside an overflowing rubbish skip a few metres away.

Wet grass enveloped her shoes, and the damp undergrowth emitted a sour aroma that was neither offensive nor pleasant. There was wild garlic growing somewhere amongst the thriving weeds, its pungency carrying on the breeze towards her every now and then.

Animal droppings were scattered everywhere she looked, and then she spotted a bevy of rabbits a few metres away, their ears twitching while they considered the intrusion to their routine before they bounded out of sight in a flurry of white tails.

Damp patches streaked the crumbling brickwork above the window lintel, its path down the wall shadowed by thickening lush green moss that appeared to be thriving in the shade thrown over the building by a neighbouring corrugated iron aircraft hangar.

'See anything?' Turpin called.

'Nope, too dark,' she said, turning away from the window before cursing under her breath as one of the nettles caught the back of her hand. 'But there's a crack of light coming in from the other side, so there might be a door or something.'

'Okay, let's take a look.'

'Are you sure it's safe?' Angling her neck to stare up at the hangar, she eyed the sheets of corrugated iron bleeding away from the steel frame and shuddered. 'You'd have thought he would have torn this down ages ago. Look at the state of it. That lot could disintegrate at any moment.'

'I'm guessing his hands were tied until the planning permission was granted. Some of these old sites are protected, after all.'

'Even so, surely the local council would be worried about the safety aspect especially if, like Belinda said, there are people breaking in and looking around.'

'More likely they wouldn't do anything until someone got hurt,' said Turpin as he led the way around the side of the building, his long legs swishing through the weeds while he held up his hands to avoid the brambles that snatched at his jacket.

'I'm guessing that Windlesham put up that fencing to protect other people as much as the property.'

The straggly grass turned to broken chunks of concrete hardstanding as they reached the back of the ramshackle remains of the officers' mess, with stubborn dandelions and groundsel reaching up between the cracks.

And there, between two windows with timber criss-crossing the broken panes, was a single doorway.

It too had been boarded up at some point during Windlesham's occupation of the site, but now three of the timber planks had been torn away, leaving a trail of splinters on the ground.

Jan emitted a low whistle as they approached it. 'Someone was determined to get in.'

'Look again,' said Turpin, 'and mind where you're stepping.'

'Glass?'

'No, evidence.'

She frowned, joining him off to the left-hand side of the doorway. 'That someone broke in, you mean?'

'Look.' He pointed at the splintered wood, then at a scrap of dark green cloth that had caught on the jagged edges of the remaining timbers before pulling an evidence bag from his pocket. 'The splinters are on the wrong side of the door if somebody was breaking in.'

'You mean…'

'I think someone was trying to break out.'

# CHAPTER SIXTEEN

Mark clutched a steaming cup of coffee and ran his gaze over the pitted cork board beside the door of Windlesham's unorthodox office.

There were the usual health and safety notices required under employment law, and an A5-sized flyer advertising the proposed development at the airfield, and then beside these were various scribbled notes in a light scrawl across yellow sticky notes. One was a Wi-Fi password, another provided the alarm code sequence to be used when leaving the office, and the rest appeared to be reminders, including phone numbers for various local contractors and a domestic cleaning service.

Moving to the right, shuffling past the compact conference table he assumed was used for occasional meetings, he took in the photographs that had been framed and tacked to the wall. These displayed the history of the site – old black and white images of fighter planes and bombers from the Second World

War, their proud crews posing beside the aircraft with folded arms and huge grins.

Mark bit back a sigh as he wondered how many of the young men had made it through the remaining war years after the photographs were taken, and instead turned to see Belinda Masters watching him keenly over a mug of sweetened tea.

'Do you think Barry was keeping someone here?' she said.

West looked up from her notebook, her eyebrow cocked. 'Do you?'

'I don't know.' Belinda took a sip of tea, then wrinkled her nose. 'This is horrible.'

'You've had a shock,' said Mark. 'The sugar will do you good.'

'If you say so.'

'How did you apply for the job here?' Mark pulled out a chair, lowering himself into it. 'And when?'

'It was through a temp agency in Abingdon, back in early February. I couldn't start until the first week of March because I was sorting out some final bits from the divorce settlement. I was already registered with them, so they phoned me and asked if I was interested before they put it online. I said yes – I just wanted something to keep me going for a few months until I started practising law again, like I said earlier.'

'What was Barry like to work with?'

'All right, I suppose. I liked him. He was no-nonsense, busy all the time. He wasn't just working on this project, you see – he had a couple of other sites that were completed recently that he used to go and check on, just for minor snagging works and things like that.'

'Where were those?'

'There's an old shoe factory out near Farringdon, and a set of six industrial units he refurbished then sold. The shoe factory was redeveloped into terraced houses.'

'We'll need the addresses.'

'Of course.' Belinda rattled off the details to West, then sat back in her chair and stared at her drink. 'This was the one he was most excited about though. He said it was going to fund his retirement.'

'He was going to retire?' said Mark. 'And do what?'

'Play golf. At least, that's what he said whenever I asked.' She shrugged. 'I overheard him saying to someone on the phone that he was looking at a villa somewhere on the Algarve though.'

'When? Recently?'

'Just after I started. I suppose the weather is better for golf there.'

'Did he ever give you cause for concern in relation to your health and safety?'

'No, never. He was really easy-going. Friendly from the start, and...' Belinda exhaled, her shoulders sagging as she looked around the office. 'He just seemed grateful to have someone come in and sort out all the paperwork. This place was a wreck when I started.'

'Do you know anything about his personal life? Was he seeing someone, or...?'

'He was divorced, no kids. His wife had an affair, so he was quite sympathetic to my circumstances. He thought it was great that I was doing this – he kept saying that maybe I should retrain and look at doing construction law instead of conveyancing.'

'Are you?'

She gave a small smile. 'No. Can't really afford the fees to be honest. Not with two kids that have hollow legs, given the way they get through food these days.'

'I can relate to that,' said West.

'So, what's the schedule of works regarding this place?' said Mark. 'I mean, if Barry were still with us and assuming the planning permission is granted.'

Belinda stood up and moved over to her desk, placing the half-finished tea beside her computer keyboard and plucking a lever arch file from a line of six before returning with it.

'It's all in here – this is my copy, so you can have it if you want. I mean, if you need it and you can give me a receipt?'

'Thanks, and yes, we will.'

She nodded, then flicked through the punched pages, eventually turning to an A3-sized document that she carefully unfolded. 'This is the current schedule. I've got it electronically of course, but I like having the real thing to look at – it makes more sense to me.'

Mark took one look at the rows and rows of text and coloured lines sprawling across the page, and frowned. 'Can you talk me through this?'

'Sure. Okay, so each row refers to a stage in the project. Online, each of these stages breaks down into incremental tasks that have to take place but to save space when printing it out, I just use the upper three levels. Then along the top, you've got the dates – again, to save space Barry just used weeks rather than days. The colours relate to each date range per task, so you can see that the whole project runs for about three years to take it from the initial concept drawings through to completion and snagging lists.'

'And there're contractors involved in every stage of the works?'

Belinda nodded. 'Pretty much. Even before he formally applies for the planning permission he'll have had to get surveys and ground probes, things like that carried out to make sure the soil isn't contaminated, that sort of thing. This folder has all the high-level documentation such as copies of heritage site applications, tree preservation orders et cetera. Some of what's in here is in the draft planning application as well.'

'And you say you can give us this copy?'

'Of course. And I'll email it to you as well if it helps.'

'Thanks. How long had the buildings around here been boarded up?'

'I'm not sure. They were like that when I got here last month, and I think Barry might've done that work himself. I can have a look to see if there's an invoice for it, but there's enough timber lying around here that he could've saved himself some money and recycled that.'

'Was he often one for doing jobs like this rather than getting someone else in?'

'That's the impression I got. He spoke fondly of his time as a labourer when he was younger – I think he still enjoyed getting his hands dirty.'

'You mentioned he thought someone was watching him two weeks ago. How often did he check the buildings?'

'Once a week. On different days though, he didn't really stick to a routine. I got the impression it was just when he had time in between site meetings and things.'

'When did he install the CCTV?'

'Last month, about a week after I started. He said it made him feel better that it was in place because I'd often be here on my own for a few hours at a time. I'm supposed to lock the door when I'm here on my own, but I forget.'

'What happens to the recordings?'

Belinda pointed over her shoulder. 'They're backed up to the computer, but he didn't want to pay for the premium service, so they're only saved to a cloud-based server for a week at a time.'

'We're going to need downloads to take with us in that case. Is that something you can do?'

'Of course.'

Mark took the lever arch file from her with a nod of thanks. 'What about visitors, rather than trespassers? Do you get many here?'

'Not really. There was a man from the council who called in about three weeks ago. He and Barry disappeared outside for half an hour or so and then sat where you are now having a coffee. They were talking about the schedule.' Belinda scowled. 'I got the impression he wasn't keen on the redevelopment of the site. He said a lot of history would be lost, and that there were a few people on the planning committee who were concerned about an increase in traffic on the roads around here.'

'Can you remember his name?'

'No, but it'll be on Barry's calendar online, and I've got access to that.' She moved back to her computer, clicking her mouse through the open tabs on her screen. 'Here you go. Felix

Darrow. He's on the parish council, rather than the local government council.'

'What did they talk about?'

'I only heard the first part of the conversation when they were here in the office. After that, they went outside – Barry gave Mr Darrow a hard hat to wear because they were going near some of the older buildings that are going to be demolished.'

'And you definitely didn't hear anything else they spoke about? What about when they came back from the site tour?'

'They didn't come back in here.' Belinda paused, her expression thoughtful. 'I *saw* them talking though, outside the door there. I couldn't hear what they were saying but their voices were carrying through the door.'

'What do you mean?'

'Well, the more I think about it, Mr Darrow seemed quite cross about something. He was pointing at Barry, who looked furious at one point. Then he calmed down and they were all smiles. Mr Darrow left after that.'

'What did Barry say when he came back in here?'

'Nothing. Not even when I asked him if everything was all right.' Belinda shrugged. 'I didn't see Mr Darrow again.'

# CHAPTER SEVENTEEN

Mark rubbed at his temples and climbed from the pool car, his legs stiff and a persistent headache needling his forehead.

West had driven the car back to Abingdon with her usual aplomb while he had worked through a series of phone calls, finishing by coordinating with Jasper Smith. He had pleaded with the CSI lead to send a team over to Barry Windlesham's site despite the caseload swamping the department's staffing levels, a request that was met with an ill-disguised sigh and a promise to do so immediately.

They had left Belinda Masters in the capable hands of a pair of uniformed constables based out of Didcot who were keen to escape the monotony of traffic enforcement duty, and who were now coordinating with the crime scene technicians.

He peered up at the sky, thankful that no rain was forecast for the next three days so the search team could work unencumbered, then rolled his shoulders.

'All right, Sarge?' West said, nodding her thanks as he opened the door into the police station for her, then leading the way up the stairs.

'Yes. Just trying to get my head around what's been going on at Windlesham's place. It's four days since he was shot at, we're two days behind any evidence that might've been available, and we're at a loss for a motive.' He exhaled and followed her into the incident room. 'We're in for a tough few weeks if we're not careful.'

'Mmm. I was thinking much the same,' she replied. 'Maybe the others have had more luck.'

'Hope so.'

Alex looked up from his computer screen when he walked over, his eyes wide. 'Bloody hell, Sarge. Every time you two go somewhere, you give Kennedy a heart attack with what you're doing to his budget figures. How many CSIs did Jasper send over to the airfield?'

'Six, which means we likely won't have any news until tomorrow or Saturday, given the state of the buildings and the size of the site.' Mark squinted against the late afternoon sunlight streaming through the blinds beside the detective constable's desk. 'How the hell can you see your screen?'

'I'm enjoying this.' Alex contemplated his pale freckled skin. 'I think I might've been a gecko in a past life. It's been freezing cold in here all day.'

'Where's Kennedy?'

'In a meeting, upstairs. He said to let you and Jan know not to disappear – he wants to catch up with us and Caroline before we leave because he's off to Kidlington first thing tomorrow.'

'Okay. Want anything from the vending machine?'

'Wouldn't say no to an energy drink, Sarge. Thanks.'

'Jan?'

'Soft drink please. I think I'm made from about eighty per cent tea at the moment.'

Wandering out along the corridor to the small kitchenette that served the upper floors, Mark tried and failed to keep the frown from creasing his brow as his thoughts tumbled over one another while he selected the numbers on the vending machine for the drinks.

'You'll give yourself wrinkles, Sarge.'

He glanced over his shoulder at Caroline's voice. 'Very funny. Want anything from this? I'm getting a round in.'

'Ooh, thanks. One of those chocolate bars will do. I'm hoping to go for a swim when we finish here.'

Mark picked out a bottle of iced tea for the detective inspector then followed her back to the incident room laden with his spoils.

Doling them out, he looked up as Kennedy emerged from his office. 'Ready for us, guv?'

'Yes, let's get on with it.' The DI took the drink with a nod of thanks before wandering over to the whiteboard. 'What's your thinking behind the officers' mess at the airfield then? Jasper said something about someone being held against their will there?'

'That's one theory,' said Mark. 'When we looked at the place, the boards across the back door were smashed outwards, and none of the ones across the windows had been tampered with.'

'Did you go inside?'

'No – called it in straight away.'

'Okay, so we're dependent on the SOCOs for now. Anything else we ought to take a look at regarding Windlesham's site?'

'Jan and I are going to go along to the planning committee hearing tomorrow night. We figured we'd get a feel for how the development proposal is being received locally given the letters we found in his safe, and what might happen now that Windlesham is dead.' He frowned. 'I'm not sure how that will work out with estate planning and business assets.'

'I've got a cousin who's a partner in a firm specialising in estate planning in Newbury, so I'll give him a call this evening to gauge his thoughts,' said Kennedy. 'At least it'll serve to give us an idea of what questions we might need to put to the sister tomorrow.'

'That'd be good, thanks. We're due to meet with her here at nine o'clock.'

'I'll give you a call later then. Moving on – how have you been getting on, Caroline?'

The detective constable swallowed the last of her chocolate bar and scrunched up the wrapper. 'We've been looking at who might've been held there against their will, if somebody was. We went through the local reports of missing persons for the past six months, guv, but there's nobody from that area on the list. There've been no kidnapping threats in the area either.'

'Okay, well pause that for now,' said Kennedy, adding her update to the board. 'Until we hear from Jasper's team about what they find – if anything – in that building, we could be looking at the wrong angle. Good work, though both of you – it's given us a head start.'

'What I don't understand, guv, is that if there was someone

held there, why didn't they come to us after they escaped?' West looked around at her colleagues, her expression baffled. 'I mean, it doesn't make sense does it?'

'Unless they weren't exactly innocent themselves,' said Kennedy. 'We also have to keep in mind that Windlesham himself might've locked someone in there.'

'But Belinda said he sounded scared the day he told her he thought he was being watched.'

'If he'd kidnapped someone, he might've been worried someone was planning a rescue,' said Mark. He turned to Alex. 'Would you mind having a look at private detectives in the area, that sort of thing? We ought to consider that if someone *was* kidnapped, their family might not want the police involved.'

'You mean like a gang-related incident?' said Kennedy, his eyebrows raised.

'Could be.'

'All right. Alex, run with that, and keep me posted.'

'Will do, guv.'

'We could also do with you coordinating with uniform to go through the CCTV files from Belinda Masters' computer,' Kennedy added. 'Those only take us back to last Thursday but we might get lucky.'

'No problem.'

Kennedy started as his mobile phone began to ring and he fished it from his pocket. 'Jasper? What've you got?'

Mark watched as the DI's face turned from interested to worried.

'Right. Thanks for letting me know. Call me if you have anything else to share.' Kennedy ended the call and looked up.

'He's just confirmed that someone was held there against their will. There are bolts in the wall, and the remains of a rope with blood in the fibres. He says it looks like whoever was there used some broken glass to cut through the rope, and then some of the larger bricks in the rubble to get through the door, although that must've taken some doing.'

'If I'd been locked up in that building, I'd have done anything to escape,' said West with a shudder. 'But it doesn't explain *where* they went after they escaped.'

'I'll ask Jasper to extend the search to the perimeter of the buildings and the rest of the airfield, even if that means his team are there all weekend.' Kennedy's thumbs were already at work on his phone. 'Just in case.'

'There's one other explanation,' said Mark, staring at the carpet. 'And it's not good.'

'What's that?'

'That whoever it was didn't make it far after they escaped from the building.' He looked up at his colleagues. 'I mean, just because the fence was cut, it doesn't mean they got away, does it?'

# CHAPTER EIGHTEEN

The next morning, Mark sat at his desk twirling a black biro between his fingers while he stared at the list of questions in his notebook.

Bright sunshine poured through the cracks in the blinds over the incident room windows, not yet strong enough to reach his desk but already warming the room with the promise of better weather over the coming weeks.

The steady purr of traffic moving to and from the industrial estate on the other side of the road carried across to where he sat despite the double glazing, while the printer whirred to life at the opposite end of the room before spitting out a steady stream of paperwork.

There was a remnant fatty smell reminiscent of the bacon sandwich that had barely lasted five mouthfuls coming from the abandoned aluminium foil scrunched up beside his computer keyboard, the grease still warm on his lips.

Ewan Kennedy had phoned him at half past eight the previous evening, the DI's cousin providing additional thoughts on the investigation in confidence, and giving his view on the implications that could arise from business assets outside of Barry Windlesham's estate planning.

The words before Mark's eyes blurred, and he rubbed his hands down his face before blinking as a takeout cup of coffee appeared at his elbow.

'Morning, Sarge,' said West. 'Tell me you weren't here all night.'

He grinned. 'More than my life's worth. As it is, Lucy's reminded me I ought to invite you and the family over for lunch soon. And Hamish was sulking by the time I got home yesterday too.'

'Aw, poor thing.'

'Don't worry. He soon cheered up after a four-mile walk. Then he spent the rest of the evening farting and snoring while we were trying to watch the telly.'

West laughed. 'Charming.'

'Good job he's cute.' Mark waited until she'd switched on her computer before passing across his notebook. 'Got anything to add to those? We've got a few minutes until Gaynor Alton and her husband get here. Kennedy's cousin provided some general background information late yesterday that might help us, so I've added some questions in relation to that.'

He sipped at the hot drink, wincing as it burned his tongue while his colleague shrugged off her coat.

Sinking into her chair at the opposite desk to his, she flipped the pages of her notebook back and forth, then gave a satisfied nod.

'I think you've covered it all, Sarge. How do you want to manage the interview?'

He placed the notebook by his computer keyboard and stared at it for a moment. 'I'd like to lead it, but as usual speak up if you hear something that we ought to delve into a bit more. I don't think we mention what we've found in the officers' mess building, not unless the conversation goes in that direction, anyway. I'd like to get a feel for whether she was of the opinion that her brother was worried about something, and what his general personality was like. From there, we can weave in some of these questions and see where we go.'

'Sounds good.' She glanced past him towards the incident room door as he heard its familiar creaky hinges, and raised an eyebrow. 'I take it that Gaynor and Oliver Alton are here?'

'They are.'

Mark turned to see Peter Cosley, the uniformed sergeant's bulk well suited for the custody suite, but perhaps somewhat intimidating for the public-facing reception desk. 'What's your first impression of them?'

'They look shattered,' came the reply. 'They arrived late last night from Wales, and apparently the traffic along the M4 by Chippenham was horrendous. Never mind that her brother's, well…'

'Where've you put them?' said Jan, before draining her coffee and dropping the empty cup into a waste bin by her desk. 'Somewhere comfortable, I hope.'

'Interview room four, the one we usually keep for juveniles.'

'Perfect, thanks Peter. We'll be right down.' Mark gathered up his notebook, two pens and adjusted his tie with a grimace. 'Let's hope Barry Windlesham's sister can shed some light on what the hell he's been up to since she last saw him.'

———

Peter Cosley had been right when he said the Altons looked tired after the previous day's journey to Oxfordshire.

Gaynor Alton's features were gaunt while she sat beside her rotund husband, his eyes troubled when he looked up as Mark entered the interview room and made the introductions.

'I understand this is a very difficult time for you, and my condolences for your loss, Mrs Alton,' he began, clasping his hands together while West set up the recording equipment at the end of the metal table. 'I take it from my colleague that you had a trying time getting here from Wales yesterday as well.'

'We did, and please – call me Gaynor.' Windlesham's sister gestured to her husband. 'Oliver and I are keen to do all we can to help you understand what happened to my brother – and find out who killed him.'

'Thank you. We'd like to record this interview if that's okay? We'll read out your rights in relation to this, but I'd like to have a chance to listen to it again and it'll serve to help me clarify anything afterwards.'

'That's okay, yes.'

Mark gestured to West to start the recording and waited while she recited the formalities, then opened the manila folder she handed to him and placed it alongside his notebook. 'Can you tell me a bit about your relationship with your brother to get us started, Gaynor?'

The woman sighed, then settled back into the plastic-backed chair and stared at a grease spot midway across the table. 'We were close when we were kids, but we drifted apart by the time I went to university. Barry's – was – two years older than me and was already earning good money as a labourer so we had less and less in common.'

'What did you study?'

'English literature. I ended up travelling for a couple of years after graduating, teaching English in different communities while I backpacked.' She managed a small smile. 'I loved it.'

'What do you do now?'

'I'm an administrator for a local private school.' Gaynor straightened. 'It's quite a prestigious place, very exclusive.'

'And, Oliver, may I ask what it is you do?'

The man leaned forward, mimicking Mark's pose, and squared his shoulders. 'I'm an orthodontist, based in Cardiff.'

'Did you get on with Barry?'

'He was a good bloke, yes.' Oliver nodded, his brown eyes downcast. 'We didn't see him as often as we'd like, but we enjoyed his company when we did. I blame my work for that. I just don't get the opportunity to take as much time away from it all as I'd like.'

'Oliver's very much in demand,' added Gaynor. She reached out for her husband's hand and gave it a squeeze. 'And he's been an absolute rock this week.'

'You've mentioned to our colleague when she phoned you

earlier this week that you last saw your brother in February,' said Mark. 'Did he seem worried about anything?'

'Not that I recall.' Gaynor sniffed, then reached out for a paper tissue from a box beside the recording equipment. 'I wish now that I'd taken more notice, but as I said on the phone, it was only a quick visit. He was on his way back from another site he was eyeing up, and the weather forecast wasn't great. He stayed overnight, and then the next day we had lunch at ours at around one o'clock. He was gone by three so he could reach the motorway before it got dark.'

'It can get quite treacherous where we live,' Oliver added. 'And the Highways Agency doesn't always grit the roads.'

'What was his mood like when you saw him?' said Mark.

'He seemed... normal.' Gaynor frowned. 'Maybe a bit preoccupied, but I put that down to him having to travel so much over that week.'

'He did keep checking his phone,' said Oliver. 'But again, I figured that was just because he was juggling all sorts of business stuff. He didn't seem to be overly concerned by whatever was on his messages, that's for sure. He was laughing and joking with us as usual over lunch.'

'You got on well with him?'

'Yes, he was like a brother to me.' Oliver swallowed. 'I don't know what we're going to do without him.'

Mark pulled a photograph from the manila folder, and passed it across. 'We found these letters in the safe in the main bedroom. Did he mention that he was being threatened?'

A gasp escaped from Gaynor, and her husband paled.

'Why would someone send him those?' she managed.

'At the moment, we're viewing these as being related to his death,' said Mark. 'Are you certain he never mentioned any concerns to you about the project or anything else in his life?'

'No…' She looked at her husband, who wore an equally baffled expression, before turning back to Mark. 'I've got no idea what's been going on, detective. And now I'm wondering if I really knew my brother at all.'

# CHAPTER NINETEEN

Mark stepped back from the kerb as a grubby white delivery van skirted the corner a little too close for comfort, and glared at the dirt-smeared rear doors as the driver hared away.

There was a freshness to the air while he walked along Ock Street, and he turned up the collar of his coat, his pace fuelled by the rumbling coming from his stomach and the paper bag in his hand that contained fresh sandwiches from one of the town's busiest cafés.

A strong whiff of foul water assaulted his senses then, and he peered farther along the road to where a pair of utilities company-owned trucks were parked on the opposite side. A work crew was setting up traffic cones and a temporary traffic light system, and he bit back an inward groan at the thought of the additional congestion it would cause.

Making a mental note to tell the team to take a diversion

from the police station for the next few days, he glanced at his watch before picking up his pace.

There were so many reports to file, so many leads to follow up from the house-to-house enquiries and CCTV that even West hadn't had time to organise sustenance.

They had arranged with Gaynor and Oliver Alton to keep them updated regarding the investigation, and in return Windlesham's sister had promised to let them know if she recalled anything from her conversations with her brother that might help explain who was threatening him.

Upon seeing the couple out to their car, he had offered to walk into town and buy West a decent lunch rather than resort to the fast-food restaurant across the road, and the look of relief in her eyes reminded him that she was juggling a busy home life on top of her expanding caseload.

He was fifty metres from the police station's front door when his phone began to ring, and he frowned at the unfamiliar number on the screen before answering.

'Detective Sergeant Mark Turpin.'

'Detective? It's Hilary Cottishall, at the hospital. We spoke the other day about a bag of clothing that had gone missing.'

'Have you found it?' Mark hurried into the station's reception area, then aimed a grateful look at Peter Cosley who stepped out from behind the desk and held open the inner security door for him. 'Where was it?'

'It's a little more complicated than that, I'm afraid.' The woman sighed. 'It appears that it's been stolen.'

'Stolen?' Mark elbowed his way through the incident room

door and walked over to West's desk, placing the paper bag in front of her. 'By whom?'

'We don't know. But we've got him on camera.'

Mark eyed the bag of sandwiches as West delved in and retrieved a thick cheese and pickle one. 'I thought you didn't have CCTV on the wards?'

'We don't. There was an altercation in the A and E department on Sunday night. All of our security guards there wear body cameras, as do any staff working in that area while they're on shift. The cameras are kept off unless there's an incident, and if something does warrant their use, the person causing the trouble is warned that they're being filmed, you see.'

'So you're saying the person who stole the clothes started a fight?'

'No, not at all – the man who did was arrested afterwards. No, the man who stole the bag appears in the background of the video. I'm looking at the recording now, and he's definitely carrying something resembling what you've told me is a dry bag.'

'What time was this?'

'The recording was taken at nine oh six. He appears in it at nine oh seven.'

'Can you email us a copy of that recording?'

'I can, yes.'

'Thank you, Ms Cottishall. That's really useful.'

'Wait, detective – there's something else.'

'What is it?'

'I've shown the recording to Selina Gunnerston – you might

recall that Emily Crake and she were on shift on Mr Windlesham's ward on Sunday night. I thought maybe he was a relative, you see, which would explain him taking the bag of clothes.'

'Right…'

'Well, Selina says the man in the background of this video is the same one who tried to visit Mr Windlesham that evening, but that when she offered to take his details and let him have an update about our patient's condition, he seemed angry about the whole situation and hurried away.'

'And Selena's sure it's the same man?'

There was a pause, then a muted conversation at the other end before she returned to the phone. 'She's here right now, looking at the screen with me, and says yes, it's definitely him.'

Mark eyed the bag of food, heard his stomach rumble loudly, then reached out and swept the car keys from the desk beside West's empty coffee mug.

'Don't worry about emailing the recording, Ms Cottishall. I'm on my way there now.'

# CHAPTER TWENTY

West zigzagged the pool car past the temporary traffic lights and muttered at the workmen lazing beside a utilities van staring at their phone screens before she accelerated past them.

A light drizzle sprinkled the windscreen, the wiper blades squeaking against its surface with a vengeance despite her repeated attempts to stop them doing so with ample applications of screen wash.

'There'd better be a bloody parking space,' she muttered.

Mark sat in the passenger seat with his phone to his ear, shovelling the remains of his sandwich into his mouth in between updating Kennedy.

'Thanks, guv,' he finished, then looked up as they joined a stream of traffic heading for the A34. 'He's stuck in meetings all day but says he'll ask Alex and Caroline to chase up the hospital to obtain copies of the ANPR images for the car park while we're interviewing Selina and getting the body camera footage.'

'Good idea – as long as our suspect drove to the hospital,' she said.

'Glass half full, Jan. Glass half full.'

'I know.'

He checked his watch. 'Selena finished her shift half an hour ago, but she's agreed to wait with Hilary until we get there so we can take a look at that recording together. Apparently she's rostered off until Tuesday.'

'Good of her to wait, then.' She shifted gears, overtaking an oversized articulated truck before stomping on the accelerator and zipping past a rusting classic sports car.

When she checked her mirrors, he saw her break into a satisfied smile as the vehicles faded into the distance, and chuckled.

'You realise we have to give this back on Monday?'

'Glass half full, Sarge…'

———

Hilary Cottishall and Selina Gunnerston were waiting for them in the legal administrator's office when Mark and West walked in.

Hilary rose from her desk and waved them inside before closing the door with a firm shove.

The nurse was younger than Emily Crake, and seemed none the worse for wear after a long shift. She had changed out of her uniform and into running shoes, sweatshirt and leggings and seemed keen to help, her gaze watchful.

Hilary made the introductions, then handed a USB stick to Mark. 'That's a copy of the recording from James Alperren's camera. He was the security guard who intercepted the man who caused the disturbance on Sunday night.'

'Do you know who his attacker was?' He pocketed the USB stick before pulling out one of the visitor's chairs for West and then leaned against one of the filing cabinets lining the office.

'No, sorry – after James had a word with him, the man left without us having to call the police.'

'No problem. Any idea what caused the altercation?'

'James told us that the man was asking one of the triage nurses about someone who had been taken into A and E that day, but was very vague and wouldn't provide a name. He simply kept saying "my brother". He started raising his voice at the nurse, so James intervened and steered the man away from the triage teams and out to the main corridor.' Hilary sighed. 'And then the man apparently decided to shove James and became quite aggressive in nature, threatening to go back into the triage area and find his brother, and then he pushed over a cart of equipment. At that point, James managed to overpower him and frogmarched him to the exit. The man didn't come back, so he didn't feel it was necessary to bother the police. I'm satisfied that James did all he could in the circumstances to contain the incident as well.'

Mark waggled the USB stick at her. 'And you say that while all this was going on, someone removed the dry bag from the sluice room?'

'Yes, that's right. I wasn't sure at first – I had to look up what a dry bag looked like, to be honest, after you were last here – but when I happened to notice it, I called Selena down here to take a look.'

'It's definitely the same bloke who came to the ward on Sunday night,' said the nurse. 'I recognised him straight away, because of the scar on his face.'

'And he didn't leave any details with you that night?'

'None at all. He just sort of made his excuses, said he'd be back the next morning, and left.'

'Did he get inside the ward area or near Barry Windlesham's bed at any point?'

'No. Definitely not.'

'Can I take a look at this now?'

'Of course. I've still got the file on my computer.' Hilary angled the screen to face them, and clicked a few times before a media file opened, and hit the "play" button. 'The recording starts as soon as James noticed what was going on – I've also put the triage nurse's body camera recording onto that USB stick for you, although I couldn't see your man with the bag in that. I just thought you might want it for completeness.'

'Thanks.' Mark held his breath as the recording began while beside him, West shifted forward in her seat.

The recording was of good quality, clear and with sound as well, and although he marvelled at the technology and the breakthrough it might provide, a rising anger touched his chest at the indignity of hospital staff having to wear the body cameras at all.

As Hilary had indicated, the man who had started the altercation was soon seen via the security guard's camera berating one of the nurses, his posture aggressive as he pointed at her several times, his face all too close to hers.

The camera moved closer as the security guard intervened, his calm voice doing little to pacify the man.

Over the man's shoulder, Mark could see one or two younger medical staff looking askance at the proceedings as they passed, and a pair of paramedics wheeling an empty stretcher who gave the scene a wide berth.

And then, off to the left of the security guard, another man appeared, his back to the camera while he walked calmly towards a closed door off to the far side of where the argument was taking place.

Mark realised he was clenching his jaw and forced himself to relax as he watched.

'Come on, turn around,' West murmured beside him. 'Let's see your face.'

Instead, the man glanced to his right as if to check if anyone was watching from that angle, then pushed the door open and disappeared.

He emerged a few seconds later, clutching a bright orange bag, his face lowered while he peered inside.

And then he looked across to where the security guard was now guiding his aggressor towards the main corridor, and in that moment Mark saw his face for the first time.

'And you're sure this is the same man that tried to get to Barry while he was on your ward?' he said, turning to the nurse while she stared at the screen.

'It's definitely him,' said Selina. She shivered. 'I'll never forget it now. His eyes were cold, like there was no feeling there, no emotion, which I thought was strange given he said Mr

Windlesham was a relative. He didn't look concerned about him at all.'

---

It was raining by the time Mark and West left the administration block of the hospital complex, and he cursed under his breath as he pushed through the exit door.

A shallow portico provided a modicum of protection and West huddled into her jacket as a nip to the air wrapped its way around the building.

'Might as well wait here for five minutes and see if this blows over,' said Mark, scrunching up his face as he eyed the blustery cloud cover. 'No sense in getting soaking wet before we have to drive over to that planning meeting.'

West checked her watch. 'It starts at four, right?'

'It'll be half past by the time they've gone through the preliminaries but I wouldn't mind getting there before it starts if we can so we can watch as people turn up.'

'Makes sense.' She tapped her toe against the concrete paving slabs. 'So, we've got a face but no name for whoever stole Barry's clothing. Do you think he went up to the ward first to see if he could find the bag there, or do you think he would've harmed him if he got onto the ward?'

'I don't know. But if it was the same person who tried to shoot him, then I think we've got to assume he wasn't there to wish him a speedy recovery.'

'It takes some brass to do that, Sarge. How on earth did he think he was going to get away with it?'

'More to the point, what was it about Barry Windlesham that someone wanted him dead so badly?'

'And his clothes were—' West spun to face Mark. 'Hang on. We were after the clothing to see if there was any evidence left on them to show that he was shot at prior to falling into the river. Why would whoever shoot him want to do the same?'

'Clearing up after the event.'

'Seems extreme – and like we've said, risky.' She jerked her thumb over her shoulder. 'All that bother, using diversionary tactics to get into the sluice room...'

'So, what are you thinking happened in there?'

'What if there was something in Barry's pockets that they were after, rather than the clothing itself?'

Mark blinked, then stepped out from the sheltered exit doors and started walking towards the car park.

West hurried after him and watched as he paused and used the toe of his shoe to prise apart the leaves on the evergreen shrubs surrounding the parking bays. 'What are you doing? I thought we were letting this rain ease off first?'

'You reckon he was after something *in* the clothing, yes?'

'Right.'

'So, I'm thinking that maybe the dry bag wasn't a priority for him.'

'Oh. Gotcha.' She glanced over her shoulder for oncoming traffic. 'Okay, you take this side, I'll take that one.'

It didn't take long. Two hundred metres from the hospital's front doors, Mark spotted a flash of colour out of the corner of his eye and called out to West.

While she waited for the traffic entering and exiting the car park to clear, he pulled on a pair of protective gloves from his pocket before stepping between two manicured rowans and thrusting his hand into an oleander bush.

He emerged with a grin on his face, holding aloft a bright orange waterproof bag, its surface scuffed and dirt-streaked.

'Bingo,' he said as she joined him, tugging a fresh evidence bag from her handbag. Sealing it, he jerked his chin towards the car. 'If we're quick, we can get that back to the station before the planning meeting.'

She already had the keys in her hand, smiling. 'Was that a challenge, Sarge?'

# CHAPTER TWENTY-ONE

Jan pulled on her suit jacket, flicked her hair over the collar and pocketed the car keys before hurrying across the narrow street to join Turpin.

There was a small convenience shop opposite where she had parked, one belonging to a well-known franchise chain, and its familiar logo was joined by that of the post office across its fascia board. A mixture of terraced and detached houses jostled for space along the stretch of road, their front doors separated from the pavement by low steps, their stonework uneven and worn from centuries of use.

In the middle of the village the main stretch of road gave way to various independent businesses that had been shoehorned into repurposed terraced cottages. A veterinary practice was next door to a thriving second-hand clothing shop, and across the street there was a small gift shop that rubbed shoulders with a beauty clinic offering waxing, manicures and other services.

Next to a bus shelter was an abandoned red telephone box that had been requisitioned for a sponsored defibrillator, the familiar green health and safety signage at odds with the old telephone handset that remained inside.

The kerbs were lined nose-to-tail with vehicles of varying sizes, makes and models and as the two detectives walked along the pavement, a steady procession of cars crawled down the village street while people found places to park.

Ravenswood village hall was tucked away along a potholed stone track that had been cut between a pretty pub with ivy-strewn walls and a thatched roof and a terrace of four stone cottages with postage stamp-sized gardens beyond a shared low flint wall.

There was a car park outside the Victorian meeting place, however Jan noted that there were no spaces available.

The publican was evidently an enterprising sort however, and had taped off his own car park and placed a sandwich board sign beside it, advertising free parking for anyone who booked a table for dinner that evening.

Jan smiled at the sight of a well-dressed couple who emerged from the pub, grumbling at the audacious tactic while hurrying to catch up with the steady line of people waiting to enter the village hall.

'Busy turnout,' she said.

'I'd imagine news of Windlesham's death has spread so I'm wondering how many of these are actually interested in the planning application process or are just here to be nosy.' Turpin jerked his chin towards a large pine tree overhanging the gravel forecourt of the hall. 'Let's stand over there until everyone's in. I wouldn't mind seeing who turns up.'

They wandered over, Jan kicking shrivelled pine cones as she went.

It reminded her of walks in Bagley Woods outside Oxford with Scott and the twins, and she realised with a start that they hadn't been there yet this year. She smiled, making a mental note to suggest it the moment this case was closed so that the boys could run amok amongst the ancient trees and busy themselves making dams over the streams that criss-crossed the walking trails.

Turning back to face the village hall, she watched while another couple – a man and his female companion in their late sixties – joined the back of the queue and greeted some of the others already in line.

'Mostly locals by the look of it,' she said.

'So far.' Turpin pulled out his phone and sidled closer so she could see the screen, then swiped through the website pages he had saved. 'This is the announcement on the parish council site for tonight's meeting. Then these are the three councillors who are on the committee. Felix Darrow – the bloke Windlesham's secretary said met with him the other week – is this bloke here.'

Jan took in the broad shoulders and low brow of the man in the photo. 'What does he do for a living?'

'It says in his biography that he runs an aggregates business the other side of Wallingford. I took a look at its website on the way here, and it's a family-run corporation – his father founded the company, and Felix took over when he retired fifteen years ago.'

'What did he do before that?'

'Business consulting, according to the professional social media pages I found.'

Jan glanced up as a newcomer arrived, this time a man on his own who wore a jacket over jeans and carried a briefcase as he hurried past. 'I wonder who that is.'

'We'll soon find out. Look, they've started letting people in.'

They waited until the queue had disappeared inside, then entered the building through a pair of heavy oak doors that had been pegged open.

Jan walked into an airy reception area with a vaulted ceiling exposing centuries-old timber beams and a wide staircase off to her right. Beyond that, she could see an open door leading into a kitchen with modern stainless steel countertops.

To her left were signs to the toilets, and another open door to what appeared to be an anteroom used for little more than storage. A jumble of stacked plastic chairs, foldable tables and boxes of overflowing Christmas decorations were scattered across the available floor space.

She turned her attention to the second set of oak double doors that led into the main hall, through which a hubbub of voices carried.

Turpin led the way and found two chairs in the back row that afforded them a view of the raised stage area.

It had long velvet curtains pulled back on each side, and in the middle was a long trestle table covered with a navy cotton cloth that obscured the delegates' legs.

A panel of six people sat behind it, and she saw Felix Darrow on the far left-hand side conversing with a woman who wore a pinched expression and watched the crowd as she listened.

In the middle were two men in business suits, and Jan squinted at the name plates in front of them, soon identifying them as two more councillors.

Another man and a woman took up the right-hand side of the table and studiously ignored each other, the woman busying herself with whatever documentation she had in front of her, a pen working furiously across the pages.

Eventually, after a further five minutes had passed, Felix Darrow bent his head to the small microphone on the table in front of him, nodded to a woman to the left of the stage who monitored a sound system, then winced at a burst of high-pitched feedback.

He recovered himself, cleared his throat and then addressed the crowd.

'Ladies and gentlemen, we're here today to discuss the impending planning proposal for the Ravenswood airfield, namely that of a partial restoration and new buildings development proposed by Mr Barry Windlesham. We've been asked to address the concerns raised by several interested parties prior to any formal application being made.' Darrow cast his gaze around the room as he spoke. 'Due to unfortunate circumstances, however, the committee are under an obligation to consider whether any application should proceed, given the recent death of Mr Windlesham.'

Silence followed his words, and Jan glanced along the row of chairs to see a line of rapt faces all watching the councillor.

'Therefore,' he continued, 'we are minded to delay

proceedings until such time as we can ascertain the legality of a future planning application, and—'

'Excuse me.'

A hand shot up halfway along the back row, and Jan leaned forward to see the suited man with the briefcase she and Turpin had spotted outside moments earlier.

He rose from his seat and buttoned his jacket. 'There won't be any need to delay proceedings.'

'I'm sorry…' Darrow looked around at his colleagues, then back to the man. 'I don't understand.'

'I'm the legal representative for Mrs Gaynor Alton, Mr Windlesham's sister. Mrs Alton wishes to proceed with the planning process as soon as possible. We'll be filing an amendment to the official paperwork first thing on Monday morning, but she wanted her wishes minuted at this meeting.'

'I… I don't see how that's possible,' said Darrow. 'Mr Windlesham was the sole director of the business.'

'Incorrect. The paperwork to add Mrs Alton as a director to the business was lodged with Companies House late last Friday. In addition, she is the legal executor for Mr Windlesham's estate,' said the man. 'Including for the business and all its chattels.'

'I'm sorry, sir, but you are…?'

'Mrs Alton's solicitor. I'm acting on her behalf in this matter with the full support of Mr Windlesham's appointed legal representative.'

'Well, I…' Darrow covered his microphone with his hand and leaned back to confer with the woman over to his left.

'We should've brought a lip reader,' Turpin muttered.

'I didn't see this coming, did you?' Jan whispered. She watched as the two panellists gesticulated furiously at each other, then glanced at her colleague. 'And Mrs A didn't say anything when we spoke to her either.'

'Makes you wonder why she decided to go ahead. I'd have thought she'd have enough on her hands at the moment.'

They turned back to the stage as Darrow cleared his throat again.

'Ladies and gentlemen, in light of this recent news, this pre-approval hearing is adjourned. We'll announce a new date when all matters are concluded and we're able to proceed.'

With that, the audience erupted.

Several attendees hurried to the door, mobile phones to their ears while they recounted events.

'Reporters,' said Turpin. 'This'll be all over the local news sites within the hour.'

'Less, if you include their social media. Do you want me to nip out and catch Gaynor's solicitor before he disappears after the meeting?' said Jan, already putting her notebook back in her bag.

'Go for it. I'll have a word with Darrow as soon as he wraps up here. Meet you back at the car.'

# CHAPTER TWENTY-TWO

Mark worked his way through a crowd that was hellbent on reaching the front doors of the village hall as quickly as possible.

Turning sideways to cut through the flow of bodies, he held his breath as he passed a man in his thirties with a sour body odour, and then a woman with an overpowering perfume.

Wiping sweat from his brow and ruing the suit jacket he wore, he shuffled ahead, determined to reach Felix Darrow before the councillor was distracted further.

The surrounding conversations reached a crescendo as he moved closer to the stage, the crowd's voices laced with indignation and confusion.

He sidestepped a woman who was furiously texting on her phone while talking to her companion, another woman who seemed only half-interested in what she was saying and was busy swiping her own phone screen instead.

Wincing as a wide man in his seventies trod on his toe, Mark watched as the planning committee members stood to one side of the stage. Darrow was trying to pacify one of the other men who had turned beetroot red at the interruption from Gaynor's solicitor.

'I'm sorry, but the rules are quite clear. I'm unable to reconvene the meeting until such time as the legalities can be explored and explained.'

'That's ridiculous,' the man retorted, sending spittle flying. 'As chairman, you have the right to overthrow the rules, don't you?'

'No, I don't, sorry. And that's the end of it.' Felix fidgeted with his shirt sleeves, tugging at imaginary cuff links, all the while wearing a benign expression until one of the female panel members started to berate him in a high-pitched voice that cut across the crowd.

'In my mind, this meeting should have been cancelled,' she squeaked. 'It was apparent forty-eight hours ago that Mr Windlesham's affairs would be tied up in probate, and yet here we are. A complete waste of time.'

'On the contrary, Charmaine,' intoned another man off to Darrow's right while he surveyed the crowd with a keen eye. 'It's allowed us to gauge interest in the project – a project, I'll hasten to add, that some of us within the community were keen to see to fruition, given how long that site's been abandoned.'

'Abandoned?' The woman's face turned puce. 'I'll have you know that at least three wildlife groups have raised objections about the proposed development, two of which have national support from many substantial donors.'

'And are any of those donors supporting your re-election campaign?' the man sneered.

Darrow held up his hands. 'Please, both of you, keep your voices down. This committee is supposed to present a voice of reason to the general public, and yet here we are squabbling like a group of kindergarten children.'

'Speak for yourself.' Charmaine huffed, before turning her back and crossing to where the other female committee member stood beside the stage curtain.

Darrow and the man turned their backs to them, lowering their heads as their voices reduced to low murmurs.

'Excuse me, Mr Darrow?' Mark palmed his warrant card, hoping no one in the departing audience would see it. 'May I have a word?'

Felix Darrow frowned. 'Police?'

'We're investigating the death of Barry Windlesham.'

The man's eyebrows shot upwards. 'He drowned, didn't he?'

'Like I said, if I could have a word?'

'Very well.' Darrow turned to the man beside him. 'Damien, would you mind giving me a minute?'

'Of course not.' The man gave Mark a look that implied the opposite, then clasped his hands behind his back and walked down the steps from the stage, joining a group of eight people who lingered.

'Right,' said Felix. 'How can I help?'

'You met with Barry Windlesham three weeks ago. Why was that?'

'I was concerned about some of the historical buildings on the site, and whether Mr Windlesham's planning application would treat them with the respect they deserve.' Darrow jutted out his chin. 'The airfield was key to this country's strategic defences during the Second World War, you see.'

'And do you have a particular interest in that time?'

'My grandfather was posted at Ravenswood as a mechanic from 1941. He was too sick to fly, but contributed a great deal to the aircraft and crew based here.'

Mark updated his notes, then glanced over his shoulder at a bark of laughter from the doors into the hall to see a broad man shaking hands with Charmaine, who visibly preened under his attention. He turned back to Felix to see him eyeing the pair with hawklike interest. 'It was my understanding that the preservation of the buildings was integral to the plans for the airfield.'

'Not the control tower, or the hangars.'

'Was that going to be the only reason for your objection to the planning application at this meeting, or…?'

'I haven't objected to the plans – the site needs renovating. It's dangerous. I simply wanted assurances from Barry that he'd try to maintain some of the historical aspects of it for future generations, or at least consider building a small memorial. And this wasn't a planning approval meeting,' said Felix. 'We haven't reached that stage yet, thank goodness. This meeting was convened as part of the *pre*-planning application process.'

'What's that?'

'Before Mr Windlesham could proceed with his application, we advised him to work with us to ensure all parties involved were in agreement with how the old airfield was going to be developed. The pre-application process takes into consideration the viewpoint of local residents, council plans and the like so the application can be better presented to committee. That way, he'd have stood a better chance of it being approved.'

Mark frowned. 'I don't understand, Mr Darrow. Why would he buy a site when he doesn't even know if he'll be allowed to build on it?'

'I presume because he felt he would get the final approval.' The councillor lowered his voice. 'The site's been derelict for nearly a decade – developing brownfield sites isn't for everyone. There are a lot of risks involved with older buildings.'

'Such as?'

'Listen, this is all rather a delicate matter, detective,' he said, his gaze furtive as he looked around at the milling crowd. 'And there are too many ears here. Perhaps we could talk at my house tomorrow?'

'Understood, Mr Darrow.' Mark jotted down the man's address. 'Nine o'clock suit you?'

# CHAPTER TWENTY-THREE

Mark listened to the car engine ticking over and gazed through the windscreen at the lush green meadow that lay beyond a metal five-bar gate.

A gold and pink glow clung to the horizon, and a thin sliver of crescent-shaped moon lounged above the Thames.

The car held an aroma of stale coffee, with two empty takeout cups shoved into the central console and remnant condensation on the inside of the window near his elbow.

He beat his fist gently against the glass while he stared, frustration nibbling at his nerves.

'So he wouldn't tell you anything else?' said West.

'Not there and then, no. I mean, he seemed keen for the site to be redeveloped in some form or another.'

'Might just be hung up on the historical aspect because of his grandfather then, like he said.'

'Surely they can't keep all the buildings though, whoever

redevelops it. You said yourself how dangerous that hangar looked.'

'True.'

He turned to her. 'What did Gaynor's solicitor have to say for himself?'

West's mouth quirked. 'Very little to start with. He was a bit cagey at first, until I pointed out to him we were trying to find out who murdered his client's brother, and until such time as we apprehend someone, it's unlikely anyone's going to approve a project.'

'Why'd she agree to take it on?'

'According to Mr Swift – the solicitor – she didn't have a choice. Barry left her the site in his Will. Swift said they only decided to announce her involvement tonight because they were worried she'd be left with a worthless piece of land otherwise. I mean, if it can't be redeveloped, she can't sell it, right?'

'So she wouldn't manage the project herself?'

West shook her head. 'Nope. Can't wait to get rid of it, apparently. She's got absolutely no interest in running that business.'

'Then why would she agree to become a director of it?'

'I asked him that, and that's when he got uncomfortable. It transpires that Gaynor hasn't told him why, just that Barry asked her and she said yes, and the paperwork was submitted to Companies House late last Friday.'

Mark stopped beating his fist against the window. 'It was two weeks ago that Belinda reckoned Windlesham thought he was being watched on site, wasn't it?'

'It was.'

'Makes you wonder if bringing Gaynor on board was a way to insure the business against anything happening to him.'

'Kennedy's next briefing is going to be tomorrow afternoon – maybe by then, Alex and Caroline might've found something via Barry's emails to help us.'

'Hopefully the forensics lot have managed to crack open that mobile phone they found too.'

'Well, if all else fails, we could always just ask Gaynor what her intentions are. Swift said she and her husband are staying at Barry's house while they're here, rather than forking out for a hotel. We're flat out tomorrow, but I could give her a call and see if she's around on Sunday.'

'Good idea.' He sighed, opening the door. 'Thanks for the lift. See you about eight tomorrow?'

'Sounds good. I'll drop off the boys and Scott to football practice round the corner and pick you up after that.'

'Great, thanks.'

As she eased the car away, he crossed to the gate then paused and rested his arms on it, inhaling the fresh air.

Across the meadow, a line of narrowboats and widebeams were strung along the riverbank, one or two bearing the markings of a local hire company, and the others a mixture of continuous cruisers and long-stay berths.

Mark's shoulders relaxed as he took in the vessel three quarters of the way along the line, eyeing the fine lines and subtle paintwork, before spotting the small black dog that was standing on the roof.

An excited bark carried across to where he stood, and he

grinned before setting off along a path that hugged the back of a row of cottages before joining the tow path.

The dog leapt from the roof to the deck and then over the gunwale before tearing through the grass to meet him, tongue lolling and tail wagging.

'Hey boy, good boy Hamish.' Mark bent over to scratch the dog between its ears. 'Come on then, home boy. Let's go. Shall we have a barbecue tonight?'

Hamish snuffled around the grass at his feet for a bit, then looked up at the cooking reference and emitted a whine.

'Yes, you can have some. Only a bit, mind. We're not doing as much walking as we both need to.'

The dog raced ahead of him, and as Mark neared the narrowboat Lucy appeared from within, adjusting a sweatshirt and pulling it down over a pair of well-worn faded jeans.

'Thought it might be you,' she smiled, kissing him as he joined her. 'Want a beer before we start cooking?'

'A beer would be good.' He followed her into the galley, dropped his backpack on the floor beside a built-in table and kicked off his shoes. 'I'll just get changed. Fancy a barbecue tonight?'

'Sounds good. I bought some fresh bread and salad bits earlier, and there are sausages in the fridge.'

'Perfect. Go on up, I'll join you in a second.'

He switched his shirt and trousers for shorts and an old burgundy sweatshirt, pushed a load of dirty laundry into the washing machine on his way back through the galley and then climbed the steps to the small deck on the back of the boat.

A light breeze ruffled the hair at the nape of his neck, and he turned to see Lucy and Hamish halfway along the roof. His girlfriend was grinning as the dog feigned indifference while another dog ran around off-leash in the Abbey Gardens on the other side of the river, until the other dog barked.

Hamish let off a short sharp yip, then stomped his feet before planting his backside on the roof and glaring at the dog's owner.

'You don't own all the land around here, mister,' said Mark, chuckling as he sat beside Lucy and taking the bottle of cold beer she passed to him. 'Cheers.'

'Cheers.' She tipped her bottle towards the narrowboat next door. 'Julie and Steve were asking if we'd like to go round tomorrow night for sundowners. I've let them know it'll depend on work.'

'Sorry.' He took a gulp of beer, smacked his lips, then took her hand in his. 'You go though if I can't make it. Hopefully I'll be back in time, but Kennedy's arranged a briefing for late afternoon and given the way this week's gone, I reckon it'll run late.'

She frowned. 'That bad?'

'Bloody frustrating.' He lowered his voice, so as not to be overheard by the other boat owners. 'We haven't had a single breakthrough yet, just more questions.'

'It goes like that sometimes though, doesn't it?' She squeezed his hand. 'And you haven't got all the information from the searches this week yet, have you?'

'Hopefully that's what we'll go through in the briefing. There's just so much information to sift through. It's times like this, I'm always worried that we'll miss something.'

He watched as Hamish stood then scurried to the far end of

the narrowboat, tail wagging as a pair of cyclists zipped past, then turned and eyed the water, mesmerised by the ripples breaking the surface as trout nipped at insects.

Frowning, Mark replayed his conversation with Darrow over in his mind as Lucy called to Hamish, and then recounted West's feedback from interviewing Gaynor's solicitor.

He choked on the next swig of beer, and beat at his chest.

Lucy turned to face him, her eyes full of concern. 'Are you okay, love?'

He already had the phone to his ear, crossing his fingers that Kennedy wouldn't object to another increase in the team's budget. 'I might be completely wrong about this, but I'm going to ask if we can get a regular patrol to go past Windlesham's house while his sister's there.'

Her eyebrows shot upwards. 'Do you think she's in danger?'

'I don't know what to think at the moment. But I'm not willing to risk it, given that Barry had some threatening letters hidden in his safe and CCTV cameras fitted at the airfield site. He was obviously worried about something. Or someone.'

# CHAPTER TWENTY-FOUR

Jan wiggled her toes, adjusted the soft fluffy cushion behind her shoulder blades and closed her eyes with a sigh.

Upstairs, the boys were playing with some old Lego that Scott had found in the loft that morning, Luke's voice carrying down the stairs every now and again with building instructions for his brother Harry. It had taken some persuasion to get them away from their computer screens, but now it seemed they had found a new focus for the evening.

The sound of a can popping and fizzing in the kitchen reached her, and she smiled at the thought of the Chinese takeaway that would be delivered within the hour.

A yawn engulfed her, the early morning start and long-hour shift finally taking its toll.

'Here you go.'

Her eyes opened to see Scott holding out a glass of lager, a grin on his face.

'You looked like you could do with it.'

'Thanks, love.'

He collapsed onto the sofa beside her and clinked his glass against hers. 'Busy day, eh?'

'Yeah. Sorry.'

'Don't apologise. After they got home from school, I had the boys help me dig over that garden border along the back we've been wanting to do for a while.' He slurped happily. 'Another session like that and it'll be ready for you to get those plants in before it's too late. They're outgrowing their pots fast.'

She rested her head on his shoulder. 'You're too good to me.'

'I know.' He chuckled, then kissed her hair. 'How did it go today, anyway? Any progress?'

'Not really. Bloody frustrating week, to be honest.' She yawned again. 'And to think, when Kennedy gave us this one we thought it was just going to be a box-ticking exercise for a delayed drowning.'

'Definitely not an accident then?'

'No, most definitely not.'

'They're not saying much about it on the news. I had the radio on while I was working on that house extension over near Garford, and they didn't mention it once.'

'That's because Kennedy and the media team haven't got anything to tell them.' She straightened, squeezed his thigh and took another sip from her can before leaning back amongst the cushions once more. 'And nobody except us and the doctor at the hospital knows about the other details – we're keeping all of that close to our chests until we know more.'

Scott smiled. 'Don't worry, I know better than to ask.'

'Hey, while I think of it – are you still playing football next week? The way this is going, I might not be able to make it.'

'No problem. It's only a dads versus lads game because there are no league matches next week. Some of their friends that are on the junior teams will be there anyway.'

'Oh, okay. Good.' Jan heard a car door slam outside, and then the front gate creaked on its hinges. 'That'll be the food. Do you want to give the boys a shout while I dish up?'

She followed him from the living room, then paid the delivery driver while Scott jogged upstairs, his voice carrying down while she took the bag of food through to the kitchen.

It smelled divine, and her stomach rumbled at the thought of a steaming hot plate of noodles, crispy seaweed and spring rolls.

Dividing the spoils between four plates, she glanced up as Luke and Harry appeared. 'Having fun, you two?'

'Yeah,' Luke said, walking past and making a beeline for the sink. He washed his hands, leaving the tap running for his brother, then wandered over. 'Which one's mine, that one?'

'No, cheeky. That's your dad's one. That's yours. Do you want another spring roll?'

'Yes please.'

'Harry – here you go. This one's yours. Can you take cutlery through for everyone?'

'Will do, Mum.'

Jan drained the last of her beer and put the can in a plastic crate with other recyclables next to the back door, then grinned as Scott reappeared. 'This was such a good idea. I didn't fancy cooking tonight, did you?'

'No – and we're going to need to do a supermarket delivery

order if you're working this weekend, too. I'm working tomorrow as well.'

'Don't worry, I'll go online after this and sort it out.'

She picked up her plate, then paused as her mobile phone began to ring where she had plugged it in to charge beside the microwave.

Scott froze, and looked over his shoulder. 'Do you need to get that?'

She saw Alex's number and padded back to the kitchen. 'Unfortunately, yes. Hi, Alex?'

'Sorry, Jan,' said the young detective. 'It's just that Becky's away for a long weekend with friends and none of my mates are around so I thought I'd work late tonight.'

'Right...'

'And so I figured I'd keep going through the ANPR images we were given. You know, the ones from the hospital car park on Sunday night.'

She put her plate on the kitchen table and picked up a spring roll, eyeing the rest of the meal with a pained expression. 'Do you need me to come in?'

'Please. I've just arranged for the man in the security guard's body cam footage to be brought in for questioning.'

'What?' The spring roll froze halfway to her mouth, and she dropped it to the plate. 'How'd you find him?'

'He thought he was being clever – he'd tried to hide his face using a baseball cap when he was driving out of the hospital car park, but the barrier took its time to raise so he craned his neck upwards to see what was going on.'

'Does Mark know?'

'I've already called him, and he's on his way in. One of their neighbours was heading into town for dinner and gave him a lift, so he said don't worry about picking him up.'

'Okay, I'll be right there.'

She caught Scott's gaze as she lowered her phone, and he raised an eyebrow.

'Got that breakthrough you were after?'

'I bloody hope so, love. I bloody hope so.'

# CHAPTER TWENTY-FIVE

The corridor leading to the interview rooms reeked of disinfectant and sweat, despite the cleaners' best efforts.

No matter whether innocent or guilty, Mark noted that the walk from the front desk and through the security door created anxiety for anyone who wasn't employed or contracted to Thames Valley Police.

The painted brick walls on either side were stained with age, peppered with faded health and safety posters that sagged at the corners, and the emulsion paint was turning scuffed and peeling where it met the fraying carpet tiles.

The lighting had a strange tone to it that yellowed the skin, making everyone look as if they were fighting off the 'flu, and no sound carried from one end to the other of the passageway, such that he couldn't tell whether the other rooms were occupied or empty.

He walked past the observation suite, and saw that West was

already stationed in front of a pair of computer screens that were linked to the cameras in the interview room, ready to take notes, then he paused and turned to Alex.

'Tell me what you've found out so far.'

The young DC stopped with his hand on the door to interview room five then walked back a few paces to join him. 'He goes by the name of Lloyd Derrie. He's been picked up by the St Aldates' lot a couple of times for aggravated assault, and his ex-wife had to get a restraining order taken out against him three years ago. He lives with his mother out near the Cowley Road, and sometimes works as a labourer. Cash in hand, that sort of stuff.'

'Social media? Friends?'

'Just the usual channels, and we haven't managed to find anything amongst his followers that's given us a decent lead about how he might be connected to the other bloke seen on the footage so far.'

'Tell them to keep digging. This is good, by the way Alex. Hell of a breakthrough.'

The young detective's shoulders straightened a little. 'Thanks. It was a lucky break though. If he'd looked up just a split second less, I'd have missed him.'

'But you didn't.' Mark closed the manila folder he had been reading through, and thrust it at Alex. 'So you can lead this one.'

'Really?' Alex took the folder as if it were lined with gold. 'Thanks.'

Pushing open the door to room five, it took Mark mere seconds and over a decade of experience to deduce that the man sitting on one side of the table was going to lie to protect the other man seen in the hospital's video.

His eyes were a dull grey, just like the sea after a squall, and he looked scared, less assured than someone who would be so bold as to fire a gun at a man and then disappear from the scene in such a practised way that nobody noticed him.

Mark's young protégé appeared to have come to the same conclusion. He cleared his throat after reading out the formal caution, took Lloyd's solicitor's business card with barely disguised disgust, and turned his attention to the man in front of him who picked nervously at a hang nail.

'Mr Derrie, who asked you to start an argument in the A and E department at the John Radcliffe hospital on Sunday night?'

Lloyd's Adam's apple bobbed in his throat before he answered. 'No one.'

Alex pulled out one of the photographs from the manila folder, an image captured from the security guard's body camera that clearly showed the thief with the bag of clothing in the background. He shoved it across the table towards Lloyd. 'How much did he pay you?'

The man's eyes flickered to the image, then back to Alex. 'I don't know him.'

The young detective folded his hands and leaned forward. 'Why were you at the hospital?'

'What?'

'Who were you visiting?'

'I... I... a friend.'

'Who? We'll need a name.'

'I can't say.'

THE ELEVENTH GRAVE    155

'Okay, well try this, Mr Derrie. We're investigating the attempted murder of a man who was a patient.' Alex paused to tap the photograph with his forefinger. 'In this image I'm showing you, this man here is taking the victim's clothing from a secure storage area within the A and E department, a storage area that would be difficult for a member of the public to access – unless the security team and staff were distracted for long enough to allow him to do so. At the present time, Mr Derrie, you're our only suspect in relation to that.'

He let his words sink in, and Mark watched with satisfaction as Lloyd paled, before leaning towards his solicitor and lowering his voice.

The legal representative kept his gaze lowered while he listened, then nodded once and looked at Mark. 'My client would like it noted on the record that he had nothing to do with the shooting.'

'Interesting,' said Mark. 'I don't believe my colleague mentioned a shooting taking place, only that we were pursuing this suspect for attempted murder.'

Lloyd Derrie looked as if he were going to be sick. He swallowed, cleared his throat, and then shifted in his seat. 'I don't know his name.'

'How did he contact you?' said Alex.

'Through an acquaintance. Someone down the pub.' Lloyd looked from Alex to Mark and then back. 'I owed someone a favour. Money. I was told if I just caused a distraction for him that they'd knock five grand off the debt.' He shrugged. 'I didn't have a lot of choice. He threatened my little girl, saying that he'd take her from her school if I didn't do as I was told.'

'Who told you that?'

'Him. The bloke in the photo.'

'Did he say why he needed you to cause the distraction?'

'No. And I didn't ask. I didn't even know what he was up to until you showed me that. What's in the bag?'

Alex ignored the question. 'Where did you meet him?'

'I got a phone call about an hour before, telling me to go to the hospital and wait in the car park until I got another call. When my phone rang, it was someone different – it was that bloke in the photo I suppose. He told me to get my arse over to the A and E department, told me what he was wearing, and said I had to walk past and ignore him, and then get into an argument with one of the security guards, making sure he had his back to that door.'

'What happened after this altercation? Where did this man go?'

'I don't know. When I turned around, he'd disappeared. Anyway, as soon as they kicked me out, I drove off, just like they told me to.'

'Did anyone contact you after that?'

'The bloke from the pub who put him in touch with me. He said the five grand had been wiped off the debt, but if I told anyone about what happened my little girl would get into trouble.' Lloyd wiped a shaking hand across his mouth. 'And then your lot fucking arrest me outside the pub, in front of everyone.'

'Where's your daughter now?' said Mark.

'At her mum's, in Newbury.'

'Can they stay somewhere else over the weekend?'

'I was going to tell the ex to go and stay with her aunt over near Reading.'

'Okay, well we'll make sure that happens.' Mark took down the woman's details, stepped outside the room and handed them to a passing junior constable. 'Get a patrol over to Newbury now, and don't hang about.'

'Sarge.'

Returning to the interview room, Mark then checked his notes. 'Mr Derrie, are you absolutely sure that you don't know who this man is, or what his name is? Lying to us in this matter would have very serious consequences for you.'

'I'm telling the truth. I'm hardly going to risk my daughter's life, am I?' Lloyd said through gritted teeth. He slid the photograph back across the table. 'The sooner you lot catch this bastard, the sooner I'll know she's out of danger.'

Five minutes later, the interview concluded, Mark led Alex into the observation suite while Lloyd Derrie was released on condition that he made himself available for further questioning. The man looked through the open door with a sullen expression as he was led past, his solicitor muttering to him as they disappeared from view.

Mark watched them go, then turned to West. 'What do you think?'

'I think he's terrified,' she said. 'That much is certain.'

'Has someone been sent over to the ex-wife's house?'

'Yes.' She saved the recording, then followed them along the corridor and towards the security door leading out to the custody suite. 'And I'll get onto St Aldate's station once we're upstairs and ask them which pub Lloyd was arrested at. Hopefully they can send over a team when it opens tomorrow and question the landlord and regulars to see who he's been talking to these past few weeks.'

Mark pushed through the door, and let Alex and West go ahead of him.

Lloyd Derrie had finished collecting his belongings from the custody sergeant and glanced over his shoulder as he headed for the exit leading onto the Marcham Road. He attempted a sneer, but the worry lines that creased his brow told another story.

Alex waited until the front door swished shut, then turned to them. 'I'll deal with the pub aspect, Jan. You're speaking to that parish councillor first thing, aren't you?'

'True, thanks.'

'When you speak to St Aldate's, get them to ask the landlord about CCTV but also whether he knows anything about this debt Lloyd was telling us about,' said Mark. 'If someone's lending money around, he might know of others in the same situation as Lloyd that can shed some light on what the hell's going on. We've got nothing to indicate that Barry Windlesham was in debt, have we?'

West shook her head. 'Caroline went through the balance sheets for the company, and there's nothing there to suggest he was in trouble financially.'

'Okay, well in that case—'

A braying horn followed by the screech of brakes carried through the reinforced glass of the front doors.

Mark was already moving, already running.

He burst through the doors, ran down the shallow steps that led to the pavement, and froze for a moment.

One of the double-decker Oxford-bound buses was slewed to a standstill a hundred metres away, its four-way indicators flashing.

'No...' He could hear Alex and West in his wake, their footsteps pounding the road as they zigzagged around the frozen traffic, skirting around motorists who were climbing from their cars, craning their necks to see what was going on. 'Stay with your vehicle, sir. Excuse me, out of the way please.'

He already knew what he would find before he reached the front of the bus.

The driver was standing in the ghostly beam of the headlights, her face pale. 'He came out of nowhere. I didn't have a chance to stop. I...'

'It's okay,' Mark put a hand on the woman's shoulder and gently turned her away, leading her towards West who, to her credit, merely nodded to him before guiding the driver towards the relative privacy of the police station.

Then he walked back to the front of the bus.

Lloyd Derrie's face had been obliterated by the impact. His broken body lay sprawled across the asphalt, his limbs splayed at impossible angles.

'Fuck,' he murmured, then turned at the sound of laboured breathing to see his younger colleague, eyes wide.

Alex swallowed as he took in the utter destruction, then managed a strangled croak. 'Was it something I said?'

# CHAPTER TWENTY-SIX

Mark shoved a mug of coffee under Alex's nose and placed a hand on his shoulder.

'Here, drink this. Plenty of sugar.'

The young detective sniffed, then did as he was told and winced. 'You weren't kidding. What happened, guv? What did I do wrong?'

'Nothing,' said Kennedy, his voice gruff. 'I've watched the replay of the interview, and it was faultless. As are you. Whatever happened out there tonight was *not* due to anything you said or did, understand?'

Alex nodded, his face glum. 'It still doesn't change the fact that we've lost our only decent lead though, does it, guv?'

'It doesn't,' said the detective inspector. 'So we'd better hope St Aldate's get some results speaking with that pub landlord and his clientele in the morning.'

Mark wandered over to the window overlooking the

Marcham Road and poked his fingers through the Venetian blind, careful not to expose his face while he peered through.

Lloyd Derrie's body had been removed twenty minutes ago, after Gillian Appleworth had attended the accident scene and signed off the required paperwork, her face grim.

Now, a temporary traffic diversion was being set up outside while a team of investigators surveyed the area in preparation for the report that would have to be filed.

The flashing blue lights of a patrol car pierced the night, casting a strobe-like reflection off the windows of the car dealership showroom on the opposite side of the road and illuminating the faces of the dozen or so people working to gather as much evidence as possible so that the road could be reopened by dawn.

Mark didn't want to contemplate the missives that would be received from Headquarters if their investigation was responsible for closing one of the town's busiest commuter routes, given that so far they had little to show for all their enquiries.

He watched as a uniformed sergeant accompanied the shocked bus driver to a waiting patrol car that would whisk her home, away from the prying eyes of the crowd that had emerged from the fast-food restaurant and petrol station to see what was going on.

A media statement had been sent out five minutes ago that was circulating on social media within seconds of being released, and Mark had phoned Lucy to tell her he had no idea when he would be home that night.

Walking over to a nearby chair, Mark sank onto it, legs weary and his eyes bleary with exhaustion as Kennedy paused beside the whiteboard.

The detective inspector loosened his shirt cuffs, biting back a yawn. 'Okay, plans for tomorrow – what are you suggesting, Mark?'

'We'll continue with our planned interview with Felix Darrow at nine o'clock to see what comes out of that.' Mark spun his chair back and forth while he contemplated the carpet tiles. 'I think from there, we interview the others on that pre-planning committee, particularly those who opposed the idea of the site being developed, and why. Alex, how were you getting on with the CCTV files that Windlesham's admin assistant sent over?'

The young detective took another swig of coffee, blinked at the sugar hit, then squared his shoulders. 'There are another twelve or so to look through but I'll get that finished tomorrow… today,' he said, glancing at his watch. 'If those don't pick up anything, I'll have a word with the service station down the road from the airfield. It's a good two miles away, but there's a small convenience store attached to it, so I figured it was as good a chance as any.'

'Good idea,' said Kennedy. 'Interview the staff as well, just in case they noticed anyone acting suspiciously or asking questions about Windlesham over the past few weeks.'

'Will do, guv.'

'What about you, Mark, any thoughts about tonight's events, and how it might tie in with Windlesham's death?'

Mark eyed the criss-crossing notes that covered the whiteboard for a moment, and sighed. 'I've got nothing, guv. Sorry. I mean, nothing we've found in Derrie's history links him to Windlesham except for this supposed person who told him to be at the hospital.'

'What about the "acquaintance" he mentioned in the interview, the bloke who put the two of them together?'

'We won't know much more until St Aldate's get back to us in the morning, guv. Their custody suite is too busy tonight to help at the moment,' said West. 'I'll ask Caroline to liaise with them so we hear as soon as they find out anything that might help us.'

'Does Derrie's ex-wife know anything?'

'No, she severed all ties with him three months before the restraining order was taken out. He only sees his daughter in supervised conditions, once every fortnight for a few hours.'

The detective inspector glared at the whiteboard, then turned back to them. 'Is Barry Windlesham a victim in all of this, or part of whatever's going on?'

'I wouldn't rule out anything at the moment,' said Mark. 'Caroline and her team are still following up with his known business associates and social groups, including his neighbours. Something might come out of that.'

'It bloody needs to.'

# CHAPTER TWENTY-SEVEN

The pool car reeked of copious amounts of spray-on deodorant when Mark opened the door the next morning.

He staggered backwards, covering his face with his forearm.

West leaned over the central console and peered out at him. 'It's not that bad. Get in, otherwise we'll be late.'

'Bloody hell, it's like a flipping perfume counter in here.' He adjusted the seat while she aimed the car towards Wallingford. 'Did the kids spill something?'

'No, they forgot to use any deodorant before we got in the car, and Scott had the bright idea of letting them use his while we were on the way. If we'd waited while they'd gone back in the house, we'd have never made football training on time.' She coughed, then lowered her window a little more. 'But on the bright side, at least we'll smell nice when we interview Felix Darrow.'

'Yes, or knock him out.'

Twenty minutes later, West turned right and drove between two concrete pillars that had been rendered dark grey.

Black powder-coated aluminium gates had been pegged open, leading to an asphalt driveway bordered by pale gravel and ornamental grasses.

The driveway was short and wide, and she pulled up outside a two-storey home that had been partially sunk into a natural bowl created by the hillside into which it nestled.

Mark got out of the car and crossed to the far left of the building where a lawn rolled away from the ornamental grasses and gave way to a sweeping view over a shallow valley. A thick line of oak and ash traced the route of the river, sunlight catching the water in places, sparkling as it cut its way southeast.

'Nice, if you can afford it,' West murmured at his elbow. 'The aggregates business must be doing well.'

'Indeed.' Mark jerked his chin as Felix Darrow peered through an upstairs window, raising his hand in greeting before disappearing from sight. 'Do you want to lead this one?'

'Okay.' She led the way round to the front door. 'What are you thinking?'

'I'd like to know more about the others involved in that planning committee who were there last night.'

'I'll see what I can do.' She winked before Darrow opened the door, then fixed a professional smile to her face. 'Morning, Mr Darrow. DC Jan West. I believe you've already met my colleague, DS Mark Turpin.'

'Indeed. Come through. We can sit in the conservatory out of the way. My wife's foolishly agreed to help with the village Easter fête, so the kitchen looks like a tornado's hit it at the moment.' He spoke without rancour while they scrubbed their shoes across a rough coir doormat, then led the way along a wide hallway. 'I've said to her every year that she should tell them she's too busy and let someone else do it, but she won't have it.'

'That's because it's fun,' called an airy voice through an open doorway.

Darrow paused at the door and gestured to the petite brunette who stood at a central granite-topped workbench, surrounded by yellow streamers. 'My wife, Alicia.'

'Morning, detectives. I'd offer you a coffee, but—' She held up hands covered in papier mâché paste. 'I'm at a critical juncture in proceedings.'

'That's fine, thanks,' said Mark. 'We'll let you get on.'

'See what I mean?' Darrow continued along the hallway, then showed them into a large box-shaped living room that opened up into a large conservatory that overlooked the valley. 'Please, take a seat.'

Mark chose a rattan armchair off to the left of where Darrow sank onto a matching sofa and watched the man while West settled into another armchair opposite the parish councillor and pulled out her notebook.

'Thanks for agreeing to see us on a Saturday, Mr Darrow,' she began. 'How well did you know Barry Windlesham?'

'Quite well, I suppose.' He leaned back on the sofa and crossed his legs, his socked foot bobbing up and down as he spoke. 'I run a profitable aggregates business, and Barry was obviously into development projects so our paths crossed from time to time. Not always in person – I have people that manage the tendering process for new contracts of course – but sometimes we'd bump into each other at local functions, that sort of thing.'

'What sort of functions?'

'Chamber of Commerce meetings in the past. I haven't been to one in years, but that's when I first met him.' He gave a benevolent smile. 'We didn't socialise or anything like that.'

'Are there any major issues with what he was proposing for the airfield?'

'There were a few potential stumbling blocks that needed to be worked through prior to the planning application being sought.'

'Such as?'

'Well, the site hasn't been surveyed for over twenty years for a start. Barry arranged for the previous owners to carry out two or three spot tests before he bought the site of course, just to check for any nasty chemicals in the soil, but nothing like the sort of research that needed to be undertaken prior to the application.'

'Why was he holding back?'

'I presume he wanted to save his money until he knew what the council's expectations would be following the pre-planning process,' Darrow said, then frowned. 'I mean, it's important for the application that we know that the land is suitable for the sort of development he was going to propose. The test surveys only included some ground probing exercises around the existing buildings because he was hoping to redevelop those. That's what was integral to his draft proposal – to utilise a brownfield site and the historical significance of some of the buildings, and then develop the surrounding airfield with new homes.'

'Did the test surveys highlight any issues?'

'Not that I'm aware of. I don't think he'd have gone ahead with the purchase if there had been. Barry was a very canny operator with years of experience delivering this sort of project.'

West nodded, paused to update her notes, then affected a frown. 'If the project was going to incorporate the older buildings, what were the objections to it? Why did Mr Windlesham have to go through the pre-planning application process?'

'Ah, that's where things get a little political,' said Darrow, his voice gleeful despite the sombre expression he tried to keep. He leaned forward. 'You see, there are some around here that believe the place ought to be kept as a rewilding project, a sort of wildlife haven. After all, the place has been more or less deserted for over seventy years, give or take some small manufacturing businesses that took up residency after the war ended. Certainly there's been very little interest in the site since the late nineteen eighties, which is why many of the hangars have fallen to wrack and ruin.'

'Who raised those objections?'

'Well, you would have seen two of them last night, albeit briefly given I had to adjourn the meeting after Mr Swift's interruption.' Darrow tried and failed to keep the annoyance from his voice. 'Charmaine Abbott is a local county councillor who's up for re-election later this year. She's under enormous pressure from her party to deliver some green objectives to offset the threat from some of the independents around here. Don't get me wrong – she's done some amazing work in the area, particularly with encouraging donations to food banks and shelters and the like, but she's managed to inveigle herself into some of the local wildlife action groups, especially those with a younger demographic, in an attempt to present a united front. Of course, one of those fronts is the objection to the airfield being developed.'

'That's a rather strong accusation, Mr Darrow.'

He shrugged. 'It is what it is. Everyone around here knows how tunnel-visioned Charmaine can be when she's got her mind set on something. She'll say and do anything to keep her job, believe me.'

'And who else on the committee raised an objection?'

'A man by the name of Adrian Mackleton.' Darrow held up his hands. 'Don't misunderstand, I like Adrian, but I believe he's misguided in his opinion that the airfield site needs to be preserved both from a historical and environmental perspective.'

'What does Mr Mackleton do when he's not objecting to building projects?'

'He's a doctor at a small clinic in Ravenswood. He's well respected within the community around here.'

'Has he been very vocal in his objections?'

'No, but very persuasive.' Darrow stretched out his legs. 'I told Barry he'd have his work cut out putting together the application in such a way that Adrian would approve it. Adrian's a lovely bloke, he really is, but he's very vocal when it comes to historical and ancient monuments and ensuring future generations can access them.'

'Were you happy for the project to proceed?'

'Absolutely.' He nodded vigorously. 'That land is going to waste, and as you know we're short of housing in the area. We need to be cognisant of current government recommendations that affordable housing be made available. Barry's project would've gone a long way to delivering that for the area, as well as bringing in new jobs during the construction phase.'

'We'd heard that you were observed having quite a heated discussion with Mr Windlesham three weeks ago,' said West. 'What was that all about?'

Mark watched with interest as Darrow squirmed in his seat, the man wincing at the memory.

'Oh, that. That was his secretary who told you was it?'

'I can't comment.'

'It was more passionate than heated, I'd say, although I can understand why she'd think differently given she could only observe, and not hear what was being said.' Darrow sighed. 'I was trying to convince Barry that maybe he should consider some of the feedback we were getting via the pre-planning process about the project. I made the mistake of suggesting that perhaps he could change the design in some way to incorporate more of the environmental aspects that were repeatedly coming up in the objections. He could be a stubborn bugger sometimes, I can tell you. Anyway, I suppose we did get a little argumentative, but it's like I said, it's only because I think we're – were – so passionate about getting it *right* for everyone involved, do you see? Anyway, by the time we'd walked back to my car I'd calmed down and Barry had assured me he would take some of the concerns into consideration before the actual application went in.'

THE ELEVENTH GRAVE    171

'Was that the last time you spoke with Mr Windlesham?'

'It was, yes.'

West glanced over to Mark, but he shook his head. She tucked her notebook into her bag and rose. 'Well, thank you for your time, Mr Darrow. We appreciate it.'

He bounced to his feet. 'Oh, you're more than welcome. And I hope my comments about Charmaine and Adrian won't be repeated beyond these four walls. You can understand why I couldn't say much last night. The project – albeit as I said, is much needed for the area – has caused a bit of division locally.'

Mark paused halfway to the door and turned. 'In what way?'

'Oh, nothing too serious.' Darrow emitted a light chuckle. 'Just a little friction, you know – placards in people's front gardens, a bit of argy-bargy down the local pub sometimes when people start talking about it after a few drinks. That's all.'

Five minutes later, West steered the car out of the driveway and switched on the wiper blades as fat raindrops began to pepper the windscreen.

'What do you think?' she said.

'I think we need to speak with Charmaine Abbott and Adrian Mackleton to close out that loop.' Mark watched the scenery flash past as he spoke. 'Particularly Charmaine, just in case some of the environmental groups she's been involved with have any troublemakers in the ranks.'

'What if—?'

West broke off as Mark's phone started to trill, and he looked down to see Kennedy's number displayed on the screen.

'Guv.'

'Have you finished interviewing Felix Darrow?'

'We've just left his place.'

'Good. Get yourselves over to the airfield. Now.'

'What's the problem?'

A shiver crept over his shoulders at Kennedy's next words.

'They've found some bodies, Mark. A lot of bodies.'

# CHAPTER TWENTY-EIGHT

Jan hitched the car's handbrake and checked her watch.

It had taken longer than she liked to reach the airfield, and although she tried to slow her racing heart rate, she knew that now more than ever, time was of the essence.

It had been almost a week since Barry Windlesham had been shot at and his fateful fall into the river, and yet they were no closer to finding out who had attempted to kill him that day, or why, leaving a grieving family with no answers, and no sense of justice for his eventual death.

She stared at a cluster of white polyester tents a few hundred metres ahead. They were positioned at odd angles, some perpendicular to others, and here and there she could see a flap opening in the side of one before a protective suit-clad figure emerged.

Grey clouds scudded across a lacklustre sky, adding to an already sombre view. Even the sheep were keeping their distance, and were huddled in a corner on the far side of the airfield.

Turpin was muttering under his breath, and then sighed. 'Eleven.'

'Bloody hell.' She opened the door. 'Let's see what they've found then.'

The wind blew her hair in her face the moment she got out, and she brushed it back while taking in the array of liveried patrol vehicles, forensics vans and – off to the side, discreet, dark grey – three coroners' vans.

The drivers stood in front of the one in the middle, stoically smoking cigarettes while eyeing the newcomers with bored expressions.

The forensic lead was already waiting for Jan and Turpin at a broad cordon staked out between spiked metal poles shoved into the soft ground, his face grim while they scrawled their signatures across a sign-in sheet managed by a uniformed constable.

Jasper held out protective bootees, then held up the tape for them to duck under. 'Kennedy's going to have a heart attack at this rate. I've had to bring in a whole new team to help with this.'

'He'll manage,' said Turpin. 'He always does. What's the latest?'

'Okay, well we weren't having any luck with extending the search for evidence around the buildings, and one of the ground-penetrating radars was playing up, so the operator wandered away from the demarcated area over there to test it on some clear ground.' Jasper pushed back the protective hood of his suit and scratched at his scalp. 'He got a blip on the radar in the grass within fifty metres of the old officers' mess, reckoned on it still being an error, and asked one of the others to do the same with theirs. That's when they found the second grave, just there, beside the old runway.'

Jan looked to where he pointed as they followed him along a path created with additional tape. 'Any chance these are historical remains? We've had this issue before.'

'Not a chance in hell.' Jasper looked over his shoulder, then continued walking. 'You'll see why in a minute.'

She fell into step behind him, casting her gaze beyond the tape to where the nearest tent had been erected. A team of three SOCOs passed in and out of the opening, the flap falling back into place and obscuring what was inside before she could catch a glimpse of what lay beyond.

'Here.' The forensic lead had stopped beside the third tent, and held it open. 'This one's more recent than the rest so it'll be easier to show you what I think we're dealing with.'

Jan's heart ratcheted up another notch before she shuffled closer and peered over Turpin's shoulder. 'Bloody hell.'

Jasper's team had cleared a shallow grave that had clearly been dug in a hurry.

The edges were jagged, the blade marks from a shovel still evident amongst the loose soil that clung to thick tangled grass roots.

The naked body within had somehow survived the trampling of sheep hooves, but had given way to insect activity and decay.

It was a man, and she reckoned he would have been no more than thirty at the time of his death, although she would defer to Gillian Appleworth's expert opinion once the post mortem had been completed. His neck was twisted in such a way that his chin fell behind his left shoulder and she could see that his eyes were missing, the empty sockets staring at her accusatorially.

And, as she circled the grave in Turpin's wake, she saw that his abdomen had been slit open, exposing the cavity within. His lower ribs had been smashed apart, leaving jagged stumps that protruded from what remained of muscle and fatty tissue.

Turpin led the way out of the tent, and turned to Jasper. 'What the hell?'

'Told you it was different.'

Jan's stomach threatened to turn to liquid, and she swallowed as she took in the other tents scattered close by. 'What about the others?'

'We're currently working through those, so I can't show you those yet but this one's the most recent burial,' said Jasper, gesturing to the other tents. 'It's hard to tell with the older remains – three of them are too decayed for us to ascertain what happened this side of a post mortem – but there's a woman over in tent three that might yield some useful clues, and another man in tent seven who can only have been in the ground for a few months.'

'What about this one?'

'We're going to get him over to the morgue right now, and I've asked Gillian if she can do the PM this weekend given the amount of decay already in place,' said the forensic expert. 'She's been over here to take a look and conduct the formalities, so she's expecting him. We'll get the others over to her as and when we've finished our assessments here.'

'What was Gillian's first impression?' said Jan. 'Did she have any theories about how he died?'

'Oh yes,' said Jasper. He glanced over his shoulder towards the closed tent flap. 'That was relatively easy. She reckons he was missing both of his kidneys as well as his eyes before he was buried.'

# CHAPTER TWENTY-NINE

Three hours later, Mark stared at the viscous liquid spurting from the vending machine nozzle, took one look at the end result, and promptly dropped it into the rubbish bin, his stomach lurching.

The reception area smelled of fresh bleach. A junior constable was using a mop and bucket to wash away vomit that had been left by a man who had started drinking at home at six o'clock that morning before starting a fight in a local gift shop – one he said was owned by his ex-wife – at eleven.

The man was now in one of the custody suites attempting to sleep off what would be an enormous hangover and several weeks of regret, and the constable whistled tunelessly while he worked, only stopping to give Mark a brief nod as he passed.

There was a stunned silence to the incident room when he walked back upstairs, a reserved quiet that spoke volumes and caused gooseflesh to pepper his forearms.

When people did speak, it was with a sombre reverence, the

shockwave from Jasper's findings casting its net beyond the team and through the entire building.

Caroline was standing beside a group of desks in the far corner, talking to four administrative assistants that she had wrangled from another investigative team whose DI had willingly told Kennedy he should take whoever he needed. Their faces were troubled while they listened to her, their voices no more than a murmur when they spoke to the detective constable. Her face was etched with a renewed determination though, and she gave him a slight nod when she saw him watching.

He walked past Alex who was staring at the CCTV images on his computer screen, and patted the young detective's shoulder without saying a word before joining West beside the whiteboard.

She flicked through a stapled document before looking up at him. 'Jasper emailed through his notes so far to give us a head start. All eleven grave sites are noted in here together with a rough sketch he's provided with regard to locations in relation to the airfield buildings.'

'Caroline? Can you get that enlarged to A3 size and pin it to the board?' called Mark, peering over West's shoulder. 'And add to that where Barry's office and the officer's mess are. It seems that he could've been right about feeling like he was being watched. Whoever's responsible for this must've had to change their plans once he started making noises about starting the planning application process and getting site surveys carried out.'

'No problem.'

Kennedy beckoned to the rest of the team to join them before walking over, his face harried. 'So we've gone from an accidental drowning death to an illegal organ harvesting scheme that's managed to operate under our noses for... how old does Jasper think the earliest grave site is?'

'He's not saying anything at the moment, guv,' said West. 'And nor will Gillian, not until the PMs are complete.'

'About those,' said Alex, hurrying over with his phone in his hand. 'She says she'll start the first one later today – that'll be for the later grave – and then she'll do the earliest victim, or what they think is the earliest victim, as soon as Jasper releases it from site.'

'Good, so we might have a rough idea of timescale by Monday, that's something at least,' said Kennedy.

'I also had a quick look at illegal organ harvesting numbers in the UK,' said the young detective. 'A lot of hospitals have tightened up their safeguarding processes after some high-profile cases in recent years, but there's still a shortage of organs—'

'And people are desperate,' said West. 'If they've got the money, they'll pay anything to save a family member, right?'

'Right, and those prosecutions have only served to drive the trade even deeper underground,' Alex added.

'Not to mention this lot are reducing their risk by ensuring none of the donors survive to tell the tale,' said Kennedy, his eyes grim. 'Let alone not having to pay them or their families. Can you go through the organ donation register and waiting lists and flag anything that gives you cause for concern as well?'

'Will do.'

'Here you go, guv.' Caroline added the A3 sketch of the airfield to the notes and photographs on the whiteboard. She had used a red marker pen to add crosses where the site office and officer's mess were located, and rapped her knuckles against the diagram. 'I checked the angle of buildings in relation to the graves – Windlesham could've only seen the airfield once he was well clear of the converted shipping container. He'd have had to have been standing beside that old hangar to see anything.'

'What about the officer's mess?' said Kennedy.

'He couldn't see that from the site office, but you can see the grave site from the front windows of the mess,' Caroline said.

'As would anyone held against their will,' said Mark. 'They would've known what was going to happen to them.'

A silence followed his words, until Kennedy cleared his throat.

'Right, moving on with the rest of today's briefing. We've got a patrol scheduled to pass Windlesham's house every two to three hours at the moment. I can't secure any more than that due to staffing constraints rather than the usual budget issues, but I want Gaynor Alton and her husband brought in for formal questioning in light of this morning's discoveries, and another search of Windlesham's home and office.'

'Are Gaynor and her husband suspects now?' said Caroline, pen poised above her notebook.

'Not yet, but gauge that during the interview and proceed as you see fit.' Kennedy updated the notes on the board while he spoke. 'And ask her why she's decided to take on the project and didn't tell us last week. You can let her know from me that we didn't appreciate yesterday's surprise announcement.'

'Will do, guv. How long can we expect the patrols to be in place?'

'Until we work out whether they're involved, in danger from

whoever *is*, or we arrest someone.' Kennedy turned to Caroline. 'And you can tell them that I would strongly recommend they return to Wales if they're not involved, just to put some distance between them and that site.'

'Got it.'

'Next, we need to follow up with the interviews from yesterday's pre-planning meeting and your discussion with Felix Darrow, Mark. What's your suggestion?'

'I think we need to start with Adrian Mackleton, guv. He's a GP, so in my mind that makes him highest on the list of potential suspects at the moment.'

'Absolutely. Do you want me to get a patrol to bring him in?'

'I'd rather interview him at home, but without giving him a chance to prepare.' Mark glanced across to West. 'I reckon we should head over to his place as soon as we're done here, and see what his reaction is.'

'Given that these people may have worked undetected for a number of years, we can safely assume they have an exit strategy in case something like this happened,' said Kennedy, pacing the carpet. 'Mackleton could be a flight risk so bear that in mind.'

'Will do.'

'Right, follow up tasks from this week,' Kennedy continued. 'Do we have the full list of formal objections to the pre-planning process yet?'

'Got it here,' said Caroline. 'Belinda sent it through from site before leaving yesterday. Aside from Adrian Mackleton, there's a Charmaine Abbott and three others who raised concerns. Barry was apparently working through those objections and in the middle of organising meetings with those people to discuss what might be done.'

'We can interview Charmaine tomorrow morning first thing,' said West. 'She was on the panel last night so she's a priority.'

'Agreed,' said the DI. 'Okay, where are we up to with the lab testing on the dry bag that was found?'

'All tests are complete, but there were no fingerprints in the system to match those on the bag,' said Alex. 'I'm also planning to arrange for the lab to run tests against some DNA that was found in the officer's mess by Jasper's team – there were some hair and clothing samples in the splintered wood in the door that might yield something we can use.'

'What about the phone that was fished from the river?'

'It's still a work in progress, guv.'

'Let me know the minute they find anything.' Kennedy paused in his pacing and faced the team. 'Well, what are you waiting for? Go, go, go.'

# CHAPTER THIRTY

There was a blustery breeze in the air as Mark and West hurried from the incident room.

The wind whipped at the navy tie Mark was fastening under his chin, flapping it over his shoulder and billowing his suit jacket before he climbed into the pool car, which smelled of fat and grease and stale coffee. When he looked down he saw several balls of scrunched up fast-food wrappers scattered in the footwell, and a discarded takeout cup shoved into the door pocket.

West muttered under her breath while she drove the four-door hatchback under the raised security barrier and out of the car park.

Mark looked up from his notes when she braked at a roundabout and then floored the accelerator to beat a grubby panel van that was avoiding the diversion still directing traffic away from the front of the police station. A pair of junior

THE ELEVENTH GRAVE    185

constables had been ordered to keep pedestrians away, and the traffic division's forensic team were working behind a screen that sheltered them from prying eyes, especially given the number of television news crews and social media vultures that were gathered on the opposite side of the road.

His colleague huffed her fringe from her eyes and swore as a car overtook them as soon as she had joined the A34, then slouched in her seat.

'You were having to give back the keys to the other one this morning anyway,' he said. 'Might as well accept the fact.'

'This has got no go in it at all,' she grumbled. 'And I can't believe that someone over at Kidlington now has the other car. We'll never see it again.'

He laughed. 'You sound bereft.'

'I am.' Her mouth quirked before she grew serious. 'Okay, so how do you want to run this interview with Adrian Mackleton?'

'Carefully.' He flicked through the notes that Caroline had collated. 'Given that he objected to Windlesham's project from the start, and that as a doctor he's got plenty of access to the sort of drugs and surgical kit that might be used to carry out organ harvesting.'

'It's a huge leap from being a GP to the sort of surgery we're talking about for a human organ transplant though,' said West. 'Even if the donors weren't expected to survive. He'd still have to ensure the recipient lived, and didn't reject the new kidney.'

'I know, so let's see what he's got to say for himself.'

'Are you going to tell him about the airfield finds?'

'Not yet, and as long as Jasper and his team can keep the place locked down, we'll keep it that way. I agreed with Kennedy last night and we've confirmed with Belinda Masters' agency that her services are no longer required so that's one less person going back and forth to that site too.'

'What about helicopters, or drones?' West checked her mirrors before overtaking an articulated truck, then swept past it, her face determined.

'I spoke with Alex before we left the station – he's arranged for a temporary no-fly zone to be set up and he's advised the local gliding club as well. I'm sure we'll get some complaints. As for drones, the team on site have been told to report any sightings, and Kennedy's somehow managed to wrangle some more manpower to patrol the perimeter of the airfield, the woodlands and surrounding footpaths to prevent anyone getting too close. Jasper reckons he'll be finished there soon.'

He fell silent as she turned down a narrow tree-lined lane that snaked through undulating woodland, the thick branches of oak and ash closing in above their heads forming a green tunnel before it gave way to a small livestock farm on one side and a large detached brick house on the other. A sign on the left-hand verge announced their arrival in Ravenswood village, and the road narrowed as older buildings jostled for space along the main street.

'Over there,' he said, and pointed to a parking space behind a mud-spattered Land Rover. As West manoeuvred the car into it, he took a last look at his notebook, and then tucked it into his pocket. Craning his neck, he spotted the doctor's surgery farther along the street and checked his watch. 'Okay, according to the website it's open until twelve. It's ten to, so he must be onto his last appointment by now. Perfect timing.'

Approaching the surgery, he noticed that the front bay window had frosted glass to prevent anyone looking in, and the front door was solid oak, much like the neighbouring properties. At some point, he reasoned, the building had once been someone's home and looked up to see a date carved into the stone lintel that was several centuries old.

Pushing open the door, he entered a wide reception room with a low wooden desk on the right-hand side, and six fabric chairs fringing the other walls, above which were healthcare posters depicting various messages from best practice for washing hands to the latest advancements in asthma drugs.

A harried-looking woman in her twenties looked up from a computer screen on the far side of the desk and frowned. 'I'm afraid we're not taking any more appointments for today unless it's an emergency.'

Mark held up his warrant card. 'We're looking for Adrian Mackleton. Is he around?'

'He's in with his last patient.' The woman's eyes widened. 'Is everything all right?'

'What's your name?'

'Sally Abordale.'

'Okay, Sally – could you let Dr Mackleton know we'd like a word with him?'

'What, now?'

'Now, yes.'

Sally's gaze shifted to the frosted window, then back. 'Would you like to come through to his office? It's more…'

'Convenient?'

'I was going to say comfortable. I'll be locking up as soon as his current appointment has left, and we tend to turn off the heaters in here to save money when there aren't any patients around. These old buildings get cold really quickly, even at this time of year. Especially the ones on this side of the street – we don't get any sunlight until later in the day.'

'Lead the way,' said Mark.

They followed Sally through a narrow doorway and along a short corridor that was lined with cardboard boxes of different sizes. Some had been opened and as Mark passed, he spotted packets of antiseptic swabs, plastic dispensing bottles, and various sealed packets labelled with health and safety warnings.

Stopping beside an open doorway at the end of the corridor, Sally waved them inside. 'Take a seat. I'll let him know you're here as soon as he's finished.'

Mark watched her hurry back to the reception area, then turned to West. 'Mind if I lead this one?'

'No problem.' She wandered over to a bookshelf that was cluttered with lever arch files and journals, some with sticky notes poking out from the pages.

Mark glanced over his shoulder before crossing to the desk and ran his gaze over the paperwork strewn across it, noting the various invoices and delivery notes associated with the running of a popular village business. He turned away at the sound of footsteps.

'This is most inconvenient.' Adrian Mackleton swept into the room, removing a protective overcoat that revealed a long-sleeved T-shirt with a cartoon cat logo on the front. He tossed the coat into a biohazard bin beside the door and glowered at them.

'I've got a full diary of house calls to make this afternoon, and I'm already running late.'

'We have some questions we'd like to ask you in relation to Ravenswood airfield,' said Mark. 'Inconvenient or not, we won't be leaving until we have some answers.'

The GP frowned. 'What sort of questions?'

'Before we begin, we would like to make this official in the circumstances,' said Mark.

'Circumstances? What do you mean?'

Mark ignored him, before reciting the formal caution from memory. He watched the doctor's gaze turn from confusion to one of intrigue. 'Mr Mackleton, we'd like to ask you some questions in relation to the death of Barry Windlesham, and to recent findings at Ravenswood airfield, owned by Mr Windlesham.'

'Okay...' Adrian moved around the desk and lowered himself into the battered leather seat. 'Go on.'

'What was your relationship to Mr Windlesham?'

'Um, there *was* no relationship, detective. I'm on the planning committee for the local council because of my interests locally and I was one of the committee members tasked with assessing Barry's pre-planning application for the airfield.'

'To which you objected, is that correct?'

'Yes.'

'Why?'

'Pardon?'

'Why did you object to the airfield development?'

'Because there are buildings there of significant historical interest that were going to be torn down, rather than preserved,' said Adrian, his tone indignant.

'Any buildings in particular?'

'The officers' mess, for a start. And the control tower. Then there are the hangars... did you know they used to fly Hurricanes out of here during the war? Imagine the stories that place could tell...'

'Those hangars looked like they were about to fall down to me,' said West. 'Surely they'd be better off dismantled.'

Adrian sighed. 'They've been standing there for over seventy years, detective. A few more years wouldn't hurt while they're made safe, and then they could be used for years to come. There are a few local flying clubs that are interested in hiring the space, and we'd be able to host historical re-enactments of all sorts there given the breadth of archaeological finds that have been made over the past four decades. There have even been Roman coins found by one amateur historian using a metal detector. They're in one of the local museums – you should take a look. It's intriguing stuff, you know.'

'It was my understanding that Mr Windlesham's application was going to include for redeveloping the control tower and officers' mess as features of the development,' said Mark.

'Exactly. All that history lost, smothered under plasterwork and goodness knows what else. Did you know there's meant to be an Iron Age settlement somewhere on that site as well? And don't get me started on the environmental impact.' Adrian sat back in his seat. 'So, I had to object. I had no choice.'

'Did you ever threaten Mr Windlesham about the development?'

'Threaten him? Good God, man – of course not. Why would I?'

'Do you know anyone who might?'

'Can't say I do, no.' Adrian frowned. 'Look, what's going on?'

'Mr Mackleton, an attempt was made on Mr Windlesham's life last Sunday. He was shot at, and although it appears he wasn't killed by that, it did cause him to fall into the river,' said Mark. 'He later died from complications from being submerged in water for a length of time before he could be rescued.'

'My God. Really?' Adrian's eyebrows shot upwards. 'The poor man.'

'Further, upon investigation at the airfield site, a number of graves have been found within the past twenty-four hours,' said Mark. 'Human graves, Mr Mackleton.'

Adrian swallowed. 'What's that got to do with me?'

'Given your objections to the site being developed, and your ease of access to the sort of drugs and surgical instruments that could kill someone, I need to know where you were last Sunday morning, and who you were with.' Mark watched while the man's jaw worked soundlessly, before a strangled sigh preceded the GP's next words.

'I think I'd like to call my solicitor.'

# CHAPTER THIRTY-ONE

It was late afternoon by the time Mark and West made their way downstairs to the interview rooms at Abingdon police station.

A deep russet hue brushed streaks across the golden sunlight hugging the horizon through the glass doors of the reception area, and Mark squinted as it caught his face when he reached the bottom of the stairs.

The doors swished open as a uniformed constable hurried inside, his hand on his radio while he nodded to Mark and murmured his thanks to West as she stood aside to let him pass.

A waft of nicotine-laden air followed through the front door in his wake, and Mark could see Adrian Mackleton through the closing doors as the GP hurriedly finished a cigarette. He was listening to another man in his early sixties who lowered his chin to speak to Adrian, their words lost through the double-glazed panes.

'That's his solicitor,' said PS Peter Cosley, looking up from his computer screen behind the reception desk. 'He just got here, and Mackleton wanted a cigarette.'

'That's ironic, given his profession.' Mark grinned, then wandered over to where West waited. 'Can you lead this one? I want to watch his reactions while you're interviewing him.'

'Sure.' She straightened. 'Any particular questions you've got in mind?'

'No, just follow your nose on this one. If I think of something you don't cover, I'll chip in.' He glanced over his shoulder as the front door opened. 'Dr Mackleton, if you'd like to come with us. Do you need a glass of water?'

'Please. Sorry, I don't usually smoke. My patients wouldn't be impressed.' Adrian cleared his throat, looking as if he was fighting down bile as well as the last vestiges of his cigarette. He gestured to the older man. 'This is my solicitor, William Hawsey.'

'We've met before,' said Mark, taking the man's business card. 'Shall we?'

He gestured to West, who was holding open the security door through to the interview rooms for Adrian, and fell into step behind the small group as she led the way down the corridor.

The solicitor walked with a stiff gait and paused to check his watch before entering the room and taking a seat beside his client. He opened a well-worn tan leather briefcase, extracted a fresh legal pad and pens, then clasped his hands on the table, his gaze expectant.

Mark switched on the recording equipment, and watched Adrian while West began by reminding the man he was still under caution following their earlier interview at his home.

The GP reconfirmed his name and other details, and tried to affect a relaxed pose that looked awkward, and fooled neither detective.

'Dr Mackleton, we asked you earlier to provide an alibi for your whereabouts on Sunday morning, which you refused to do when we were at your home. Would you like to change your statement from that time?' West said.

'I would, yes.' Adrian shot a sideways glance at Hawsey, who gave the briefest of nods. 'I'd spent the night at a hotel outside Henley with a woman who's still married – she's waiting for her divorce to go through, but until it does, she doesn't want her husband to find out. She's afraid he'll try to use that to gain more control over their two children.'

'We'll need a name,' said West, her tone dispassionate.

'It's Marie. But if you could please be discreet and not leave messages on her phone, we'd both be grateful,' said Adrian, before taking his phone from his pocket and setting it on the table. He swiped it open, then read out the mobile number from his contacts list. 'I was with her until eleven on Sunday, then drove home.'

West finished writing, then walked to the door and handed the page to the uniformed constable waiting outside. She eyed the doctor when she returned to her seat. 'What were your movements for the rest of that day?'

'I caught up with some reading after a light lunch, then went for a bike ride in the afternoon.'

'Who did you go with?'

'No one. The usual crowd I cycle with go out in the mornings and usually ride out to a café somewhere, so I just did a twenty-five-mile loop to stretch my legs.' Adrian leaned back in his chair. 'And I had to have an early night because I was due up at five in the morning to get ready to drive over to one of the training colleges in Oxford to deliver a guest lecture first thing, so once I'd had dinner I went up to bed about nine o'clock and read for a while – oh, and I texted Marie. Here.'

He spun the phone around to face Mark and West, and scrolled through an encrypted message service until he found the one he wanted. 'See?'

Mark bit back the rising disappointment in his chest, but kept his face passive while West jotted down the time that the message had been sent.

'When was the last time you visited the airfield?' she said.

'Back in February. Around about then. I'd heard someone had bought the site and wanted to see whether any immediate changes were apparent. Barry had set up that shipping container he used as an office by then, but he wasn't around. His mobile number was on a sign on the door, so I phoned him there and then – he was out meeting a site surveyor about the project, but said I was welcome to have a look around if I wanted to.'

'And did you?'

'I did, yes – only around the outside of the old officers' mess and the control tower. Barry had boarded up the old doorway to that by then – you used to be able to go inside it, but I guess his insurers probably advised him to block it off in case anyone fell out the top of it.'

'How long have you been a GP?'

'Over twenty years now.'

'Any problems during that time?'

'What do you mean?'

West looked at him patiently. 'Any complaints about your work?'

'No, not at all. The practice is well respected in the area.'

There was a knock at the door, and West opened it, her murmured reply to the constable inaudible to Mark. She gave him a slight nod as she returned.

Mark eyed him for a moment, then opened the manila folder and crossed his hands on top of the documents inside. 'Dr Mackleton, it appears that your alibi checks out, so I'd like to thank you for bearing with us. Perhaps I could impose on your professional knowledge to assist us further?'

'In what way?'

'Okay.' Mark pulled out a sketch of the airfield site from the folder and slid it across the table.

Adrian pulled the sketch closer, and frowned. 'This is Ravenswood airfield, isn't it? What are these markings beyond the old runway?'

'That, Dr Mackleton, is our crime scene,' said Mark. 'And so far, we have eleven victims that we believe were kept against their will in one of those buildings at the airfield before they were murdered.'

Adrian paled. 'Eleven? Even one victim doesn't bear thinking about.'

'I agree,' Mark said. 'Which is why I want your help in finding out where these murders may have been taking place.'

'How?'

'I realise that operating on people is very different to treating them, but I wonder if you could tell me what we would need to look for in relation to the sort of place where illegal operations could take place?'

'Illegal operations?' Adrian frowned. 'What's that got to do with—?'

'If you could just answer the question please.'

Adrian leaned back in his seat and stared at the table for a moment, drumming his fingers on the surface. He looked up eventually, his hand falling still. 'Um, well. You'd need sterile surgical instruments, obviously, and somewhere the recipient could recover – and they'd need access to ongoing care. I'm no expert, so that's the bare minimum of requirements. You'd need to speak with a surgeon to understand the details.'

'What about—'

'Excuse me, Sarge.' PS Peter Cosley peered around the interview room door, his entrance preceded by a brisk knock. 'Sorry to interrupt, but DI Kennedy would like a word with you and DC West.'

Mark gave the sergeant a curt nod, then turned back to Adrian Mackleton. 'Dr Mackleton, you're free to go but if you think of anything else that might help with our enquiries, please contact me on this number. Interview terminated at four oh thirteen.' He shoved his business card across the table, and signed off on the recording. 'Sergeant Cosley will see you out.'

West led the way back to the incident room, taking the stairs two at a time before thrusting open the door on the landing and hurrying along the corridor.

Kennedy was waiting for them, his jaw set. 'There's been a fire at an industrial unit over near Ravenswood. A patrol car's in attendance, and given what they've found, they've requested we take a look. You'll need to report to the fire chief, Bradley Holbrook, when you get there.'

'What have they found?' said Mark.

'The remains of any evidence that might've helped us find out who's responsible for the organ harvesting.'

# CHAPTER THIRTY-TWO

'Fuck.'

Jan rested her hands against the steering wheel and glared through the windscreen.

A pall of smoke was misting upwards from the twisted girders and cinderblock walls of what was once a row of three industrial units. The one on the far left had borne the brunt of the inferno, with its front windows exploding out across the concrete hardstanding and the large powder-coated aluminium warehouse door crumpling from the heat.

The middle unit had fared little better, with the fire tearing across the roof of the first unit and ripping its way through the ceiling of the next before taking hold in the upper offices and spreading downwards as it gathered force.

Only the third unit on the end bore any resemblance to an office, and that was just on the lower floor. Like its neighbours, its roof was missing and the upper storey bore a blackened and smudged façade.

Two fire trucks were still on site, and one of the crew was keeping a steady stream of water from a hose aimed at the base of the first building. Another man wearing the insignia of a crew manager paced the hardstanding, his gaze intent on what remained of the structure.

A single patrol car pulled away as Jan crawled the car to a standstill between a lopsided wooden fence that separated the small industrial estate from the road and a row of three industrial-sized clothing donation bins. She raised her hand in parting to the uniformed constable in the passenger seat of the patrol car as they passed, then braked and watched as the fire crew manager took photographs on his mobile phone, his face grim.

Despite the car windows being closed, her throat rasped with the stench of remnant smoke.

Turpin barked a cough, then: 'Shit.'

'According to Alex, the fire was reported at four o'clock this morning by a woman who lives along the lane there,' said Jan. 'She got up to let out her dog and smelled the smoke, then saw the glow from the flames through the trees. By the time the first crew got here, the end unit was long gone.'

'Shit,' he repeated, then sighed and reached for the door. 'Okay, might as well go and see what they can tell us.'

She followed Turpin across to a thin rope that had been strung between two temporary posts to prevent anyone getting too close to the buildings, and waited while he took a clipboard from a young uniformed constable and signed them both in. As he scrawled his signature, the crew manager turned away from the last building in the row and spotted them, lowering his phone.

'Turpin and West?' he said, tucking the phone into his fluorescent jacket as he walked over.

'Yes,' she said. 'We got here as soon as we could.'

'I'm Brad Holbrook,' he said, then hitched his thumb over his shoulder. 'Best get suited up if you want to take a look inside.'

Jan glanced at Turpin to see him wearing the same perplexed expression she was sure she wore. 'I'm sorry, why? We thought there was just some remnant evidence to gather up.'

Holbrook looked at them both, his face grim. 'We found two bodies at the back of the building ten minutes ago, inside the one on the end here that's been destroyed.'

'Jesus, were they trapped inside?' Jan swallowed as she looked past the crew manager to the blackened interior.

'Not exactly.'

Her attention returned to Holbrook. 'What do you mean?'

'One of them was dead before the fire was started, that much is likely. We're not sure about the other one.' He peered over his shoulder. 'Have you got any protective coveralls in your car, or do you want some of ours?'

'We've got some.'

'Come over as soon as you're ready, then. Forensics are on their way, and so is the pathologist.'

'Christ, now what?' Turpin said as they walked back to the car.

'I hate to think,' Jan replied. She opened the boot, handed him a sealed plastic bag and split open an identical one before extracting a set of coveralls with matching booties. Balancing on one foot while she pulled the coveralls over her suit, she eyed the skeletal remains of the industrial units. 'Do you think this is where the illegal organ harvesting was taking place?'

'Maybe.' Turpin stepped into the bootees, then glanced up as a goods train rattled past the back of the buildings. 'And that racket would help stop anyone hearing what was going on inside the building, wouldn't it?'

'Yes.' She locked the car as a grey panel van drove through the entrance, closely followed by Gillian Appleworth's car. 'Well, we're about to find out.'

They walked back to where Bradley Holbrook was waiting for them, and Jan greeted Jasper and the pathologist as they donned protective coveralls before turning to the fire crew manager. 'We're ready.'

'Okay, we'll be entering through the fire exit door at the back,' he said, already ushering them past the industrial unit on the far left before directing his commentary towards the forensic specialist. 'I've set out a demarcated path for you as far away from the bodies as I can so these two can see what we're dealing with – is that all right?'

'Yes, but if you can let me go first, then Gillian.' Jasper glanced over his shoulder. 'You two hold back until we call for you, okay?'

'Sounds good,' said Turpin. 'And thanks for letting us tag along.'

The smoke had dissipated, but the stench still clung to the air and Jan could hear the sound of running water now that the hose had been turned off. Water trickled from what was left of the upper storey and dripped over the lower floor, washing away embers and ash across the concrete hardstanding before it pooled beside an overflowing storm drain a few metres away.

'Here we go.' Holbrook stood next to an open fire-resistant door that had done its job for the first sixty minutes before the flames had taken hold. It had been wrenched off its hinges by the fire crew in their haste to check the building for survivors, and the broken remnants of wooden door frame now lay in splinters on the wet concrete.

Despite the paper mask she had donned before following the others, Jan wrinkled her nose at the pungent stench of smoke and burned flesh that caught on the breeze and smacked her in the face. Once identified, it could never be forgotten, and she had seen the aftermath of what fire could do to a human body too many times before.

Holbrook and the others stepped one at a time over the remains of six steel girders that had collapsed, and despite trusting the crew manager's judgement she looked up to check that there were no remaining beams that could fall. Exhaling, she moved in Turpin's footsteps, the plastic bootees slippery on the wet surface.

'Through here,' said Holbrook, pausing beside a blackened filing cabinet. Its drawers were open, the contents mere ash, but as he moved aside, Jan saw the curled-up remains of a human on the floor at its base. The mouth was open in a rictus snarl of agony, the head thrown back.

An overpowering stench assaulted her senses, and she took a step back.

'You'll have my full report in due course, but it's my view that this person was the one who started the fire,' said Holbrook.

'You can smell the accelerant, for a start, and it's my belief that this lump of plastic here is the remains of the petrol canister used.'

'Perhaps he started the fire to hide any evidence, then,' said Turpin, looking around. He sighed, his paper mask billowing. 'Which he seems to have succeeded in doing.'

'Not necessarily,' said Holbrook. 'Gillian, Jasper, are you okay to come back to this one? There's something else I want to show you first, and then you can get on.'

'Of course,' said the pathologist. 'Jasper, that okay with you?'

'Go on.'

Holbrook nodded. 'Thanks. Come with me.'

He ventured farther into the building, using a gloved hand to balance himself as he climbed over the remains of a plasterboard wall, and pointing out where he deemed it safe for them to tread. Then he branched off to the left, and walked beneath a supporting beam under which a doorway had once been. 'I think this was a sort of store room at the back of the unit, or what would have been used for warehousing if it had been that sort of business.'

'What sort of business *was* here before the fire?' said Jan.

'I'm not sure.' Holbrook shrugged. 'Two of your lot out there are interviewing the neighbouring business owners at the moment.'

'Okay.' She followed the others after him, finding herself amongst the twisted and crushed remains of wall-to-wall steel shelving units.

'Careful, there were scalpel blades stored here – some are

scattered on the floor, along with all that glass over there.' Holbrook moved farther into the room. 'Here we go.'

He stepped aside, revealing a long grey chest freezer, the lid open.

Jan swallowed, already knowing what she would see, but nevertheless horrified when she peered in and saw the man's body.

His face was turned away and his left arm was twisted over his cheek, obscuring his eyes and nose. A blue hue covered his cheekbone and neck, and days-old stubble clung to his jawline. He was wearing jogging bottoms and nothing else, his legs folded such that he could fit in the freezer. His fingers and toes were frostbitten and ice clung to his hair and eyebrows.

'May I?' Gillian said to Jasper.

'Go for it – we can't do anything until you're done here anyway,' came the reply.

The pathologist moved closer, obscuring Jan's view of the chest freezer while she worked. 'Can you give me a hand turning him?'

Jasper manoeuvred himself until he was leaning over the man's head and shoulders as Gillian wrapped her hands around his ankles, and then they rolled the body towards them.

Jan watched, observing the way the two specialists worked with a practised ease while affording the victim a modicum of respect as they gently moved his arms and legs away from the ice that clung to his skin and clothing.

That done, Jasper stepped back with a sigh. 'Looks like he put up a fight, given those bruises to his face.'

Intrigued, Jan moved closer and peered in. 'Bloody hell, Sarge – it's the bloke from the hospital.'

'What?'

'The one we saw in the security guard's body cam footage,' she said. 'The bloke who stole the kayaker's dry bag while Lloyd Derrie was creating a distraction.'

Her colleague closed the gap between them in two long strides and stared at the man's features. 'Shit. How long do you think he's been in here, Gillian?'

'Hard to say until I get him back to the morgue and defrost him. I'll take a body temperature reading now and continue to monitor it.'

'So, what do we think? Did he jump inside this to escape the fire, only to suffocate?' said Turpin.

'Maybe,' came the muffled reply. The pathologist's suit crackled while she continued to move around the freezer, her gaze never leaving the remains inside as she continued her assessment. 'Ah, perhaps not.'

'What've you got?' Jan took a step closer, leaning over the demarcation line to better see what the pathologist was doing.

'There's an incision in his abdomen, similar to what we've seen in the bodies recovered from the airfield site so far.' Gillian turned, her grey eyes keen. 'I think he was dead before he was placed in here.'

'Which might go some way to explain why Lloyd Derrie was so scared when we brought him in for questioning, and then decided that running out in front of a bus was a better option than this lot catching up with him,' Turpin said, frowning.

'Anything else for us at the moment, Brad?' said Jan.

The fire officer aimed his thumb over his shoulder. 'We're still processing down here, obviously, and we'll take a look at what's left of the upper storey once it cools down. In the meantime, I've got a couple of people dampening down some industrial waste bins out the back that also went up in smoke. As soon as they deem it safe, I'll hand them over to Jasper's team to go through.'

Gillian turned away from the chest freezer. 'So I'm wondering if perhaps whoever was carrying out the illegal organ harvesting and transplant operations was keeping donors hidden in the officers' mess building before the surgery took place, then storing the bodies here until they could be buried at the airfield. I mean, this place is only fifteen minutes away from the site, isn't it? A bit risky though, moving them twice.'

'True, but it's probably a system that worked well,' Jan said.

'Until Barry Windlesham's death,' added Turpin. 'And then the discovery of the graves at the airfield.'

'If we're right about that, then there's still a gaping hole in our theory,' Jasper said.

'He's right.' Turpin wandered a few paces away, his face pensive as he took in the ruined building.

'What's that?' asked Jan.

He turned back to her. 'Where the hell did they carry out the operations? And how did they transport the bodies once they were done?'

# CHAPTER THIRTY-THREE

The next morning brought a cloudless sky and the promise of warmer weather.

Mark left his jacket on the back seat of the car and followed Jan along East St Helen Street, treading carefully so as not to twist his ankle on the uneven pavers and exposed cast iron drain covers. Their route took them to the end of the street, and then along the river wharf. He glanced at the open door to the pub on his right, mindful that on any other Sunday, he and Lucy might have walked there from the narrowboat with Hamish tagging along.

Instead he was here, ready to interview another potential witness in what was becoming a desperate need for a breakthrough.

The previous evening had been spent going through the evidence to date, including the preliminary report from Bradley Holbrook's assessment of the fire at the industrial unit and a running commentary from Jasper over text messages while the forensic team sifted through the debris.

Gillan was already at the morgue this morning, working with Clive to carry out the post mortems of the two bodies discovered following the inferno.

Mark turned away from the pub, his focus turning to where a pair of women were conversing at the far end of the wharf, their backs turned to the approaching detectives.

'Who's that with Charmaine Abbott?' said Mark.

'It's her campaign manager, Judy Sarsgold. Her photo is on Charmaine's campaign website, along with a couple of assistants.'

'She can afford assistants?'

'She's a very successful business management consultant away from politics,' said West. 'And not cheap, if the micro company accounts that have been filed on the Companies House website are anything to go by.'

'Good to know.' Mark raised his voice as they drew near. 'Charmaine Abbott? Detective Sergeant Mark Turpin, my colleague DC Jan West. We were advised we should meet you here, rather than at your house.'

'That's right.' The woman was a full head shorter than him, but was wearing three-inch heels and lifted her chin by way of compensation, her gaze steady. 'Hope that's okay?'

'No problem at all.' He glanced at the other woman who was standing a few paces away, her ear to her phone while she watched them with interest. 'As long as it is with you?'

'Oh, sure. Judy's been looking after my business and personal affairs for a number of years, and I have no secrets from her. I presume this is about Barry Windlesham? I saw you both at Friday's pre-planning meeting, didn't I?'

'You did. We were hoping—'

'Hang on. I need to do a quick piece to camera to post on my social media so Judy can schedule it to go out in half an hour. I was meant to do this yesterday, but something cropped up,' Charmaine said, turning away and hurrying across to the wrought iron railing that bordered the river. 'Don't get in the background, will you? You'll spoil it.'

'Flipping heck,' West muttered while they watched the woman fix a broad smile to her face, angle her body sideways to her phone and flick her hair over her shoulder. 'Felix Darrow wasn't kidding about trying to get in with the younger demographic of voters, was he? I mean, listen to her.'

Mark did, suppressing a smile.

Charmaine opened her spiel to camera with a breezy hello, gestured expansively to the scenic watercourse beside her, then frowned and went on to say that the local environment was in constant danger, and she was its champion. She ended her video with a call to her followers to take action, clearly aimed at those undecided about which way to cast their vote in the coming months, then lowered the phone and hurried over, thumbing the screen as she approached. 'Judy, I've just sent that to you so you can head off if you want?'

'Thanks.' The other woman checked her phone. 'Okay, so once you wrap up here, you need to get yourself over to the airfield to meet with Gaynor Alton's solicitor and reiterate your opposition to the proposed development. He's only going to be there until half eleven,' she added, with a pointed look at Mark and West.

'No problem.' Charmaine turned to them. 'I noticed that access has been blocked to the site this morning. What's going on?'

'Routine enquiries,' Mark said. 'We'll have it open again as soon as possible.'

'You'll need to.' Judy glanced at the politician. 'We're planning to record a video later in the week to show the sort of wildlife that can be found there – we'll miss the opportunity to film the hares that've been seen otherwise.'

Charmaine smiled at the two detectives. 'One of our charity contacts told us he's seen hares boxing on the fringes of the woodland, and Judy thought it'd make a great analogy about the fight we've got on our hands to protect the area.'

Mark said nothing, while West looked away, her jaw clamped shut. Despite that, he could see the threatening smirk on her lips.

'Right, Charmaine – I'll let you get on,' said Judy. 'I'll call you later to confirm the meeting with that woodland charity near Wallingford. Pencil in this Thursday at five o'clock.'

With that, Judy gave a satisfied nod, and waved her farewell.

'Sorry about that,' said Charmaine, turning her attention back to Mark and West. 'We're trying to capture as much as possible of my campaign on video at the moment, and what with that and attending all the usual meetings... We ran some analytics last week and it seems most of my voters prefer to hear from me mid-morning on weekends so we need to keep everything as fresh and relevant as possible. Every vote counts, after all, especially now that we're only a few months away from the re-election. My party are obviously very keen for me to stand again, and I'm keen to represent them locally, you see. I'm a safe pair of hands being a long-term resident and business owner.'

Mark waited until she paused to gulp a breath. 'We'd like to speak with you about the death of Barry Windlesham, Mrs Abbott, particularly your objections to the airfield development.'

Her perfectly arched eyebrows shot upwards. 'Why?'

Mark looked over his shoulder, checked there were no passers-by, and then guided Charmaine over to one of the wrought iron and wooden planked benches under the trees beside the river. 'Let's talk over here, out of the way.'

The woman sat at the far end of the bench, watching West while the detective constable pulled her notebook from her handbag and stood equidistant between her and Mark. 'What's going on? Barry drowned, didn't he? What's this got to do with me?'

Mark took the other end of the bench, adopting a casual pose. 'How long had you known Mr Windlesham?'

'Not long, I suppose. A few weeks, that's all.'

'Was that before or after you became aware of his plans for the airfield?'

'I heard someone had bought the land, so I made enquiries.' Charmaine's shoulders relaxed a little as she warmed to her subject. 'Of course, I wanted to make sure the new owner understood and appreciated my constituents' concerns about any redevelopment of the land, given the exquisite flora and fauna there, and so I introduced myself as soon as possible.'

'In person, or over the phone?'

'I asked Judy, who you just met, to get in touch in the first instance. I was surprised when Barry suggested we meet on site so I could show him in person what my concerns were.' Charmaine's brow furrowed. 'And yet, despite my showing him the different orchids and insect life that was in abundance there, he still went ahead with the proposal. So frustrating.'

'Did you meet with Mr Windlesham at any time after that first visit?'

'Oh, yes.' Charmaine nodded. 'There were a few meetings within the context of the pre-planning process over the last few weeks. I mean, he did make some concessions to which parts of the airfield he would develop but the eventual result would be the same – a lack of protection for the environment. He just wasn't prepared to preserve enough green space within the housing plans.'

'Did you ever socialise with him?'

'No.' She frowned. 'Why would I?'

'So you never met with him to discuss the proposal outside of any official meetings?'

'No.' Charmaine glanced at West, then back. 'Listen, what's going on?'

'We have reason to believe that someone attempted to murder Mr Windlesham on Sunday, and that his drowning wasn't an accident,' said Mark. 'Did you ever get the impression in your meetings with him that he was under duress, or any stress regarding the project?'

'Not at all, no.'

'Did you ever send threatening letters to his home address?'

'Good God, no. Why would I? All of our conversations were extremely civil, even if we did disagree.' Charmaine shook her head. 'I mean, I didn't see eye to eye with Barry, but for someone to do that... He was a good man, just misguided in his attempts to do something with the old airfield site.'

'What would you do to the site?' said West. 'If you had the chance?'

'Oh, that's easy – I'd raise money to rewild the entire place,' said Charmaine, beaming. 'Can you imagine? We could integrate an educational centre for children, introduce bushcraft courses, things like that. The whole place could remain protected while still bringing in jobs for the local area. It'd be so much more beneficial to the environment than another housing estate in an area that lacks the infrastructure to support such a project.'

'So, you might benefit from Mr Windlesham's death?' said Mark.

Charmaine's jaw dropped. 'You can't seriously be suggesting I had anything to do with that. I mean, I hardly knew him for a start.'

'But you've said yourself that you could benefit from a different approach to the site.'

'Detective, I resent your accusation,' Charmaine hissed. She stood, checked around to make sure no one was within listening distance of the bench, then glared at him. 'I've worked bloody hard to achieve what I have in my political career, and I'm not about to let the police screw that up for me. I had nothing to do with Barry's death.'

'Understood,' said Mark, raising his hands to placate her. 'But you do understand, we had to ask.'

She reached into her handbag, pulled out a business card, and thrust it at him. 'The next time you want to speak to me, you can do so through my solicitor. And be warned – if any disparaging rumours about my supposed involvement in your investigation reach the media, I'll be reporting you to your superior officers. Goodbye, Detective Turpin.'

With that, she strode away from them, turning the corner to East St Helen Street without a backward glance.

'That went well, Sarge.' West finished her note-taking and moved closer. 'She looked like she'd sucked on a wasp.'

Mark smiled. 'I had to ask her.'

'Agreed, but I think your people skills still need some refinement.' She frowned. 'You didn't tell her about the graves we found.'

'No.' He leaned back on the bench and eyed the fast-flowing river as it lapped at the grassy bank on the opposite side. 'She said herself – she wants the site redeveloped, just not in the way Windlesham had planned. She wasn't interested in preventing it being used for something else.'

His colleague emitted a frustrated sigh. 'Back to the drawing board then, Sarge.'

# CHAPTER THIRTY-FOUR

When Gaynor Alton opened the door to her brother's house, she wore a crumpled pale blue shirt over jeans and a wary expression.

'I thought you might be in touch,' she said, standing to one side to let Mark and West pass.

'And I thought you might've informed us about your intentions to take over your brother's business after his death,' said Mark. He could smell the remnants of a recent meal – garlic, onions, mixed with beef and something else, green vegetables perhaps. 'Sorry if we're interrupting lunch.'

'You're not,' she said, closing the door. 'I was just stacking the dishwasher.'

There were two suitcases and a navy canvas sports bag on the marble tiled floor at the base of the staircase, together with a tan leather handbag and an empty laptop case.

'Are you leaving?' said West.

'In a few hours. We thought we'd dodge the worst of the traffic on the M4 if we left after five. I was going to phone—' Gaynor sighed. 'I'm sorry, I couldn't tell you about the directorship of Barry's business before that pre-planning approval meeting, and I was bound by a non-disclosure agreement until the final papers were signed.'

'Nevertheless, we need to talk,' said Mark. 'And this time, it'll be on the record.'

'Oliver's in the study catching up on paperwork. Do you need to speak to him as well, or just me?'

'Just you, unless his name is also now linked to the business.'

'Come through to the living room then.'

When they walked in, there was a classical radio station playing softly via the large television on the wall, and after directing them to the six-seater sofa in front of it, Gaynor reached for the remote control, silencing the music before she perched on the end cushion.

After reciting the formal caution, Mark eyed the woman carefully. 'Apart from Ravenswood airfield, what other sites does the business have by way of investments?'

'None, just that one,' she said. 'And before you ask, I've got no intention of continuing with the project. I've instructed Max Swift – my solicitor – to find a buyer.'

'But your solicitor told me on Friday that you'd be moving forward with the planning application,' said West. 'And that was less than forty-eight hours ago. What's changed?'

'Nothing. You're mistaken – I am letting the planning application process continue, but only so that the site can be sold as a going concern for a new developer.' Gaynor sighed. 'It's not worth much otherwise, according to Max. And I've got no intention of moving here to oversee something like that. I've got a career, as has Oliver.'

'So why agree to become a director of the company two weeks ago?' Mark said.

'Barry could be very persuasive. And I was intrigued. He told me at the time that I wouldn't have to do anything, just sign off on occasional formal paperwork such as the yearly accounts, tax statements, that sort of thing. He hasn't got children or heirs, and he said this way, if something happened to him I wouldn't be exposed to so much inheritance tax because I'd receive the business assets instead.' Her hands trembled as she wiped at the tears forming. 'If only I'd thought to ask... He didn't sound worried about anything, he was just his usual self when he phoned up to ask me.'

'So you didn't meet in person to discuss any of this?'

'No, like I told you last week, the last time we saw Barry was in February. But he left a message for me two weeks ago saying he wanted a quick word – that was the exact phrase he used, so I didn't think it was urgent – but when I called him back during my lunch break he said that taking on a huge project like Ravenswood made him realise that he should build some contingency into both the business and his personal affairs.'

'Contingency?' said West. 'How much collateral did you have to put in to become a director?'

'Only a nominal five hundred pounds,' said Gaynor. 'Just to put some equity in for accounting purposes. And until Barry's death, he only had me on board as a non-voting director.'

'But you became the sole voting director on your brother's death,' said Mark.

The woman's gaze snapped from West to him, and a snarl crossed her lips. 'I didn't kill my brother, Detective Turpin. Nor did I have him killed, before you accuse me of that as well.'

He held up his hands. 'We've already established your alibis following our last conversation, Mrs Alton. Who did Barry buy the airfield site from?'

'Apparently it belonged to a wealthy woman nearby,' said Gaynor, pushing herself off the sofa and crossing to the patio doors. She folded her arms and gazed out across the lawn. 'It was previously farming land that'd been passed down through three generations. The Ministry of Defence took over the place in 1941 like a lot of land at the time, but luckily for the family it was handed back in 1962. The woman who sold it to Barry last year was in her late fifties. The MoD passed it back to her father.'

'Was?'

'She died in August, according to Max.'

'What was her name?'

'I don't know off the top of my head. I'd have to ask Max.'

'We could call him, if you're heading back home today.'

'Of course.' Gaynor crossed to the coffee table, picked up her phone and read out the solicitor's number from her contacts list.

'Do you know if the woman who sold the site had any children?'

'Two daughters. They both live locally – one is an industrial chemist, and the other's a sculptor. I remember that much. Neither were interested in hanging onto the land – the younger one who's the chemist wanted the money to pay off her university debts and they both planned to buy houses after the deal was completed. Max said they couldn't understand why their mother held onto it – it wasn't being used for farming or earning money in any other way. It's just been sitting there.'

'Any idea what the mother did for a living if she didn't use the land for anything?'

'No, but apparently she retired early and lived well. Barry told me that her house was advertised for nearly a million pounds after she died. I suppose she had some good investment advice given that she wasn't concerned about selling the airfield. She simply left it there to rot.'

# CHAPTER THIRTY-FIVE

Mark popped the lid on the can of energy drink, wrinkled his nose at the sickly sweet aroma that escaped, then took a slurp and suppressed a belch.

He ran a hand over tired eyes, biting back a yawn.

The past three hours had been spent reviewing all the investigation notes to date, including a further review of the house-to-house enquiries that had taken place around Ravenswood airfield and those from Barry Windlesham's friends and family.

Gaynor and Oliver Alton had returned to Cardiff, leaving a key to Windlesham's house with DI Kennedy with confirmation that the place would be sold as soon as the investigation was concluded and probate matters settled.

In the meantime, West had left a message with Gaynor's solicitor, asking Max Swift to phone them as soon as he got in to his office the next day. When Mark walked back upstairs to the incident room, she was focused on her computer screen, her jaw set.

'There's very little in the local news about the sale of the airfield to Windlesham last year,' she said. 'Just a few snippets here and there that he was buying to redevelop it. Most of the articles talk about the history of the place during the Second World War, and there are one or two articles that mention the way nature's taken over the place since. Oh, and there was a letter to an editor of one local newspaper from last July that talks about the dangerous state of the old aircraft hangars.'

'Do any of them mention that woman, the seller?'

'No, nothing. There is one that mentions that the seller was represented by a firm of solicitors in Oxford though, so I've left a message for them as well.' She closed the web browser as he passed her a chocolate bar from the vending machine. 'Thanks. If neither solicitor gets back to me by lunchtime tomorrow, I'll chase them up.'

'And if that doesn't work, tell me and I'll phone them.' Kennedy's voice carried across the room as he emerged from his office. 'It's been a week since Windlesham was shot at, and we've still got no idea who wanted him dead, even if we do know why.'

The detective inspector crossed to the whiteboard, gave a low whistle to attract the attention of the rest of the team, and waited while they gathered around. Despite it being a weekend, there were still more uniformed officers than the roster indicated, with several of them opting to take overtime or cancel personal engagements to lend their support to the enquiry.

Kennedy checked his watch before he began. 'Gillian

Appleworth has arranged to video call me in fifteen minutes, and she's agreed that it would be useful for all of you to hear her findings from the first post mortems that she's carried out this weekend, rather than wait for her reports given the urgency of the situation. Where's Tracy? Can you set up the call on this laptop here?'

The team's administration officer elbowed her way between PS Peter Cosley and a uniformed constable with a determined expression. 'No problem, guv. I've just had an update from Will Trelawny over at digital forensics – he's been working on Windlesham's mobile phone this weekend and has some news too. Do you want me to give him a call and put him on speaker phone while we're waiting for Gillian?'

'Please do.' Kennedy waited while she dialled the number, then turned up the volume. 'Will? It's DI Kennedy at Abingdon. I've got you on speaker so the rest of my team can hear you. Tracy says you've got an update for us.'

'Thanks, Ewan. Afternoon, everyone.' The forensic specialist cleared his throat. 'Okay, so the phone fished out of the river at Culham wasn't damaged thanks to Windlesham putting it in a waterproof bag first. We've managed to unlock it but there's nothing on it to suggest it belonged to Windlesham himself. None of the numbers in the recent calls list match any of the ones that his admin assistant passed on to us, and there are no names saved to the contacts list.'

'Got any good news for us, Will?' Kennedy growled, his chin in his hand as he listened.

'Actually, I do.' Mark could hear the smile in the other man's voice. 'Whoever's phone this is, they were sent a text message three weeks ago with details of a train going to Didcot station. Nothing else, just a time and the date. That could be related to someone arriving or someone departing, but…'

'If we have that, we can check it against CCTV images from the station and see if we recognise anyone on the platform,' Kennedy finished, writing down the text details on the whiteboard. 'That's a good lead, Will. Anything else?'

'No, sorry.'

'Never mind. Good work. I'll let you get on, thanks.' The DI ended the call and turned his attention to Caroline. 'Can you follow up that CCTV footage and get someone to review it with you as soon as possible?'

'No problem, guv. I'll phone them after the briefing.'

'And what about Windlesham's car? Any luck?'

'Not yet, guv.' The detective constable frowned. 'None of his neighbours have seen it, and it hasn't been found abandoned anywhere yet.'

'Keep looking.'

'Guv?' Tracy called over from the neighbouring desk. 'I've got Gillian on video conference ready for you.'

'Thanks,' said Kennedy, turning the laptop to face the team. 'Gillian? Good to see you – thanks for doing this. Makes a lot of sense in the circumstances.'

'No problem,' said the pathologist. 'I can imagine you're as busy as I am, so I won't hang around. If you're all ready, I can begin.'

'We're ready,' said the DI, casting his gaze around the team as a few stragglers found seats and opened their notebooks. 'Over to you.'

'Thank you.' Gillan was sitting at her desk, and settled into her seat as she began. 'I concluded the post mortem on the most recent victim found at the airfield site, and I passed on DNA swabs to Jasper yesterday. In the meantime, I can confirm there are no trauma wounds to bones, apart from a broken toe that looks to be several years old. I've concluded that given the rate of decomposition, he's been in the ground for no longer than four weeks. Normally, that would mean a lot of evidence would already be lost, but the soil around here is heavily clay-based, which slows down the decomposition rate a little. So, although his organs have started to decompose, I was able to ascertain that he had both kidneys removed.'

'Any chance you can tell us the cause of death?' said Kennedy.

Gillian's mouth twisted. 'I've sent some samples for analysis, but it's going to be difficult Ewan, given the state of the remains. As I said, there are no blunt trauma wounds.'

'Damn. Okay, how does that one relate to the other graves?'

'The others are older, with the next recent being under a year old I think – I'll have to run some more tests before I can corroborate that though, so that's off the record for now.'

'And the oldest grave?'

'Give me a chance, Ewan. It's only been two days.'

A ripple of laughter flittered through the incident room as the DI gave the pathologist a rueful smile. 'It was worth a shot.'

'Shall I move on to the next report?' Gillian said. 'I think the findings from this might help shed some light on how the victims at the airfield died.'

'Please do.'

'Okay, so the man found in the chest freezer – he had a similar incision to his abdomen, which upon examination proved that he'd had his kidneys removed recently. Again, there's no sign of a typical blunt trauma wound.' Gillian leaned closer to the screen as she warmed to her subject. 'There are signs of damage to tissue, and a couple of broken fingers but that's likely due to the way he was crammed into such a tight space – he was quite a tall man.'

Mark swallowed, his mouth dry. 'Gillian, were there any signs of a struggle, or him being overpowered?'

'None at all,' replied the pathologist. 'Which makes me wonder, were these victims led to believe that they would survive these procedures?'

'As soon as we're able to identify the victims, we'll be able to look into their financial history,' said Kennedy. 'At least that way, we'll be able to see if any large sums of money changed hands, and perhaps trace the source of that income.'

'Unless they were paid in cash of course,' said Gillian. 'That way, the money could be easily retrieved once the donor was dead.'

Mark ran his thumb down his notes, then frowned. 'Gillian, you said there were no signs of a struggle, and that there were no obvious trauma wounds to bones. How are you suggesting that this man was killed?'

'An overdose,' came the reply. 'Due to the preservation of his remains, I was able to run some tests. I'm willing to posit that this man was killed by a massive overdose of barbiturates, probably whilst under the effects of a general anaesthetic. It would have been quite simple to have simply turned up the dosage once the organ harvesting was complete. It would be easier to pacify them that way, and – forgive me for sounding crass – better for the harvesting of vital organs if adrenaline levels were kept to a minimum.'

'But this bloke wasn't a donor, was he?' said West, looking at Mark. 'We know he was the bloke who took the dry bag from the sluice room at the hospital, and may be the same man sent to kill Windlesham. So why kill him and put him in the freezer? Why harvest his kidneys? They wouldn't do that without making sure he was a suitable match for a donor, would they?'

'Maybe it was to teach him a lesson,' Kennedy murmured, his face troubled.

'And maybe,' said Mark, 'given that the grave site had already been discovered by us, the industrial unit was meant to be a temporary measure.'

'Why, if they had a donor lined up ready?' said Jan.

'Because maybe they didn't,' said Mark. 'Maybe they decided to kill him because he was deemed a risk, and then auction his kidneys. Maybe we're not just dealing with one illegal organ harvesting group, but a network of them.'

# CHAPTER THIRTY-SIX

A shocked silence followed Turpin's words.

Jan could hear the awkward shuffle of feet across the carpet from the young uniformed constables standing at the back, the clock ticking on the wall above the whiteboard, and the purr of traffic beyond the incident room windows. She looked around at her colleagues' faces, and saw each of them wearing a sickened expression at the reality of what they were hearing, each of them meeting her stare with the briefest shake of the head, or lowering their gaze to the floor while they absorbed Gillian's findings.

Then the pathologist's voice pulled her attention back, and she tightened her grip on her pen once more.

'I've got my findings from the post mortem of the other body found at the industrial unit, too,' said Gillian. 'The one found burned. If, that is, you're ready?'

Kennedy cleared his throat. 'We're ready.'

'Okay, so obviously this victim was in a greater state of

decomposition due to fire damage so I'm limited with what I can tell you. However, I have passed on DNA swabs to Jasper and the lab and requested that they undertake urgent tests. If you don't hear anything by tomorrow afternoon, Ewan, you might want to phone them.'

'Noted,' said the DI. 'Go on.'

'I believe that this victim was killed by a blunt trauma wound, but it's towards the top of his skull, which has splintered from the impact. I found traces of wood and metal in amongst the bone, so I'm inclined to suggest that he was killed as a result of the building collapsing before he could escape. Jasper will have more information for you, but from my conversation earlier with him, and from what Bradley Holbrook told us on site, it may be the case that this is the person who started the fire.'

'Can you corroborate that?' Kennedy said.

'I will do, within my final report and after I've heard back from Jasper to confirm my opinion.' Gillian leaned back from her screen. 'That's all I have for you at the present time. The other remains from the airfield will be examined over the course of next week, so if I learn anything else from those that will help you with the investigation, I'll be in touch.'

'Thank you,' said Kennedy, and ended the video call. He turned his attention to the team. 'I'm sure I'm not the only one who needs a five-minute break after that. We'll reconvene at six thirty. Don't be late.'

———————

Jan stood on the landing between the ground floor and the incident room, ignoring the foot traffic passing on the stairwell behind her, and gazed at the softening amber hues from the setting sun beyond the windows.

Indigo clouds smudged the horizon, and a thin sliver of crescent moon shone above the trees lining the industrial estate beyond the main road.

'I'm sorry, love, but you can still go to see the film with your dad, right?'

Her heart tugged as her eldest twin, Harry, sighed at the other end of the phone. 'But we've planned it for weeks, Mum.'

'I know, but a man died last week and I'm helping to find out who hurt him to help his family.' She lowered her voice as a pair of uniformed constables thundered down the stairs, watching until they were out of sight and the security door through to the reception area slammed shut in their wake. 'I'll just have to catch it when it's on one of the streaming services – that'll only be a few weeks away, won't it? No spoilers in the meantime, though.'

'I should tell you the ending,' he grumbled.

She could hear the smile in his voice despite the threat. 'Don't you dare, you little toe rag. Tell you what, keep your dad company tonight because I know he's been looking forward to it just as much as you and Luke, and I'll treat us all to a day out as soon as this case is closed. Sound good?'

'All right. Love you. Gotta go. Here's Dad.'

'Hey, love.' Scott's voice cut through her exhaustion, his soft baritone soothing her fatigue. 'I take it that it's going to be a late one for you?'

'We're only halfway through the briefing,' she said. 'And

we're not even close to finding out who did this, so it's going to be one of those weeks.'

'Sorry to hear that— Hang on. Shhh, Luke. Let me talk to your mum. No, I don't know where your trainers are. Have you looked under your bed? Sorry, love. How are you? Do you need me to drop anything off to you on our way out?'

She smiled. 'No, but thanks. Hopefully I'll be back before ten. I reckon this briefing will go on for a bit and then Mark and I will probably stay on to try and get a head start on the paperwork before tomorrow.'

'While I think of it, and only if you can, did you ask if he and Lucy want to come along to the dads versus lads football match on Friday night?'

'Oh, Christ, I'd almost forgotten with everything else going on here. What time's kick-off?'

'Six o'clock.'

'Okay, I'll ask him tonight before we leave.' She glanced over her shoulder as the door at the top of the stairs opened and Turpin peered out. He beckoned. 'I've got to go, looks like Kennedy's ready for round two.'

'I'll see you later, love.'

'Love you. Enjoy the film.'

She ended the call and hurried up the stairs, smiling her thanks to Turpin as he held open the door for her and fell into step beside her as they headed back towards the incident room.

'Everything all right at home?'

'Yes, thanks – and before I forget, Scott's asked if you and Lucy would like to watch him and the boys play football on Friday night. Six o'clock kick-off.'

'I'll check with the social secretary but I'm sure we'll be okay for that. Drinks afterwards?'

'Sounds good, Sarge.'

They found their seats at the front of the gathered officers, and fell silent as Kennedy waited beside the whiteboard, his hand hovering above the desk phone once more.

'Everyone here?' he barked, stopping to crane his neck over the team for any stragglers, then: 'Good. Okay, next up – Jasper's on the line ready with what he's managed to find to date. Jasper, you there?'

The call connected, and the forensic specialist's dulcet tones filled the room. 'Evening, all. If you're all sitting comfortably, then I'll begin.'

Jan settled into her chair and readied her notebook and pen.

'I thought I'd give you all an update this evening rather than tomorrow because I've just heard from the lab,' Jasper began. 'I called in a favour with someone there who's been working over the weekend, and they've come through with some results for us.'

As one, the team fell silent, with any remnant conversations frozen on the air.

'Go on,' said Kennedy, his gaze boring into the phone.

'Okay, well to put it simply, they've got a match between the DNA swabs we took from the officer's mess, and that from the latest victim uncovered at the grave site.'

The DI exhaled. 'So whoever he is, he managed to break out of there, only to be recaptured. Are you sure about the testing, Jasper?'

'They double checked everything before phoning me with the results. The swab was taken from some clothing that had caught on the door splinters. There was some blood mingled with the threads so whoever he is, he caught himself on the door when he escaped.'

'I wonder where they put him once they caught him?' said Jan. 'I mean, it'd have been too risky to put him back in the officers' mess, and the other buildings are open to the elements.'

'I might be able to shed some light on that,' said Caroline, raising her voice from the back of the room. She moved to where Kennedy was standing. 'If I may, guv?'

'The floor's yours,' he said. 'What've you got?'

'I've been spending the day reinterviewing the other business owners at the industrial estate where the fire was,' she said. 'Although no one could tell the officers that carried out the initial interviews yesterday who ran the business where the fire started, I've just taken a call from the bloke who owns the welding place opposite. He said that he'd seen occasional deliveries by a white van at odd hours. Apparently, he's an insomniac and sometimes works late at night to keep on top of things.'

'Did he see who was driving the van?'

'No, guv – but he did say that three weeks ago, he saw two men meet the van and help unload it. He said it looked like a heavy, long object because it took two of them to carry it into the building.'

'Did he see any identifying markings on the van?' said Kennedy.

'No, there's no lighting on the industrial estate in that corner so it was too dark for him to see. He did say that on one of those occasions, they took a bag from the van over to the charity clothing bins next to the perimeter fence.'

Kennedy's eyes widened as he listened. 'Sounds like he's our only witness to bodies being taken from wherever the operations were carried out and being stored prior to burial.'

'And perhaps using the charity bins to dispose of the victims' clothing after they'd been killed,' said Turpin.

'Why not destroy the clothing instead?' said Jan.

'Maybe they couldn't, or didn't want to risk remnants showing up,' said Turpin. 'And passing on the clothes to charity shops would mean they'd get washed and mixed with other people's DNA over time. It'd be impossible to trace back to any of the victims.'

'It's genius. Bastards.' Kennedy turned back to the phone. 'Did you get all of that, Jasper?'

'I did. Can you get a patrol over there now to tape off the bins and I'll meet them there? We didn't have any luck with the bin right outside the industrial unit, but this sounds promising.'

'It does. Before you go, have you got anything else for us?'

'Not yet – we've retrieved the remains of some of the items that were in the industrial unit and damaged by the fire, and we're working on processing as much as we can from the airfield graves that have been exhumed so far to get results to you as soon as possible, so I'll phone you with another update late tomorrow.'

'Thanks.' Kennedy turned to the team after Jasper hung up. 'Caroline, can you liaise with the patrol going over to the industrial site to ask them to find out the name of the organisation that collects from those charity bins, then phone them? We need to find out what happens to those clothes, and when the last collection was made.'

'Will do, guv.'

He turned to the youngest detective. 'Alex, can you make a start going through the missing persons database as soon as Jasper sends the DNA results through? If these donors were held against their will, we need to consider that they were vulnerable to exploitation.' The DI turned back to the phone as it rang once more. 'Are you expecting anyone else to call in, Tracy?'

'No, guv.' She hurried over and peered at the screen. 'That's the internal number from CrimeStoppers.'

He snatched up the phone. 'DI Kennedy. Right. Yes. Is that so? Got a number? Thanks.'

'Now what?' Turpin murmured.

Jan's skin prickled as Kennedy returned the phone to its cradle, his eyes gleaming. 'Guv?'

'Apparently, CrimeStoppers took a call ten minutes ago from the father of two boys who were out cycling near Culham village last Sunday,' the DI said, a grin forming. 'And he says they've caught a man on their phone cameras who I reckon might be Windlesham's attacker. Mark, Jan – make sure you interview them after school tomorrow.'

# CHAPTER THIRTY-SEVEN

The next morning, Mark jumped the mountain bike's tyres from the road onto the pavement, thanking a dog-walker who stepped aside to let him zip past, and changed gear as he pedalled through the back lanes that ran parallel to Ock Street.

His backpack was heavier today, laden with the laptop he'd taken home to catch up on emails and a plastic container filled with ginger biscuits that Lucy had baked the previous evening. His suit had been carefully rolled up to avoid as many creases as possible, and somewhere within the main compartment was a can of energy drink he knew he would need within the hour.

He wore a T-shirt and shorts, relishing the fresh air that carried from the river and washed over him, and he was already invigorated by a run with Hamish an hour ago that had seen them take in the Abbey Gardens and Meadows before returning to the narrowboat out of breath and gasping for water.

After a hurried goodbye to Lucy, he had set out again, a renewed determination surging through him.

The revelations from yesterday's briefing had been shocking, and he was under no illusion that it would take the investigative team all of their efforts to trace whoever was responsible for the horrific crimes.

Checking over his shoulder, Mark braked to let a double-decker bus pass and then swung his leg over the bike as he braked to a standstill beside the police station car park's security barrier.

'Morning, Sarge,' Alex called. He waited by the back door, holding it open as Mark locked up the bike and then followed. 'Good ride?'

'Yes, thanks. How was your evening?'

'Quiet.' The detective constable gave a shy smile. 'I kind of needed it after this week, and Becky had been with her friends all weekend so we crashed on the sofa.'

'Sometimes you need to do that. I'll grab a quick shower and see you upstairs.' Mark slid the box of biscuits from his backpack. 'Hand those out while you're up there – Lucy's been busy again, and my waistline won't thank me if I eat them all. Have you seen Kennedy yet?'

'His car's parked in the usual place, but the engine was still cooling down when I walked past.' Alex checked his watch. 'He wasn't planning on a briefing this morning, was he?'

'No. We'll catch up later if any of us manage to find out something to help us along. Catch you in a bit.'

Mark took five minutes to shower, towelled his hair dry and applied a liberal amount of deodorant and ten minutes later walked into the incident room to find Ewan Kennedy pacing the carpet beside his desk, his face thunderous while West tried to hide behind her computer screen.

'What happened, guv?'

'Someone managed to film what was going on at the airfield this morning,' the DI growled. 'And I'm going to fucking string them up when I find out who. It's been posted to social media within the last fifteen minutes.'

'Can't we get it taken down?'

'We're already onto the person who posted it, but you know what it's like. I've asked the media team to get a press release out before nine o'clock but we're in damage limitation mode now.'

Mark kicked his backpack under the desk and moved around to West's computer.

She had a download of the offending video playing, and he groaned when he saw the zoomed-in images of the white tents and figures walking back and forth in protective suits. 'Bugger. We're not going to be able to downplay that, are we?'

'We can say it's an ongoing investigation that hasn't yet determined whether the remains are historical or otherwise,' said West. 'That's what we're going with at the moment anyway, until we've heard back from Kidlington.'

Mark raised an eyebrow at Kennedy. 'The top brass are involved?'

'You bet they are,' the DI said. 'And I don't need to tell you that it's going to cause us all sorts of problems. They'll be sending someone over within the next day or two to audit the investigation at this rate.'

'Fuck. We don't need to lose that sort of momentum now.'

Kennedy glared at him. 'So why are you two still here when there are leads to follow up?'

———————

'I don't envy Alex and Caroline being stuck in the incident room this morning,' said West, her heels clacking on the asphalt as they made their way towards the pool car. She aimed the key fob at it, then opened an empty plastic bag and emptied the passenger footwell of crisp packets and a crumpled soft drink can. 'Honestly, you'd have thought by now that Alex would clean up after himself.'

Mark smiled, despite the gloomy start to the day. 'You can lead a horse to water...'

'It's like having a third kid around sometimes,' she grumbled. She tied off the ends of the bag and carried it over to a nearby wheelie bin before returning. 'And I didn't get to tell you my news thanks to Kennedy being in a foul mood.'

'What's that?' He caught the keys she tossed to him and got in, starting the engine. 'And what leads did Kennedy mean? I thought we weren't interviewing those teenagers until later today.'

'I got a phone call last night from Max Swift, Barry Windlesham's solicitor.'

'Really? What did he want at that time of night?'

West waited until they had passed under the security barrier. 'Head towards Wallingford. Swift said he was prepping for a probate hearing first thing today and came across some paperwork from when Barry purchased the airfield site. He confirmed it belonged to an elderly woman, a Mrs Sofia Cartney-Bowler, who left the site to her two daughters in her will. Neither of them wanted to keep it – from what Swift said, it seemed to me like they couldn't wait to get the deal done and spend the money. Anyway, he gave me the daughters' details and I spoke to them as soon as Max hung up. The eldest one is on holiday in Scotland at the moment, but the youngest daughter has agreed to speak with us – she works in Wallingford and said she can squeeze us in before a meeting this morning.'

'Couldn't we have spoken to her over the phone?'

'We could,' said West. 'But in the circumstances, I thought you might want to meet with her face-to-face.'

'Why?'

West gave a grim smile when he glanced over. 'Apparently, her mother used to be an anaesthetist.'

# CHAPTER THIRTY-EIGHT

Sofia Cartney-Bowler's daughter was waiting for them outside a café on the fringes of Wallingford.

She had her gaze lowered to her phone as they approached, her thumbs working frantically across the screen, and she seemed oblivious to the other customers who side-stepped past her to get to the front door.

'That's her, right?' Mark murmured, slowing his pace.

'Yes, Marion's her name,' said West. 'She's worked for a local chemical sales company since finishing her degree, and said she's planning to move back into the area now that she's paid off her uni debts.'

'Where does she live at the moment?'

'Thatcham – she commutes here every day.'

The young woman looked up at the sound of their footsteps, frowned, then her shoulders sagged and she tucked the phone away. 'You must be the detectives, right?'

West smiled. 'Thanks for seeing us at short notice. I'm DC Jan West, this is DS Mark Turpin. Did you want to talk here, or...?'

'Not really.' Marion glanced over her shoulder. 'I thought it might be quieter by now, but...'

'We could go for a walk,' said Mark. 'The castle gardens are open, and probably not too busy at the moment. Sound good?'

Marion nodded. 'Let's go. I've got forty-five minutes until my next meeting and my car's parked over there anyway.'

She set off, her shoulders slightly hunched as Mark and West followed. She was clearly unwilling to talk on the way, and instead waited until they were through the castle's public entrance and following a meandering path alongside a budding shrubbery.

Pausing beside a wooden bench, she stopped and turned, her arms crossed. 'Okay, what did you want to ask me that we couldn't deal with over the phone?'

'Tell us about your mother's reluctance to sell the airfield site,' said Mark.

Marion rolled her eyes. 'Honestly, I think that place was the single thing that caused friction in our relationship with Mum – I'm including Ellie in that, because she'd suggested to Mum early last year that she sell the place. She hadn't even visited it for nearly eighteen months.'

'Why did she keep the land?'

'I don't know,' Marion sighed. She sank onto the wooden bench and gazed at the lush green turf that lined the opposite side of the path before it abutted the castle's thick stone wall. 'For years, she told us it was because it had always been in the family

– she was proud of its history, and she used to tell us stories about some of the aircraft that flew from there during the war. When we were little, she used to take us there for picnics and things and we'd muck about in the old buildings.' She frowned. 'That all changed about six years ago.'

'Why?'

'Apparently, she'd received some advice that said the buildings were dangerous, and she said we weren't to go to the site anymore. Not without her, anyway.'

'Did you go back there with her?'

'No. The first time I went back was when Barry Windlesham approached us via our solicitor with an offer to buy the land in January. Ellie and I met with a surveyor who helped us understand how much the place was worth, and we had a wander around with him then. Barry bought the land soon after, so I haven't been back since.'

Mark waited while West updated her notes, then turned his attention back to Marion. 'How did news of the sale go down with the villagers?'

She wrinkled her nose, then shaded her eyes as she peered at him. 'Some of them weren't impressed. I suppose they were used to it being abandoned, and were worried what Barry was going to do to the place. There were one or two threats—'

'Threats?' West's eyebrows shot up. 'From who?'

'Not sure.' Marion shrugged. 'Ellie's car got scratched with a key or something when we were clearing out Mum's house, and someone put a note through the door saying we should reconsider – although it was a bit more pointed than that, and given I was living there for a couple of weeks on my own while we sold the furniture I was worried for a while, but nothing came of it. I suppose once the wheels got rolling on the sale, whoever it was doing that realised it was out of our control. We'd kept the whole thing quiet until the last minute anyway. I think we anticipated some sort of stink about the sale, but I think if it had dragged out, things might've taken a turn for the worse.'

'What makes you say that?' said Mark. 'Did the threats increase?'

'Not exactly.' Marion shivered. 'I just got the impression in the last few days that I was being watched all the time. When I was at the house, I mean. I couldn't wait to leave.'

'You mentioned on the phone to me that your mother worked as an anaesthetist,' said West. 'When did she retire?'

'Last year.'

'Forgive me for being rude,' said West, 'but how old was your mother when she retired?'

'Fifty-two. She had the airfield of course, and some good investments that Dad put into place before he passed away when I was eighteen – he had lung cancer – so she said taking early retirement suited her,' said Marion. 'Mind you, Ellie and I were surprised.'

'Why?' said Mark.

'Because she'd never mentioned it up until the week it happened. One minute she was working all hours and I barely saw her when I was home from university, and the next she had stopped.'

'What did she get up to after she retired?' said West. 'Did she have any interests or social groups she belonged to?'

Marion looked baffled. 'Come to think of it, she didn't *do* anything when she first retired. I mean, I'd have thought most people in her financial position would've taken a holiday or something, travelled the world or done a cruise, but... no, she didn't. Whenever I asked what she was doing or how she was spending her free time, she simply changed the subject. I figured she was just embarrassed that she'd gone from having a busy career to nothing in the space of a short time and that it'd take a little while for her to adjust.'

'And did she? Adjust, I mean,' said Mark.

'No, not as far as I'm aware. I mean, she was an incredibly clever woman so Ellie and I couldn't understand why she didn't put up a fight about the early retirement – or look for consulting work elsewhere. I mean, she could've written a book with all the knowledge she'd gained over the years, but even that idea didn't interest her.'

'Where did she work before she retired?'

'Her last role was at that private hospital the other side of Didcot, the one—'

'I know it,' said West, closing her notebook and turning to Mark. 'Sarge, I have an idea.'

'So do I,' he said, handing over a business card to Marion. 'Thanks for your time. That's my direct number. If you think of anything else about the airfield, could you let me know?'

'Okay.' She waited until they were a few paces away before calling after them. 'My mother was a good person, detective. She saved a lot of lives.'

# CHAPTER THIRTY-NINE

Mark's first impression of the private hospital where Sofia Cartney-Bowler had worked was that it was either doing a brisk trade, or had several generous benefactors.

Maybe both.

Located a few miles north of Ravenswood airfield, it had once been a Georgian manor house, with sandstone columns each side of the enormous oak front door framed by a decorative fan of glass above it that was etched with leaves.

The old stable buildings on each side of the main house looked as if they had been converted into offices and outpatient clinics, and the gardens were enclosed within privet hedges that shielded the clientele from prying eyes while they relaxed with visitors or convalesced in quiet groups.

The front door was open, and as Mark hurried through it after West, he saw that the original entrance hall had been converted into a welcoming reception area for patients and their family members. There was an elongated staircase that swept upwards from the chequered floor tiles on the left of the hall and led to an open landing, and Mark could see several works of art on the panelled wall beyond the balustrade and guessed that – unlike the bucolic prints that lined the walls of many hospitals – these were, in fact, original.

A man was working at a computer behind the reception desk and peered over it, his eyes curious. 'Can I help you? Visiting hours have nearly finished until this evening.'

Mark flashed his warrant card. 'We'd like a word with James Rasper please.'

The man's eyebrows shot upwards. 'I'm sorry, but as our CEO Dr Rasper is a very busy man – he's chairing a meeting with our trustees in the morning and is currently preparing for that. You can't just turn up expecting to speak with him. That's just not possible.'

West leaned on the counter and glared at him. 'We can speak to him here, or take him back to the police station. Up to you.'

The man swallowed before he pointed at a sofa that had been placed on the far side of the hall, and reached for his phone. 'Take a seat. I'll have to see what I can do.'

'Thanks.'

She winked at Mark and led the way over to the sofa, both of them choosing to remain standing rather than take up the receptionist's offer.

After ten minutes, Mark had read through all the glossy brochures about the private hospital and was about to march back to the reception desk when footsteps at the top of the stairs caught his attention.

He looked up to see a man in his early sixties descending, buttoning his jacket and wearing a harried expression. The man cast his gaze around the hall, seemed relieved nobody else was in sight apart from the receptionist who stared at them with ill-disguised interest, and hurried over.

'Detectives, I'm James Rasper. I believe you've already been informed how busy I am today. A phone call would've been much better for me.'

'But not for us,' said Mark, holding out his warrant card. 'And not in the circumstances. We need to talk to you about Sofia Cartney-Bowler.'

Rasper stiffened. 'She hasn't worked for us for over a year.'

'We're aware of that. We're interested in finding out why she retired early from a role she was clearly committed to.' Mark looked around at the ornate surroundings and spread his hands expansively. 'Especially from such an exclusive place as this.'

'Come with me,' said Rasper, glancing over his shoulder. 'We can talk in one of the consulting rooms.'

Mark nodded to the clearly disappointed receptionist as they followed the CEO out of the hallway and along a corridor to a room that had a vaulted ceiling and bespoke bookshelves. There was a mahogany table over in one corner and four chairs, and Rasper pulled out one for West.

'This used to be the library when this was still a manor house,' he said. 'We use this and the old dining room next door for consulting rooms.'

Mark waited until the doctor was sitting in a chair opposite West. 'How long have you worked here?'

'About fifteen years.' Rasper's chest expanded. 'I started as one of their leading cardio specialists, rather than carrying out surgery. I've been CEO for the past four years.'

'Was Mrs Cartney-Bowler here when you started?'

'No, Sofia came on board about twelve years ago. She'd previously worked at a large private hospital in London but said she wanted a quieter life for her daughters. They were nearly teenagers back then, and I think she was worried about the sort of crowd they'd started hanging around with and wanted to move them out of the city.'

'Did you interview her?'

'I was one of a panel of three who interviewed her for the role, yes.'

'What were your impressions of Sofia over the years?'

'She was a very capable anaesthetist, and extremely good at calming nervous patients.' Rasper drummed his fingers on the table, his gaze moving to a spot over Mark's right shoulder as he spoke. 'She was dependable, and often helped train new members of staff, as well as sitting on different committees over the years that helped shape what the hospital is today.'

'When did it all go wrong?' said Mark.

The finger drumming stopped, and Rasper's Adam's apple bobbed in his throat. 'Pardon?'

'Something went wrong here, didn't it?' Mark repeated. 'Someone of Sofia's calibre doesn't suddenly decide they want to retire. Not when they have no interests outside of work. So, what happened?'

'I-I...'

'Must've been pretty bad,' said West, relaxing in her seat while Rasper squirmed. 'But also managed internally by the trustees, because we haven't found anything in the news reports from last year.'

'If it was that bad, the General Medical Council would've carried out an investigation,' Mark added. 'Unless it wasn't reported to them. Unless it was covered up.'

'Look here,' said Rasper. He clasped his hands on the table and cleared his throat. 'Yes, it's true that we had to ask Sofia to take early retirement afterwards. But it was an accident, I can assure you.'

'Can you?' Mark pulled out one of the chairs from under the table, dragged it closer to Rasper and sat. 'What happened?'

'Please bear in mind that she was one of our top staff members. Very professional. Dependable, great with patients—'

'What happened?' Mark repeated.

'It was the last operation of the day, one that she and the operating team had carried out many times before... They had had a long day because of a complicated hysterectomy that had been scheduled for the afternoon... Anyway, a problem arose during the final surgery, and – for whatever reason – maybe she was tired, Sofia... God, it pains me to say this. From what we can gather, while the patient and his donor were anaesthetised and the surgery was underway, she... she adjusted the dosage, and the patient's donor died.'

'She killed him with an overdose, you mean?'

'Yes.' Rasper looked miserable. 'For someone of her calibre to make such a fundamental error...'

'I don't recall this being raised with us as a formal enquiry,' said West. 'Was it reported?'

Rasper's face flushed crimson. 'We discussed it with the

donor's family. They're overseas – he flew in especially for the donor process. They're rather well-to-do, so rather than have the British media all over the story, they opted for a significant compensation payout instead. And, of course, Sofia's immediate dismissal.'

'What sort of operation was it?' said Mark. 'You mentioned a living donor.'

'A kidney transplant. They're quite popular with our overseas clients.'

'What happened to the patient who received the donor kidney?'

'Oh,' said Rasper, leaning back in his chair with a look of relief. 'He made a full recovery. He's back at work in... the country where he resides... and leading a full and healthy life. Of course, he'll be on medication for the rest of it, but—'

'At least he can afford it,' West finished.

'Who was the surgeon that carried out the operation?' said Mark.

'Dale McArthur. He was one of our most esteemed staff members.'

'Was? Has he retired as well?'

'No. Sadly, Mr McArthur was killed in a hit and run accident near his home in Aylesbury last September. They still haven't caught the driver.'

# CHAPTER FORTY

The rest of the investigative team were already huddled around the whiteboard when Jan and Turpin walked back into the incident room.

Twenty or so heads turned to watch them while they hurried over and found seats, and as Jan scanned the updating bullet points that Kennedy had scrawled within the past fifteen minutes, she realised there had been some sort of breakthrough.

'Apologies, guv,' said Turpin. 'We got caught in traffic after interviewing the schoolkids who had the video once we'd completed the interview at the private hospital.'

'Any luck with that?'

'Yes, they've managed to get clear images of Barry Windlesham walking along the track towards the bridge, followed a few moments later by another man, about six foot two and wearing a dark coloured jacket and jeans.' Turpin pulled out a USB drive from his pocket. 'It's a copy of the video the boys took.'

'Give it here.' Kennedy took it and plugged it into his laptop, spinning the screen around to face the team before pressing "play".

There was some shaky camerawork and a lot of laughter as the two teenagers hared around the track and surrounding scrubland that fringed the fields, but then they paused, pulling the bikes over to one side while the phone continued recording.

'Thanks,' they heard a voice say, and then Barry Windlesham hurried past, his hands shoved into his jacket pockets and his head down. He glanced over his shoulder a few metres from the boys, then picked up his pace and followed the fork in the track that led to the bridge.

Moments later, a second man passed the boys, ignoring their antics while he hurried in the same direction as Windlesham. At that point, the boys took off once more, heading for the top of the track near the village before turning around to face the river again. Here, they paused for a drink of water from bottles they pulled from their backpacks, all the while debating what to do next while the video continued to record.

Jan thought she heard a muffled *crack* in the distance, but couldn't be sure, and the boys didn't comment on it either.

And then, ambling along as if he had all the time in the world, the man in the jacket and jeans returned, his shoulders hunched as he walked up the track towards the boys.

He said nothing as he passed, although she heard a noncommittal "all right?" from one of them, and then the image shook as the teenagers set off again.

'Got you.' Kennedy reached out, rewound the recording, and froze it on the man's face before looking over his shoulder at them. 'Anyone recognise him?'

His question was met with muttered responses, none of which were helpful.

'All right – get this image circulated throughout the division and we'll see if anyone else does. Anything else? How did you and Jan get on at the private hospital, Mark?'

Jan listened while Turpin updated the team about their conversation with Sofia Cartney-Bowler's employer.

'It might be the case that the surgeon who carried out the operation was also murdered,' he finished, 'so you might want to bring our counterparts in Aylesbury into the loop, guv. We might be able to share information with them.'

Kennedy nodded. 'Will do. What's your thoughts regarding the error Sofia made?'

'We were talking about that in the car coming back here, guv,' said Jan. 'We were thinking that if she was helping to carry out the illegal organ harvesting on top of her day job, she'd have been exhausted. She might've forgotten where she was, zoned out or something and automatically killed the donor, as if she had been at one of the illegal harvesting operations instead of at the private hospital.'

'Something we might also have to consider is that the surgeon's death has nothing to do with our investigation,' said Alex. 'If the donor's family received compensation for what Sofia did, they might've felt it wasn't enough, and that they felt the surgeon's oversight in managing Sofia was to blame as well. Eye for an eye, and all that.'

'Good point.' The DI updated the whiteboard, then called over his shoulder. 'Caroline – what's the latest regarding those charity bins at the industrial site?'

The detective constable pushed herself away from the wall she had been leaning against and raised her voice to be heard over her colleagues. 'We located the company who runs the service, and it's going to give us a list of charity shops in the area that receive clothing donations from them. I should have that in the morning. I think the best thing we can do in the circumstances is to ask those shops to cease selling any men's clothing they've received in the past month until Jasper and his team have time to sift through it all for DNA matching that of the man in the freezer, or the most recent burial at the airfield. Our other option is to tell them to close down until those tests have been carried out, but I'm concerned that might alert our killers that we're onto them.'

'I'm inclined to agree with you, Caroline. Do as you suggest and tell them to cease selling men's clothing and to use gloves to bag up everything until Jasper's team collect it.' Kennedy's phone rang then, and he pulled it from his pocket. 'DI Kennedy. Yes? Right... Is that so? Please, yes. I'll have two of my team drive over to her house now. What's the address? Thanks.'

Jan glanced across to her colleague and saw him leaning forward on his chair in anticipation. Her heart rate quickened as Kennedy ended the call and turned to them.

'We've received an update from the Missing Persons team,' he said. 'A family member got in touch about someone who was thought to have been visiting friends in Oxford three weeks ago by the name of Patrick Westington. The family have been trying to phone his number with no response, but finally managed to get in touch with one of his friends. That friend has told them that Patrick never made any arrangements to stay with them, and seemed surprised that he would do so. Patrick hasn't been seen since he left home that day.'

'So, are we looking for another body?' said Jan.

'I don't think so. I think he's already in Gillian's morgue,' said Kennedy. 'His number is the one that received the text on the phone Barry Windlesham dropped in the river.'

# CHAPTER FORTY-ONE

Mark shrugged his jacket over his shoulders and eyed the darkening grey clouds that bustled above the rooftops.

The houses along the lane were large and set back from the road behind laurel or rhododendron hedges, broken only by electronic gates built from thick wood or powder-coated aluminium. The names of the properties echoed the neighbouring countryside, with a nod to the animals that still occupied the woodland behind them.

On the other side of the lane, the trees had been thinned out over time, providing a sweeping view across the Berkshire Downs. A breeze had settled across the fields, riffling through the yellow oil seed crops that brightened the hillsides around Pangbourne, and as he cast his gaze over the undulating landscape he focused his thoughts on how he would tell Patrick Westington's parents that their son would never return here.

'Ready?' West peered over the roof of the car at him. 'As we'll ever be, anyway.'

He grunted in reply, then followed her across the driveway's moss-speckled gravel to the front door of a detached two-storey house that had recently been rerendered in a pale grey.

Underneath a shallow wooden portico that had been painted a contrasting matt black, a pair of discarded walking boots had been kicked off to one side of a coir doormat. The soles were slicked with dried mud and grass, and a shabby golfing umbrella had been propped up in the corner of the portico, its edges frayed with use. A single pane of frosted glass was set into the door, and after West rang the bell, Mark saw movement.

The figure hesitated halfway along the hallway, lowered their head for a moment, and then appeared to square their shoulders before opening the door.

A man in his fifties peered at him, worry lines creasing his forehead. He had a sadness in his eyes that was devoid of hope. 'You're the police, right?'

'Detective Sergeant Mark Turpin, and my colleague DC Jan West.' Mark tucked away his warrant card. 'Mr Westington, may we come in?'

'Aaron, please. We're in the sitting room, through here.' The man closed the door and gestured to a room off to the left of the hallway.

Mark walked into a space that was light and airy, with a vaulted ceiling and a wrought-iron spiral staircase on the far wall that led up to a gallery taken up by bookshelves, a sprawling six-seater sofa and reading lamps. The living room was a cluttered space that exuded desperation and neglect – a clutch of missing persons flyers were lying on a low wooden table stained with coffee mug marks, the ends curling on the uppermost posters and the wan face of a man in his early twenties peering out from a photograph.

He bore a striking resemblance to his father.

A woman rose from one of two sofas that bookended the table and held out a slim hand. 'Detectives? I'm Helena Westington.'

Her hand was cold to the touch when he shook it, and she was trembling.

'Thank you for seeing us,' said Mark.

She nodded, then wiped at fresh tears as Aaron put his arm around her shoulder. 'We're expecting the worst, detective. Now that you're here.'

His heart twisted at the remark, and he thought of his two daughters, both of whom were living with their mother. 'I'm so sorry. Shall we sit?'

Helena flapped her hand towards the sofa nearest to West while she retook her seat and pulled a cushion over her chest. She held tightly onto her husband's hand as Mark joined his colleague. 'Where's our son? Where's Patrick?'

'May I get to that in a moment? If that's okay?' Mark said. 'I understand from your message that you last saw your son three weeks ago. Could you tell me about that day?'

'It was a Monday, because I was working from home,' said Aaron. 'I only have to travel into the City on Thursdays for executive meetings, and Patrick wandered in here just before a video conference call I had scheduled at eleven o'clock. He had a backpack with him, and was wearing an old burgundy sweatshirt that he's had since playing hockey at secondary school—'

'It's falling apart,' said Helena, her voice wistful. 'I've been nagging him for years to get rid of it.'

Aaron sniffed, blinked, and then continued. 'He had that on over jeans and he was wearing his old walking boots. He asked if he could borrow fifty quid because he was heading off to Oxford to catch up with friends and hadn't been paid yet – he has a part-time job while he's studying, over at the garden centre. I grumbled a bit – he and his sister, Beth, are always scrounging off me—'

'It's because they know you're such a soft touch, love,' Helena murmured.

'It is.' Aaron gave a rueful nod. 'Anyway, I didn't have time to transfer the money into his account, so I gave him forty quid in cash instead, and asked him how long he'd be away.'

'He told us three weeks,' said Helena. 'I was sitting here, listening to the pair of them talking, and I told him there were some clean clothes in the tumble drier if he wanted those. He told me not to worry. He said a bunch of them were thinking of heading up to the Lake District to go hiking so he wanted to travel light.'

'Can you describe his backpack?' said Mark.

'It's a navy blue one with grey straps, thirty litres in size,' said Aaron. 'It's an old one of mine he nicked off me when he started at university.'

'These friends in Oxford, have you met them?' said West.

'Oh, yes – they've stayed here before when we've had barbecues in the summer,' said Helena, a faint smile passing her lips at the recollection. 'They're a rowdy lot, but courteous with it. Fun to be around.'

'It's why we didn't worry… to start off with,' said Aaron. 'Patrick's often gone away with them, so we didn't think anything of it until the end of the second week. Then I texted him to see how things were going, where they'd climbed – I enjoy a hike when I have time, and it was me who introduced Patrick to the Lake District when he was fourteen. We used to go away at weekends together, and Helena and Beth would do something different at the same time.'

'Beth isn't much of a walker,' Helena explained. 'She prefers shopping and spas.'

'How old is she?'

'Nineteen. Three years younger than Patrick.'

'So Patrick left uni… last year?' West ventured.

'That's right, yes. He got a job working for an engineering company straight out of uni, but they lost a big contract just after Christmas and he was made redundant. The garden centre job is just something to tide him over until something else crops up.'

'When did you suspect something was wrong?' said Mark.

'A couple of days after I tried texting Patrick and hadn't got a response, I phoned one of his friends,' said Aaron. 'As Helena said, they're often around here over the summer so I had their numbers. Charlie was surprised when I called, and said he hadn't seen Patrick since early March when they went to a mate's engagement party. That's when we got in touch with your lot.'

Mark let the man's words sink in for a moment, seeing the desperation in his eyes, then swallowed. 'Aaron, Helena, I'm so, so sorry to tell you this but based on the phone number you've given our colleagues for Patrick, we're very concerned for his wellbeing.'

Aaron paled. 'What do you mean? What have you found?'

'Please understand, we're unable to confirm anything until we can prove otherwise,' said Mark. 'Could I ask you, did Patrick ever break his toe?'

'Oh God.' Helena wailed, burying her face into her husband's shoulder. 'Oh God.'

'You've found his body, haven't you?' Aaron managed, his voice strangled. 'What happened?'

'We're working to ascertain the circumstances,' said Mark. 'I'm sorry, but until we're sure I can't share anything further with you. Please understand that. Before we make any assumptions, I'd like to ask you if we could take some swabs for DNA testing. Do you have a comb, or perhaps something else that we could test?'

Aaron wiped his cheeks with his hands and rose on unsteady feet. 'Come with me.'

Leaving West to comfort Helena, Mark followed Patrick's father upstairs and along a carpeted landing that stretched the width of the house.

Ignoring the first three doors, Aaron pushed open the one at the far end and stepped aside to let Mark pass. 'This is Patrick's room.'

'Did he have a spare toothbrush or anything in the bathroom?'

The man managed a sad smile. 'He's only just out of his teens, detective – what do you think?'

'Ah.' Mark looked around the room, at the balled-up clothing that had missed the wicker laundry basket by the door, and then at the contents of a cluttered bedside table. 'Do you mind if I take a look around?'

Aaron flinched as Mark pulled on protective gloves, then nodded. 'Take whatever you need to find who harmed my baby.'

With that, he turned on his heel. Moments later, Mark heard the sound of a door closing farther along the landing before a loud sob reached him.

# CHAPTER FORTY-TWO

'Here, boy.'

Mark gave a short, sharp whistle then waited as Hamish bounded from the hawthorn bushes lining the path that ran alongside Barton Lane.

It was early, an hour after sunrise, but Mark had been unable to sleep and rather than disturbing Lucy, he had opted to go for a walk to try and calm the jumbled thoughts going around in his head. The small dog needed no persuasion, and they had taken a leisurely route across the weir at Abingdon lock before following a national cycle route to Radley Lakes and circling back.

A lean man on a road bike zipped past, his blue mirrored sunglasses catching Mark's reflection as he and Hamish stood to one side, and then he was gone, his bright Lycra shirt making him stand out as he disappeared into the distance.

After glancing at the time displayed on the screen, Mark

shoved his phone back into his pocket and picked up his pace. There was a warmth to the air at long last, the mere whisper of a breeze creating wavelets on the Thames, and the sweet smell of blossom from the different trees and shrubs he passed.

And yet...

Mark had found an old baseball cap in Patrick Westington's bedroom yesterday, a faded navy blue one with a yellowing logo. It was well worn and, upon closer inspection, had trapped a straw-coloured hair within its seams, a hair that matched the photographs the young man's parents had tearfully provided. Not wishing to prolong their agony any further, he had driven the sample to the testing laboratory while West sat in the car's passenger seat, filling out the required evidence log and paperwork and swearing under her breath every time he hit a pothole.

Jasper and his team were now tasked with testing the DNA sample against the clothing found in the charity bins next to the industrial unit that was set alight and the fabric remnants found caught in the jagged doorframe of the officers' mess at the airfield.

Until then, all that Kennedy's investigators could do was wait.

Mark sighed, clipped the dog lead to Hamish's collar and took the fork in the path that crossed the weir.

Part of him wanted an answer from the samples, and the other part dreaded it. One way or another, he would have to deliver devastating news to Patrick's family. Either the man was dead, or still missing.

Meanwhile, Caroline and Alex were working through his social media profiles, speaking with friends and old work colleagues in an attempt to understand – if the testing proved to be a positive match – why Patrick might have agreed to donate a kidney without discussing it with his parents.

Hamish strained on the lead as a couple with an older mongrel ambled towards them.

'Easy, boy,' Mark murmured. 'He might not live on the river like you do, but he's got every right to be here.'

Hamish grumbled, then promptly passed the other dog with his nose in the air.

'Morning,' said Mark to its owners, who nodded in response before continuing their conversation. He frowned as he rounded the slight bend in the river and the row of narrowboats and widebeams came into view.

Lucy was standing on the gunwale of their boat, waving to get his attention, then pointed at a lone figure on the riverbank.

West was pacing back and forth, her phone to her ear.

'Come on,' said Mark, breaking into a jog. 'I think we're wanted.'

Hamish gave a low *woof* under his breath and kept pace, tongue lolling as they drew near. He was panting by the time they reached the boat, and as soon as Mark unclipped the lead the small dog leapt on board and buried his face in his water bowl.

West finished her call. 'That was Kennedy,' she said. 'He wants us to head straight into the incident room – someone's come forward with information about what Barry Windlesham was doing in Culham last Sunday. Morning, by the way.'

'Morning.' Mark glanced sideways as Lucy disappeared for a

few seconds, returning with foil-wrapped packages in her hands. 'What's that?'

'Bacon and egg butties,' she said. 'Eat them on the way back to the car. I'm guessing you two aren't going to get another chance to eat today by the sound of it.'

# CHAPTER FORTY-THREE

The man waiting in interview room number four was standing
with his hands behind his back and reading a health and safety
poster when Mark and West walked in.

He wore a three-quarter length beige raincoat over a green
checked shirt and jeans, with greying hair that touched his collar
and curled under his ear lobes. He turned and looked over half-
moon glasses that had drifted to the end of his nose, pushed them
up with a finger that in other circumstances would have been
rude, and then blinked.

'Are you the two I'm meant to be speaking to, or are you
going to offer me another cup of tea?' he said.

'Sorry to keep you, Mr...'

'Gregory Lesk.'

Mark introduced himself and West, then gestured to the four
aluminium chairs surrounding a metal table against the far wall.
'Would you like another drink?'

'Not unless you want me interrupting every five minutes to ask if I can go to the loo, no.' Lesk flapped the back of his coat before sitting, and then crossed his legs.

'Thanks for coming in, Mr Lesk.' Mark took the seat opposite him and opened his notebook, West doing the same. 'I understand you have something for us that might help with our enquiries into the death of Barry Windlesham?'

'I do, yes.' Lesk narrowed his eyes. 'What happened to Barry? All it says in the news is that you're investigating his death. He died in hospital, didn't he?'

'He did, and I'll explain in due course. What's your association with Mr Windlesham?'

'We were at school together. Played on the same football team, got into the same fights. When he went into construction, I took myself off to university, but we stayed in touch over the years.'

'What is it you do, Mr Lesk?'

'I'm a lecturer at Oxford.' The man picked at a loose thread on his coat cuff for a moment, his eyes shifting from West to Mark, then back. 'And I'm trying to understand why on earth Barry would send me a USB stick while I was on holiday, and then go and get himself killed.'

'I don't believe we said he'd been killed, Mr Lesk.'

'You didn't need to, detective. It's quite obvious that if you're involved, something's wrong. You're the one whose narrowboat went up in flames a year or so ago, aren't you?'

Mark sat back in his seat, holding the man's gaze. 'I am. What's this about a USB stick?'

Lesk rummaged in his shirt breast pocket and withdrew a

slim black plastic stick and a car key fob. He held them up, then slid them across the table. 'Those were in an envelope addressed to me, sent by Barry. His car was parked on my driveway.'

'When did the envelope arrive?'

'I don't know. I've been on sabbatical in Tuscany for ten days and only got back last night. When I opened the front door, it was on the mat.'

'Did you keep the envelope?'

'It hadn't been posted, detective. Barry had stuck it through the letterbox himself.'

'Then how do you know it's from Barry?'

'Because there was a note in the envelope with those. It says to tell you lot that he's hidden a mobile phone in the river at Culham, next to the bridge, and that he was planning on coming to see you but he reckons he left it too late.' Lesk unfolded a piece of paper from his pocket and passed it across before pointing at the USB stick. 'And that shows the airfield site where he's been trying to get that blasted housing development off the ground, and I think it's from one of the security cameras he had fitted just before I went away.'

Mark turned the USB stick between his fingers. 'Why would Barry send this to you?'

'Because it shows a young bloke at the window of the officers' mess building,' said Lesk. 'And I know Barry had that place boarded up to keep out urban explorers or kids in case somebody got hurt. So, who is he?'

'Where do you live, Mr Lesk?' said West, ignoring his question.

'In Culham, just around the corner from the church.'

'When you returned home from your sabbatical, were there any signs of an attempted break-in?' Mark said.

'No, there weren't – and believe me, after finding Barry's envelope on the doormat the same thought crossed my mind.' Lesk picked at the loose thread again. 'I couldn't see that anyone had tried to tamper with the doors or windows though.'

Mark glanced at his colleague before turning back to the other man. 'I don't suppose you have security cameras at your home, do you?'

'No, never seen the need to. It's a quiet village, and my road doesn't get too much through traffic, so I've not bothered.' Lesk held up his hand as Mark emitted a frustrated sigh. 'But my neighbour does, and he's often said that the camera on his garage captures my driveway as well. He checked with me when he installed it, in case I wanted him to change the angle to retain my privacy. I couldn't see any harm in it, so I told him not to worry.'

Mark smiled. 'I'd like the name and phone number for your neighbour, please.'

# CHAPTER FORTY-FOUR

There was a frantic level of activity within the incident room when Mark held open the door for West and followed her across to their desks.

Warming afternoon sunlight pierced the window blinds at the far end of the room and the air conditioning created a gentle breeze across the back of Mark's neck as he walked beneath a ventilation grill.

More officers had been drafted in from other investigations to assist with the burgeoning amount of evidence being produced from the airfield and industrial unit crime scenes, and Mark noticed that a second whiteboard had been wheeled next to the original one at the far end of the room, its surface already covered with Kennedy's sprawling handwriting.

Every member of the team either had their gaze glued to their computer screens or phones to their ears, and the level of conversation created a dull hum throughout the room.

Two further photocopiers were churning witness statements and briefing agendas into neat stapled piles over near the water cooler, and he wandered across to where Tracy kept a wary eye on the process, her movements brisk as she separated the documentation ready for distribution.

'Hey, Tracy – where's Caroline?' Mark asked, craning his neck to see over the throng. 'Is she around?'

'She's overseeing the collection and storage of all the clothing from the charity shops,' the administrative officer said without turning around. 'She'll be back later today.'

'Any news from her yet?'

'Nothing yet. I'll give you a shout if I hear anything though.'

'Thanks.'

He turned away, careful not to let the disappointment show. Sitting at his desk, he wiggled the mouse to wake up his computer, logged in and sifted through the emails that had arrived since he had left the previous evening. Ruing the offer of coffee he had declined from West as they walked past the vending machine downstairs, he tried to ignore the wave of frustrated exhaustion that threatened and turned to the list of recent updates in HOLMES2.

'Sarge?' Alex wandered over, murmured a greeting to West, and shuffled his feet. 'I think I might've found Patrick on CCTV.'

Mark spun his chair around to face the young detective. 'Where?'

'Didcot station. A few weeks ago. The date ties in with when Barry Windlesham was said to have thought he'd seen someone at the airfield site.'

West was already out of her seat and on her feet. 'Show us.'

They followed Alex over to his desk, Mark hovering at the man's shoulder while he cued up the footage on his screen.

'I figured Patrick would've caught a train from Pangbourne, given that he didn't have a car. I discounted any trains that didn't stop there on the way to Didcot the day that was mentioned in the message on that phone Windlesham hid in the river,' he said. 'And just to make sure, I checked the whole morning, not just the time in that message in case there'd been a change of plans.'

'Good thinking,' said Mark, biting back his impatience. 'Do you want to play the footage?'

'Oh. Sure. Here you go.' Alex turned back to the screen. 'Here's the train pulling into the station – it's not too busy so he's easy to spot. Here he is, getting out of the third carriage. See?'

Mark watched while the young man on the screen hefted a backpack up his arm and glanced over his shoulder as he ambled along the platform. He looked a little lost, his head turning this way and that, and he slowed before reaching the stairs leading to the underground pedestrian exit that was at the bottom of the screen.

'He's looking for someone,' West murmured.

Mark nodded. 'I think you're right.'

'You both are. Look.' Alex paused the recording as a figure appeared on the staircase, his back to the camera, and wearing a dark-coloured baseball cap.

'Please tell me he turns around,' said Mark.

'He does.' Alex started the video once more.

The man held out his hand, whereupon Patrick handed over his backpack. They spoke for a moment as the train pulled away from the platform, and then the stranger hitched his thumb over his back. Patrick nodded, and then the man turned back to the stairs.

His face was in shadow, obscured by the baseball cap he wore.

'Fuck.' Mark clenched his jaw. 'Any other angles?'

'Two more.' Alex's fingers flew over the keyboard and then a second video screen appeared. 'This one's from the underground concourse as they're heading for the Station Road exit.'

'That's the way to the car parks,' said West. 'There's a short stay car park along the road on the same side as the station, and a longer stay one opposite.'

Mark grunted a reply, his gaze on the screen. The video only lasted eight seconds. It captured the two men as they emerged from the stairs and then walked side by side under the CCTV camera set into the low concourse roof. And again, the stranger's face was obscured. The camera shook a little as a train passed overhead, and then the two men were gone.

'He kept his chin down too, did you notice?' said West. 'Please tell us you've got some good news.'

'The next clip is from the camera overlooking the bus terminal outside,' said Alex, pressing "play" once more.

Mark held his breath. As the video started, Patrick and the stranger walked out from the station, across the asphalt apron of the bus terminal. There, they paused as cars shot along Station Road, both men turning their heads this way and that as they waited for a break in the traffic before darting across to the other side and disappearing from view.

The video stopped and Alex held up his hand. 'Before you say it, Sarge, I know where they went. Just a sec.'

The young detective moused over his screen, clicked on a different folder and opened a fourth video file. He hummed under his breath while he worked, his movements methodical. Mark glanced over to see West clenching her jaw. She caught his gaze and mimed putting her hands to the back of Alex's neck to strangle him.

'Ah, here we go,' he said, oblivious to his colleagues' growing impatience. 'This video's from a CCTV camera on a lamp post opposite the train station, next to a pub.' Alex looked over his shoulder. 'You can stop that, Jan. I can see your reflection in the screen.'

West blushed, and Mark laughed. 'Get on with it.'

'Right-o, Sarge.' Alex turned back to the computer and hit "play". Within seconds, he pressed pause and jabbed his forefinger at the screen. 'That's them, there.'

'Dammit, we still can't see his face,' said West as she peered closer at the frozen image.

'No, but that's good work, Alex. Get yourself over to that pub and ask them for any security footage they've got showing the street angles, would you?'

'Will do.'

Mark looked down as his phone started to ring. 'Jasper? Jesus, that was quick. Yes, okay. Right. I understand. Yes, I'll let Kennedy know. Thanks, I'll tell him that.'

West was staring at him, eyes hungry as he ended the call. 'What did he want?'

'He's just finished speaking to the laboratory we sent

Patrick's DNA samples to this morning,' he said. 'They put a rush order on it given the circumstances.'

'And?' prompted Alex.

Mark glanced over his shoulder as the door to the incident room swung open and Kennedy stalked in, his mobile phone to his ear and his face harried. 'The guv's going to have to break it to Patrick's parents that their son is our latest victim in the airfield graves.'

# CHAPTER FORTY-FIVE

Mid-morning the next day, Ewan Kennedy called Mark and West into his office and closed the door.

The hubbub of activity in the incident room became muted, and as Mark sat in a worse for wear visitor's chair opposite the DI's computer, he noticed the dark circles under the man's eyes and the lines that were becoming more pronounced across his forehead.

'How did it go with the parents yesterday, guv? You okay?' he ventured.

'I am, they're not,' Kennedy said. He gave a slight nod. 'Thanks for asking.'

Mark watched while the DI busied himself for a moment, shuffling paperwork to one side, signing documents and reports, and sat patiently. Each of them dealt with the severity of a case such as this in different ways, and Kennedy had the additional pressures of managing a team within an expected budget as well as the ongoing political ramifications if they didn't resolve the case soon. 'Were his parents able to provide any ideas about why Patrick might have agreed to sell a kidney?'

Kennedy dropped his pen and leaned back in his chair with a sigh. 'No, so I asked uniform to interview his friends. That has produced some answers, although not ones his parents are going to like, so I'm in a quandary about how much to tell them at this point in time.'

'What answers, guv?' said West, inching forward in her chair.

'It seems that Patrick had voiced some concerns about how to pay off his university debts given he was made redundant and only has part-time work at the moment. An ex-girlfriend who stayed friends with him said that Patrick told her he felt trapped living at home and guilty for relying on his parents for his upkeep. Plus, he wanted to travel – loved it, she said. And then another friend told us that Patrick felt stifled at home, that he owed his parents money and that although they told him it was okay, his mother in particular would constantly ask him how his job hunting was going and that he couldn't let the debt slide because it had come from his father's retirement savings. It seems Patrick felt an enormous amount of guilt about a situation he couldn't control.'

'Which possibly made him vulnerable to the sorts of people we're looking for in relation to the organ harvesting,' said Mark. 'Were any of his friends able to shed light on that?'

'I issued instructions to uniform not to allude to the kidney donation,' said Kennedy. 'Too risky at the moment, given that the media haven't got wind of it yet. Instead, Patrick's friends were asked if he had mentioned any new connections, associations or suchlike. That ex-girlfriend of his said that he'd told her he was planning to go away for a few weeks and not to worry, but that's all.'

'Thereby excusing the fact that he thought he would need time to recover after donating his kidney,' said West. 'Poor bugger believed he was safe, didn't he?'

Kennedy nodded in response. 'And it also means we're no closer to finding out who's responsible. Not until we can identify the man who met Patrick at Didcot railway station.'

'I can't work out how Windlesham ended up with Patrick's mobile phone though,' said West. 'Because we haven't found his clothing or backpack yet, have we?'

'Maybe Barry found it when he was checking around the buildings the day he thought he was being watched,' Mark suggested. 'If whoever's behind all of this kept Patrick there under duress, it makes sense that he would have had his belongings taken from him before being locked in the officers' mess. It's definitely him on the security footage that Barry posted through his friend's door before he was shot at. If Patrick put up a fight or realised his life was in danger he might have had a chance to toss away his phone before anyone noticed.'

'And perhaps Barry realised after finding it and suspecting something was wrong at the airfield that the phone was important, hence why he chose to hide it in the river rather than posting it through Gregory Lesk's letterbox along with that memory stick containing the camera footage,' said Kennedy. 'He split up the evidence.'

'A shame he just didn't come to us with it,' Mark replied.

'Instead, someone suspected him of taking Patrick's phone and followed him, then tried to shoot him.'

'He might've been too scared to come to us,' said West.

'True. It seems as though the bloke who stole the dry bag from the hospital expected the mobile phone to be with Barry's belongings, though, so whoever shot him didn't see him putting it in the river,' Kennedy mused. He glanced over Mark's head at a knock on the door. 'Come in.'

'Sorry to interrupt, guv.' Caroline huffed her fringe from her face. 'Got some news you might want to hear though.'

'Go on.'

'I've taken a call from uniform – they reckon they've found Barry Windlesham's clothing that was removed from that dry bag in one of the shops we're investigating.'

'Really?' Mark straightened. 'Where?'

Caroline smiled. 'The second-hand clothing shop in Ravenswood village.'

# CHAPTER FORTY-SIX

West braked hard, slapped the car into reverse and executed a nimble parallel parking manoeuvre that had Mark clutching at his seatbelt before she had finished.

After ratcheting the handbrake, she looked at him in bewilderment. 'Something the matter?'

'I think I just got a whiplash.'

'Don't be a drama queen.' She checked her blind spot, then opened the door. 'You'd have moaned if I'd ended up parking at the other end of the village.'

He bit back a smile, climbed out and eyed the sign for the charity shop a little farther along the uneven cobbled pavement.

There was a peacefulness to Ravenswood that belied the reason they were here. The flower baskets dangling from wrought iron brackets outside the beauty clinic twisted lazily in the breeze, the displays of Spanish bluebells and primroses jostling for space. In the distance, the pub was preparing to open and Mark could see a man wiping down a pair of wooden picnic benches before disappearing back inside.

A group of four pensioners – Mark guessed two couples – were gathered outside the village shop and post office, their laughter filling the air while one of the men looked on as his wife regaled their companions with a snippet of gossip about someone who worked in the pub. The other man peered past the wife then frowned after Mark gave him a curt nod, and the group's voices reduced to a murmur while they watched the two detectives approach the charity shop.

There was a "closed" sign on the door, but when he leaned against the handle, it swung open easily. Mark heard the tinkle from a cluster of small bells that were dangling from a thin rope attached to the back of it, their brass surfaces clinking against the woodwork. West followed, closing the door behind him and leading the way between rails of coats, trousers and T-shirts to the counter.

It was an old teak dresser that had been bashed and chipped away at over the years, its once polished surface now cluttered with a till, receipt book, charity tins and various items of jewellery for sale displayed on velvet-lined trays that were fighting a losing battle with dust.

There was a woman sitting on a chair behind the dresser who looked up from a dog-eared paperback historical novel, peered down her nose at them and then called over her shoulder. 'Constable Fields? I think these people are for you.'

A curtain was shoved aside, revealing an inner doorway, and a petite blonde woman in her twenties appeared, her ponytail a little dishevelled and her face flushed. Her uniform shirt sleeves had been rolled up to her elbows, and she wore protective gloves.

'Good, you're here,' she said. 'Do you want to come through here, Sarge, and I'll show you what we've found?' She held open the curtain and stood to one side. 'And, Sarah – can you relock the front door please? No one else is to enter now.'

'Fine.' The woman stood up and placed her paperback upside down on the counter, her tone petulant. 'I might as well not be here.'

PC Alice Fields gave a patient smile to the woman's back as she stomped away. 'I'll let you know when you're free to go.'

Once the curtain dropped behind them, Mark turned to her and lowered his voice. 'Does she know?'

'No, haven't said a word, Sarge.' Alice grinned. 'Figured this place leaks like a sieve as far as gossip goes, so we've kept her out there.'

'Good. Where'd you find Windlesham's clothing?'

'In one of the bundles that hasn't been processed for sale yet. Through here.' Alice beckoned them through to an anteroom off the narrow passageway where another uniformed constable was squatting beside a cardboard box full of shoes.

Grant Wickes glanced up at their arrival, his face resigned. 'We're not going to be popular with the forensics lot, are we?'

'None of us are, Grant,' said West. 'So you might as well get used to it.'

'This is Barry's clothing, isn't it?' said Alice, holding up a pair of labelled evidence bags. 'We're not wrong, are we? I mean, Grant said the kayakers' witness statements listed what they took off him, and these match the description so we figured we'd best call it in.'

Mark heard the nervousness in her voice. 'Let's take a look, shall we? Better to be safe than sorry, so there's no harm in you asking us to come out.'

He slipped on a pair of protective gloves that West produced from her handbag, waited while she donned another pair and then took the evidence bags from Alice.

Unzipping the first one, he extracted a pair of jeans and underpants. The underwear comprised a simple pair of black cotton boxer shorts, but the jeans bore the insignia of a named brand and the label inside stipulated the same sizing that Barry Windlesham wore, and a small ragged hole had pierced the material where his hip would have met the fabric. Mark tucked the clothing back into the bag and unzipped the second one. Inside was a navy sweater and grey long-sleeved base layer. The sweater was well worn with a hole forming in one elbow, and again the sizing was right.

'What do you think?' he said, turning to West.

'Could well be,' she said. 'I reckon we should get these run past the Middletons to see if they can confirm this is the clothing they placed in the dry bag after rescuing Barry though, just to be sure. And then we can ask the lab to test it against his DNA in case there are any traces left.' She put the sweater close to her face and sniffed. 'Smells like a river to me though. God knows I've had to wash it out of the kids' clothing often enough over the years.'

'How much more have you got to sift through?' said Mark,

eyeing the piles of clothing. 'Any sign of Barry's work boots yet?'

'No,' said Grant, 'but we haven't started on the bins outside the back door yet.'

'Bins?'

'There are rubbish bags within a locked cage just outside the back door,' said Alice. 'So we're going to be here for a while yet.'

'Show us,' said Mark. 'Maybe I can ask Kennedy to send over an extra pair of hands.'

He and West followed the young constable out the room and along the corridor to a fire exit door. Alice pushed it open and waved her hand towards a large wire mesh cage with a tarpaulin flung over it that served as a makeshift roof. It had been weighted down with chipped red house bricks at each corner, and inside the cage were bulging black plastic bin bags, recycled supermarket carrier bags and various plastic archive-style boxes.

'Apparently these were delivered last week but haven't yet been processed,' Alice said. 'The shop's run by volunteers and most of them are part-time so it takes a while. The one we found Barry's clothing in came from this pile so we reckon his boots must be in here somewhere too.'

'Makes sense,' said Mark. He pulled out his mobile phone. 'True. Okay, Alice – I'll give the DI a call and ask him if he can spare an extra pair of hands.'

'Thanks, Sarge.'

'Jan, do you want to— Jan?' He turned to see his colleague standing with her back to the cage, oblivious to his question. 'Jan? Everything okay?'

She turned to face him, a shocked expression in her eyes, her cheeks devoid of colour.

'Are you okay?' He lowered the phone. 'What's wrong?'

A worried frown creased West's brow. 'What if they were using an ambulance to move the bodies, Sarge?'

'An ambulance? Even if it were privately owned, it'd be difficult to hide I would think. I mean, there'd be all sorts of logistical issues wouldn't there?'

She jerked her head towards a white van parked a few metres away outside another of the old terraced houses that had been converted into a successful business. Its liveried sides matched that of the vet practice next door, the colourful logo depicting a cartoon dog with a bandaged paw.

Her frown became a sly smile. 'What if they were using a pet ambulance?'

# CHAPTER FORTY-SEVEN

Leaving Alice to keep a close eye on the liveried van in the yard behind the terraced buildings, Jan and Turpin walked back through the charity shop and along the cobblestones to the independent vet surgery.

The front door opened into a light and airy reception area that smelled of disinfectant and dog biscuits. There were posters on the walls warning pet owners about the various health risks associated with ticks, fleas and other untreated ailments, a selection of pet products and toys arranged across three shelves against a wall, and a battered wooden reception desk with a bowl of water next to it.

There was a woman behind the desk with a phone tucked between her ear and shoulder while she struck her computer keyboard with talon-like fingernails. She looked up as Jan approached, kept talking to the frantic owner on the other end of the line, and assured them that their dog, cat, goldfish – Jan tried and failed to guess what kind of animal was being discussed – was booked in for a five-thirty appointment. That done, the receptionist put down the phone and narrowed her eyes.

'Are you something to do with the police next door?' she said.

'We are.' Jan produced her warrant card and introduced Turpin. 'And you are?'

'Julia Barkham,' came the straight-faced response. The woman glared at Jan, as if daring her to comment on her last name.

Jan didn't smile. 'There's a white van parked out the back of your premises with the practice logo down the side of it. Who owns it?'

'The practice. I mean, Doug does. He's the vet. Is there a problem?'

'Is Doug here?'

'He's with a patient at the moment.' Julia's gaze flicked to a closed door off to the right of the counter that displayed a sign that read "consulting room". Murmured voices could be heard through it, a baritone providing much of the conversation. 'He'll be at least another five minutes I think. And then he's got an appointment he has to go out to – it's been in the calendar for weeks.'

'He'll have to cancel it,' said Turpin. 'Best make a note in that calendar of yours to reschedule.'

'I can't—'

'You can.' He turned away and began contemplating the posters.

Julia stared helplessly at Jan for a moment, and then the

consulting room door opened and the vet appeared, wearing dark jeans and a pale green scrub top, the collar of a polo shirt poking out from the neckline. With his back to Jan and Turpin, he ushered a woman clutching a kitty carrier back into reception before he sensed the presence of additional people in the reception area.

He turned, shock registering in his eyes when he saw Jan and Turpin, and then the professionalism was back as he glanced over his shoulder. 'Julia, could you sort out Mrs Aberdale's bill and make sure she takes some of those antiseptic swabs we've got on the shelf there? I've put through the prescription on the system so everything should be in order.' That done, he focused his attention on the two detectives. 'Would you like to come through?'

The moment the door to the consulting room was shut, Turpin leaned against it and produced his warrant card before making the introductions. 'In the circumstances, Mr...?'

'Doctor. Doctor Douglas Holton. Or Doug to most people.'

'Dr Holton, we're going to make this formal.' With that, Turpin recited the standard caution and Jan watched as the vet's face turned from one of intrigue to fear.

'What's going on?' he said. 'Why are you here?'

Turpin ignored the question. 'Can you confirm that the white van parked outside the back door to this practice belongs to you?'

'It does, yes.'

'Where are the keys?'

'Hanging up next to the back door, where they always are. Why?'

'When was the last time you drove it?'

'April, last year.'

Jan looked up from her note-taking and saw confusion cross Turpin's face.

'Last year?' he repeated. 'Are you sure?'

The vet straightened, some of his candour returning. 'I am, yes.'

'Do you have an alibi?'

'I don't need one, detective.' Doug smiled patiently. 'I lost my licence on the eleventh of April last year due to early onset Parkinson's. I'm not allowed to drive.'

Turpin's eyes narrowed. 'Then who *does* drive it?'

'My assistant, Tom.' Doug shrugged off his scrub jacket. He hung it over a chair behind the consulting table, then sat. 'I employed him in February last year when I began to suspect I wouldn't be able to carry out my duties for much longer. Tom took over the day-to-day responsibilities such as the operations and house calls. I just tend to animals that require general healthcare, tick treatments, that sort of thing. I still help out during the operations from time to time but my surgery days are over, just like my ability to drive.'

'Where's Tom now?'

'There's a farm over near Benson with a herd of cows that are overdue for tuberculosis testing.'

'Phone him and tell him you need him back here now,' said Turpin.

'I—'

'Phone him.'

Doug glared at Jan instead. 'We've got a duty to—'

'So have we,' said Jan. 'So you might as well make the call. Otherwise your farmer is going to wonder what's going on with this practice of yours when our lot turn up, isn't he?'

Doug blanched. 'Look, are you going to tell me what's going on?'

'We're investigating the suspicious deaths of at least thirteen people,' said Turpin. 'And we want to question your assistant, Tom, in relation to our enquiries.'

'Okay, okay. I'll phone now.' The vet's hands trembled noticeably as he slid a mobile phone from his jeans pocket and swiped the screen. He put the call on speaker, and the dull dialling tone echoed off the walls. There was no answer. 'He's not picking up.'

'Phone the farmer.'

Doug nodded, turned to a laptop open on a small desk beside the consulting table and moused through different windows until he found the details he was seeking. 'Hello? Martin? It's Doug Holton. Is Tom there?'

Jan held her breath.

The vet's brow furrowed. 'Didn't he phone you? I'm so sorry. Look, I've got something on here at the moment but I'll give you a call as soon as I'm done and we'll get something sorted out. Okay, thanks. 'Bye.'

'What's wrong?' said Jan.

'He's not there. Apparently, he didn't show up.'

Turpin frowned. 'Was he here earlier?'

'No – he uses his own car to do the rounds sometimes before coming in here, especially if those appointments are first thing

THE ELEVENTH GRAVE   293

and we know he won't need the ambulance – that thing isn't cheap to maintain.'

'When did you last see Tom?' said Jan.

'Monday morning,' said Doug. 'He was out early – he said someone's dog had a suspected tick bite. When he came back, he helped me with neutering a cat, and then I had a doctor's appointment so I left him to finish the day's appointments and close the surgery. Julia only works until three o'clock. Tom had a day off yesterday.'

'Why?'

'I don't know. It was very last minute and Julia had to shuffle some appointments around, but we made it work for him. He's so dependable, despite working and studying all hours, so I didn't feel that I could say no.'

'We'll need his contact details and address,' said Turpin. 'Right now.'

The vet blinked, then acquiesced. 'Of course.'

He reached down and unlocked his desk drawers, then rummaged through the lower one and produced a flimsy file that he flipped open. 'There you go.'

Jan snatched the folder from Doug and headed for the door, ignoring his surprised squeak. Stepping outside his office and checking that the door to reception remained closed, she hit speed dial.

'Tracy? I need a patrol to check out this address. We think—'

'You must be psychic or something,' said the administrative assistant, her voice strained. 'How quickly can you get back here?'

'Why, what's wrong?' Jan said.

'Just get here as soon as you can. Kennedy's orders.'

# CHAPTER FORTY-EIGHT

Mark raced up the stairs to the incident room, hearing Jan's belaboured breathing over his shoulder as she hurried to keep up with him.

Face flushed, his colleague smoothed down her blouse when they reached the landing, then followed him along the corridor. Three uniformed constables paused in their conversation and stepped to one side to let them past, their faces grim while static and barked commands from their radios echoed off the walls.

Mark heard sirens wail into action as a patrol left the car park, the sound increasing the sense of urgency that seized at his chest. His grip tightened on the copy of the personnel folder for Tom Mildenhew that Doug Holton had provided, his mind already turning to the different steps that would have to be taken to track down the vet.

There was a frisson of excitement in the incident room when

he walked in, borne from the adrenaline rush of a potential breakthrough.

And yet, that energy was tinged with a renewed desperation.

A shiver crossed his shoulders, despite a trickle of sweat that dribbled down his spine thanks to the sprint from the car park, and when he eventually spotted Kennedy on the other side of the room talking with Alex and Caroline, the DI's face was grey.

'What's the matter, guv?' called West. 'You've heard we've got a potential suspect, yes? Surely that's good news.'

'It is, but we've got a bigger problem. Come here.' Kennedy beckoned them across to where Alex was sitting with his gaze focused on his computer screen. He didn't look up as they neared, and Caroline hovered at his elbow, her jaw set. 'Alex, show Mark and Jan what you've just found.'

The younger detective rewound the video he had been watching and rolled his chair back a little. 'Here you go.'

Mark heard the angst in the man's voice and leaned forward, resting his hand on the desk as the replay began.

It was a CCTV image from the same camera above the platform at Didcot railway station that they had watched while tracing Patrick Westington's movements before his death, and as Mark's attention flicked to the top left-hand corner of the screen, he saw that it was dated that Monday, and time-stamped just after seven thirty in the morning. A high-speed train arrived, spewing its guts onto the platform the moment the doors opened. Passengers hurried away, a determination in their stride, with some elbowing others out of the way as they hoisted backpacks over shoulders or carried scooters.

At seven thirty-five, Alex stopped the playback and looked up at him. 'That's why everyone's worried.'

Mark blinked, then looked at Kennedy. 'What am I looking for, guv?'

'We think they've got another victim.'

'What?' Bile churned in his stomach, and Mark's eyes widened.

'It's why we've sent a patrol over to the train station now,' said Caroline. 'We can get the recordings remotely, but we need statements taken from staff members as soon as possible.'

'How did you find this?'

Kennedy jerked his chin at Alex, pride in his eyes. 'This one decided to take it upon himself to monitor the same daily train time arrivals as Patrick Westington's, just in case.'

'And it paid off,' said Caroline, giving her colleague's shoulder a gentle slap. 'He's even got an image of our suspect's face.'

Alex shrugged, a flush to his cheeks. 'I just thought maybe they make sure the donors are picked up at a busy time so they can blend in with all the other commuters. We've only just worked out what they're up to, so I thought maybe they haven't had time to cancel any operations that have been paid for, and that maybe they'd keep to the same routine or days to meet donors.'

'Jesus, that's bold of them.'

'Bold, or are they desperate because we're onto them?' said Kennedy. 'If they're charging the sort of money our financial team think they might be for this sort of thing, then they've got clients with clout. Clients who might not appreciate being told the deal's off.'

'True,' said West. 'I mean, the sort of people who are willing to pay a lot of money for a black market kidney aren't going to be the sort of people we'd invite to the office Christmas party, are they?'

'Are we sure it's the same bloke that met Patrick?' said Mark.

Kennedy nodded. 'I'm sure. Play it again, Alex – and this time, can you splice in the other footage from the station concourse as well?'

On the video, a steady stream of commuters poured down the concrete steps from the platform, then filtered along the underground passageway that led to the ticket office and car park. Some paused to exchange a parting comment with their fellow passengers before splitting like tributaries across the station forecourt, hurrying to work before the forecasted rain shower smothered the town.

And, amongst these, was the man seen previously with Patrick Westington, except this time a woman in her early twenties was hurrying to keep up with him, her face determined.

'Shit,' West said. 'That's Tom Mildenhew, the vet. There's a photo of him in his personnel file.'

Mark turned to Kennedy. 'We have to find that woman. Now.'

# CHAPTER FORTY-NINE

Kennedy had ordered the four detectives and a group of uniformed personnel into another room that was partitioned from the main investigation team.

It was bright in here, sunlight dazzling Mark's eyes while he pulled down each of the window blinds, shutting away the outside world.

The air conditioning was grumbling through ventilation shafts above their heads while it attempted to lower the temperature in the stuffy meeting space, not helped by the number of people now pulling out chairs around a hastily constructed conference desk that constituted eight tables borrowed from various other rooms.

Mark loosened the top button of his shirt, tucked his tie into his trouser pocket and took one of the manila folders that was being passed around by Caroline with a murmured thanks. Opening it, he saw she had copied Tom Mildenhew's personnel file and added screenshots of the scant social media profiles she could find, including one that was for professionals seeking work.

None of the profiles had been updated for the past fourteen months. Not since Tom had started working for Doug Holton.

To his left, West sat stony-faced as she stared at the captured image of the young woman. 'Does anyone know who she is yet?'

'We've worked with British Transport Police to trace her movements,' said Peter Cosley, pushing his glasses up his nose. 'She boarded that train at Tilehurst, west of Reading, and we've got CCTV images from a convenience shop and a pub that shows her walking there from a nearby housing estate. Two patrols are currently doing house-to-house enquiries to find out where she lived, supported by officers here. As soon as they find out who she is, they'll let us know.'

'Thanks, Peter.' Kennedy turned to another uniformed sergeant on his right. 'Michael, what about Tom's family?'

'We're unable to trace any close relatives, guv,' came the reply. 'We went to the flat he's renting and spoke to his neighbours, but they said they haven't seen him in the past three days.'

'We do have some information about his pre-work life, guv.' PC Marie Collins raised her hand. 'One of his uni alumni we interviewed said there were some issues while they were in their second year, but couldn't provide any more information – apparently it was all discussed behind closed doors. I spoke with Tom's lecturer at university to find out what those issues were, and it turns out that some of his peers thought he might've been torturing animals rather than treating them, and reported their concerns. Nothing happened – it couldn't be proven – but she did say that Tom became more withdrawn after that. He passed his finals with no issues. But I can't find out anything about him prior to starting uni.'

'Keep digging,' said Kennedy. 'Mark, what about you?'

'Jan and I worked through his personnel record and spoke with the two vet practices he worked at before starting at the one in Ravenswood,' said Mark. 'Both employers said that although he was good at what he did, he lacked any of the typical empathy that comes with dealing with animals and their owners.'

'Why did he leave his last job?' said Kennedy.

'He told them he was going travelling for a while,' said Mark. 'That was two months before he started working for Doug Holton.'

The DI looked around the room. 'Anyone know where Mildenhew was during those two months?'

'I checked his passport records, guv,' said Michael. 'He went out to Thailand for six weeks. We've got no trace of him there, and we can't get hold of any bank statements for him in the timeframe we need today to see what he might've spent his money on while out there. When he returned, we believe he stayed with a friend in Maidenhead until he moved to Ravenswood to start working with Holton two weeks later. He used the friend's address on his job application.'

Kennedy jabbed a finger at the sergeant. 'We need to find that friend, now.'

'He went missing a week ago, guv.' Michael let his news sink in before continuing. 'I've asked a local Maidenhead patrol to go door-knocking and interview the man's family and friends…'

'But it doesn't sound good, does it?' Kennedy sighed. 'Okay, next steps. What about Holton's van that he says Tom's been driving?'

'Jasper's lot are there now,' said West. 'They're planning to work their way through the operating room at the surgery, looking for any trace evidence to link the place to the illegal organ harvesting, as well as the van for anything that might suggest it was used to transport Patrick Westington and any evidence that might help us find that woman. Holton told us that Tom used it on Monday morning before he came to work but had a day off yesterday. And just because the van was parked outside when Doug and his receptionist turned up to work this morning doesn't mean Tom hasn't used it again so we're waiting for ANPR camera footage from around the area to clarify its movements for the past three days.'

'Good, thanks. Caroline, when that footage comes in can you get a team of officers to go through it?'

'Will do, guv.'

'Are we all of the opinion that Tom might've been using the operating room at the vet's to conduct the organ harvesting?' said Kennedy, looking around the gathered officers.

'It seems our best bet at the moment, guv,' Mark ventured. 'It's a sterile environment, and although it's nowhere near ideal for a surgical procedure like that, it's tucked out of the way – and until now, convenient for the burial site at the airfield. Tom could have used it after hours, because there are no residential buildings overlooking the back yard area where the ambulance was parked – it's all small artisan businesses along that short stretch of the village. Gillian's over at the vet's at the moment

THE ELEVENTH GRAVE 303

working with Jasper to see if there's anything at the practice that shouldn't be there – I mean, anything that wouldn't typically be used on an animal patient. Jasper's going through the whole place looking for trace evidence too so we can try to work out who might've been helping Tom as well.'

'Okay, well there's nothing further we can do until we hear from them and the house-to-house enquiries,' Kennedy said, shuffling through the stack of papers in front of him. 'Moving on to patients – Marie's done some quick research and anyone who's received one of these kidneys is going to require ongoing medication to make sure those organs aren't rejected. That's going to cost upwards of twenty thousand pounds a year, probably more on the black market so Peter, can you work with Marie to open up a file on that and talk to the financial investigation team at HQ to see if they've got anything that might help us?'

'Will do, guv.'

'I want formal interviews carried out immediately with anyone who fits the profile.'

'Got it.'

Mark waited until Peter and Marie had left the room, then turned to the DI. 'Guv, do you want myself and West to head back to the vet clinic? At least that way, we can action anything Jasper and Gillian find out the moment they've got something.'

'Do it,' said Kennedy, jerking his chin towards the door. 'And if you find anything – *anything* – that indicates where this bastard has taken this woman, you let me know straight away.'

# CHAPTER FIFTY

Mark found a parking space at the far end of Ravenswood's narrow main street, and ended up with the pool car squashed bumper-to-bumper between one of Jasper's plain grey panelled vans and a landscape gardener's pickup truck.

West was already marching towards the vet's surgery, stepping off the pavement to skirt around several locals who crowded the cobblestones in small groups, their voices no more than a subdued murmur.

They fell silent and stared at Mark when he passed, then after he gave them a curt nod, they turned their backs and whispered.

Outside the pub, the landlord watched, arms crossed and his jaw set. 'Oi,' he said as Mark hurried by. 'Any idea when they're going to be finished? They're putting off my clientele.'

'No idea,' said Mark, and kept walking.

There were four patrol cars now taking up the spaces outside the charity shop and the vet's, and both premises were cordoned off with crime scene tape accompanied by temporary signs that directed pedestrians across to the other side of the road so no one could peer through the open doors. Just in case that didn't work, one of Jasper's team was fixing plastic sheeting as a temporary curtain across each doorway.

A steady stream of protective-suited forensic technicians moved in and out of the charity shop carrying bags of second-hand clothing, and another two were talking in low voices at the entry to the vet's.

Mark flipped open his warrant card to one of them. 'Any idea where Gillian Appleworth is?'

'In there,' said the shorter of the two. He eyed Mark up and down. 'Got suits, or do you need a pair?'

'If you've got some spare...'

'Here you go.'

'Thanks.' Mark slipped them over his clothes, adding the plastic bootees over his shoes while West did the same. That done, he signed the clipboard that a uniformed constable held out. 'Okay for us to come in?'

'All yours.' The forensic technician lifted the tape for them to walk under. 'Stay on the demarcated path, and follow the corridor that leads off to the left of the reception area. You'll find Gillian and Jasper down there.'

'Thanks.'

Mark stepped aside to let West go first, the protective suit crinkling as he moved. It was already itching his scalp, while the plastic material was creating sweat patches under his arms.

All of the surgery lights had been switched on, and at the end of the corridor he could see that bright LED lights had been removed from the forensic vans and erected to aid Jasper and his team while they worked. When he walked into the operating theatre at the rear of the practice, he blinked to offset the glare from the stainless steel table and equipment that filled the space.

The floor tiles were polished to a high sheen, and when he inhaled, there was a strong aftermath of bleach in the air. A forensic photographer nudged him out of the way before crouching beside a two-door stainless steel cabinet, angling the camera lens so it captured the floor tiles beside the cabinet as well. Over in the far corner, one of the forensic technicians was removing files from a cabinet, while her colleague took swabs from a laptop that had been left open on a desk.

There were two other people dressed head to toe in protective suits standing beside a trolley laden with surgical equipment, their attention on a locked wall cabinet while the taller of the two tried to prise it open.

'Jasper?' Mark ventured.

The lead forensic technician stepped back as the cabinet door sprang open, then turned. 'We're going to be a while here.'

'I know.' Mark gestured to West. 'Kennedy thought it'd be a good idea if we were here though. Got much to go on?'

'Lots of blood trace,' said Jasper, 'but that's to be expected. The place has been thoroughly disinfected. Holton says it was last washed down by Tom Mildenhew on Monday, according to the cleaning schedule, and no procedures have taken place within the past forty-eight hours. However the lights have picked up traces around the fringes of the drain and there's some splatter on the corner of that floor cabinet over there, so all the swabs we're taking will be tested to check if any of those are human blood or other fluids and tissue.'

The shorter suit-clad figure turned, and Gillian Appleworth's eyes bored into Mark's over the top of her protective mask. 'There are some instruments on the trolley there that beg the question what they're doing in a vet's surgery as well.'

'Really?' He wandered over, keeping his hands clasped behind his back while he peered at the various drills, saws, pliers and scalpels. 'How can you tell?'

Gillian huffed behind the mask. 'Because I can.'

Mark held up gloved hands. 'Is there anything you'd like us to do to help?'

'Yes,' she said. 'Get out of the way.'

She brushed between him and West, crossed over to where a glass-fronted cupboard had been fixed to the wall above a small refrigeration unit and began sifting through packets of surgical wipes and sealed needles. Jasper winked at Mark, then dropped to a crouch beside the filing cabinet and started to lift piles of documents from the hanging files inside.

'Shall we head outside?' West murmured. 'We could have a look at the receptionist's statement and see if Alice and Grant have found anything else.'

'Okay. Perhaps if we—'

'Oh no.'

He turned to see Gillian standing beside the open refrigerator door, her movements careful.

'Oh, that's not good,' she said.

Mark moved closer, West at his side. 'What've you got?'

By way of answer, Gillian swivelled around and held up a glass jar, its contents bloodied. 'This.'

He frowned. 'Sorry, I don't know what that is.'

'They're kidneys, Mark. Human kidneys.'

'Sarge, got a minute?'

Biting back a rising anger, Mark turned at the sound of PC Grant Wickes's voice. 'What is it?'

'We managed to break open the back of the van, Sarge.' The constable's face was grey. 'There's a dead woman inside.'

# CHAPTER FIFTY-ONE

By the time Mark and West walked out the back door of the vet's surgery and into the yard, a small crowd of forensic technicians had joined the two uniformed constables that stared at the white van.

Gillian led the way, her manner brusque until she reached its open rear doors. Then she paused for a moment, and Mark ventured a few steps closer. Over her shoulder, he could see the crumpled form of a young woman, her naked body part-covered by an old wool blanket that had fallen aside to reveal her leg bent at the knee and her arm flung out to the side. If it hadn't been for the slashes in her lower abdomen and the sickening alabaster sheen to her skin, she might have been sleeping.

'You poor thing,' said Gillian, her shoulders slumping. 'You poor, poor thing. Do you know who she is?'

'Not yet.' Mark blinked. His own daughters were only a few years younger than the woman who lay dead before them, and his chest tightened. 'But we'll find out, and when I get my hands on Tom Milden—'

'What the bloody hell took them so long to get this thing open?' Kennedy said, hands on hips as he glared at the forensic technicians working their way along the inside of the van.

Mark glanced over his shoulder. 'I didn't know you were on your way, guv.'

'I'm getting too many phone calls from HQ on this one, especially after I've told them we've lost our main suspect, so I thought I'd come down and take a look for myself.' The DI jerked his chin at the van. 'I thought Doug Holton had the keys?'

'So did he,' said Jasper. 'It turns out they weren't on the peg in the office where they normally are, so after he spent nearly an hour trying to find them, we had to break it open. Hence the delay.'

'Right, where's Grant?' Kennedy turned and whistled to the constable, waving him over. 'Get onto control and tell them to hurry up with the all-ports alert I've requested for Tom Mildenhew, and make sure it includes any working airfields around here – especially Kidlington. Ask them to get all data relating to flights out of the UK since Monday evening as well. Caroline and Alex are already trying to find out if Mildenhew is using his own car so as soon as they've got any information relating to that, they'll be updating the alert.'

'Guv.'

Mark watched the young officer hurry away with his radio to his lips while he relayed Kennedy's instructions, then turned back to the DI. 'If Tom brought her here, guv, someone was expecting to receive at least one of those kidneys.'

'Grant!' Kennedy shouted. 'Tell them to check incoming domestic flights as well, and check them against that register of people who are waiting for donations.'

The constable nodded in reply before turning back to his radio.

'They could've driven, guv,' said West. 'I mean, I know it's not helpful, but…'

'It's a good point. I'll have a team check vehicle registrations against the waiting list as well and see if we get any matches before we see if there are any hits on the ANPR around here.' He squinted into the back of the van. 'Gillian, any thoughts about how he killed her?'

The pathologist backed out of the van on her hands and knees, then looked at the woman's body that was now being swabbed and photographed by two of Jasper's team. 'He didn't bother with anaesthetising her.'

Mark swallowed. 'Christ, he didn't cut her open while she was still alive, did he?'

'I don't know.' Gillian sighed. 'Not until I do the post mortem, but she's got one hell of a crack to the back of her skull which would've knocked out an ox.'

'What about her clothes?' said Kennedy.

'Alice Fields has two probationers helping her to go through the charity shop donations in the cage over there again,' said West. 'If anything looks remotely like what our victim was wearing in the CCTV footage from the train station, they'll bag it for testing.'

'Good. Anyone interviewing the charity shop volunteer?'

'She's next on our list,' said Mark. 'She's already been

interviewed by Alice and Grant regarding Patrick Westington's clothes and denies any knowledge of how those ended up in the shop, but we'll ask her if Tom was seen hanging around the back of the shop within the past forty-eight hours.' He pointed to the fire exit door of the shop where a small camera faced the cages. 'And we'll chase up the CCTV footage that Alice requested as well.'

'Okay, thanks.' Kennedy turned his attention back to Gillian. 'If no donor was here, why continue with the operation?'

'Kidneys will keep for twenty-four to thirty-six hours if stored correctly,' said the pathologist. 'It wouldn't be ideal, but if the donor wasn't able to get here until after Mildenhew killed this woman, then they may still be en route.'

'Or waiting nearby in case he finds somewhere else to carry out the operation,' said Mark. He sighed, and gestured to all the police and forensic teams working in the yard. 'And anyone who was meant to be meeting him here will have been alerted to all of our activity by now, I'll bet.'

'There's another possibility, too,' said West, her voice bleak. 'If we're dealing with a network of people dealing in illegal organs, then they might be trying to sell those kidneys to someone else online.'

# CHAPTER FIFTY-TWO

Jan broke off a corner from a chocolate bar and tossed it across her computer screen to where Turpin was sitting.

He caught it one-handed, shoved it in his mouth and mumbled his thanks, his gaze never leaving his own work.

Behind her, she could hear the rest of the team on phones or talking in small groups gathered around each other's desks, all working through the growing list of tasks that Kennedy had passed around at a hurriedly organised briefing.

The detective inspector stalked the carpet outside his office, his phone to his ear while he coordinated with HQ, his face haggard.

Checking the clock in the corner of her computer screen, she saw it was after 2AM and rubbed at tired eyes. And yet she wasn't exhausted, not yet. Instead, her mind turned to the scanned list of documents she had been sifting through for the past hour.

Tom Mildenhew's history had been updated as the statements from the house-to-house enquiries were collated, and she was gaining a better understanding of the man's upbringing.

Thankfully, the housemate Tom had rented a room from on his return from Thailand had emerged unscathed, phoning the incident room upon arriving back from a university alumni event in Edinburgh. The man had been surprised by the interest in Mildenhew, but had provided valuable information about the young vet when Jan had spoken with him.

'Hey, here,' she said, handing over the rest of the chocolate bar to Turpin. 'You can get the next one.'

'Thanks.' He bit off a corner. 'How are you getting on with Tom?'

'Slowly. I'm going to work my way through some emails that came in late afternoon while we were over at the vet's surgery, but so far I'm not seeing anything that can help us. The bloke over at Maidenhead confirmed he knew Tom from university but had lost touch after they graduated – he pursued a career in pharmaceuticals while Tom was studying to become a vet. Apparently Tom got in touch out of the blue to ask if he could stay with him for a couple of weeks while he found somewhere else to live.'

'Any red flags?'

'Not that he could remember, no.' She closed the document she had been reading and turned to the growing number of emails, biting back a groan. 'And I spoke to someone at the Home Office who confirmed there was nothing untoward noted in relation to Tom's passport while he was out in Thailand, either.'

'Maybe he was keeping his head down until he got back here,' Turpin said, tapping his pen against his nose while he stared at his screen.

'Or, I wondered if he was making his own enquiries into illegal organ harvesting while he was out there,' said Jan. 'He might have been on a fact-finding mission to see if it was something he could replicate once he was back here.'

Turpin grimaced. 'Good point. Christ, it doesn't bear thinking about, does it?'

'And yet, here we are.' Kennedy clapped a hand on Jan's shoulder. 'How's it going?'

'Getting there,' she said, opening each email in turn and scanning the contents.

Then Turpin sat upright and reached for his desk phone. 'Bloody hell.'

She looked up to see him clutching a witness statement in his other hand. 'What've you got?'

'Hang on.' He paused while the call connected, then: 'Hello? Is that Sarah? It's Detective Sergeant Mark Turpin. Sorry for the late call, but I'm just going through the statement you gave earlier today to one of my colleagues, and I have a few questions I wondered if you'd mind answering? Thanks. You've said here that the CCTV camera on the back of the shop facing the yard doesn't work, and that it's just a deterrent to stop anyone breaking in. When PC Fields asked you whose decision it was not to fit real cameras, you told her the woman who's one of the charity trustees said it was a cost-cutting exercise, and that because not much cash was kept on the premises, real cameras were an extravagance. Is that correct?'

He nodded while the woman on the other end of the phone spoke, and Jan held her breath. Kennedy went to lean against her desk, then changed his mind and paced back and forth instead.

'Okay,' said Turpin, returning to the caller. 'Thanks. Who *is* the trustee that told you the cameras weren't required? Really? Is she very involved in the day-to-day running of the shop? Right. Right. No, that's really helpful, thank you. Yes, I've got her details, and I'll give her a quick call now. Thanks for your time.' He ended the call, his eyes sparkling. 'We've got a breakthrough, I think.'

Kennedy stopped pacing. 'Well, spit it out.'

'The trustee who nixed having real CCTV cameras at the back of the charity shop is Judy Sarsgold.'

Jan frowned. 'Charmaine Abbott's campaign manager?'

'I'm wondering if maybe Judy is overseeing the charity shops to get rid of victims' belongings,' said Turpin. 'And, maybe it was Judy who persuaded Charmaine that it was a bad idea to let Barry redevelop the airfield site so she could prevent the graves being discovered.'

Kennedy checked his watch. 'It's almost three o'clock. I'll send uniformed patrols to pick up Judy Sarsgold. We'll start the interviews at eight o'clock this morning to give her time to organise legal representation. If you want to go home and shower, and get a few hours' sleep, then do so. You're all going to be busy today.'

# CHAPTER FIFTY-THREE

Mark yawned, his eyes adjusting to the bright sunshine that dappled the water and cast sparkles of light across the river. Beyond the boat, downstream from where he stood, a lone kayaker approached, his face determined as he dug in his paddle left then right to offset the current.

He raised his half-empty coffee mug in salute as the man passed, then looked through the hatch into the galley at the sound of footsteps.

'You off in a minute?' Lucy said, rubbing at wet hair with a towel.

'In a sec, yes. Just waiting to spot Jan's car.' He squinted across the water meadow to the car park. 'She won't be far off, just stuck in the usual morning traffic.'

He wrapped an arm around his girlfriend as she joined him on the deck at the stern of the boat, burying his nose in her hair. 'You smell nice.'

'Thank you.' She smiled up at him before her face grew serious. 'So this is it, do you think, a breakthrough at last?'

'I hope so. I don't want to find any more bodies.' He shivered, despite the suit jacket he wore. 'We let her down, you know. If we'd moved quicker, if we'd asked the right questions…'

'No, you didn't let her down.' Lucy laid a hand on his chest. 'There's nothing you could have done for her, Mark. But yes, you can try to stop him killing anyone else. That's what you need to focus on today. Find the answers you need.'

He blinked, then pulled her into a hug. 'You always know what to say.'

'Sometimes.'

A car horn beeped twice, and he looked over her head to where a silver hatchback pulled into the car park. 'I have to go.'

Lucy stood on tiptoe and kissed him. 'You've got this.'

'I bloody hope so,' he murmured, then climbed over the gunwale. 'I'll call you later if I get a chance.'

She waved in response, then hugged her arms around her waist and pulled her cardigan close as he turned away and set out for the waiting car.

When he climbed in, West handed him a foil-wrapped bacon sandwich that was still warm to the touch. 'Thanks, although between you and Lucy I'm going to have to really get back into running with Hamish at this rate.'

'You can put it back in the bag down there if you don't want it.'

'Bugger off,' he said, unwrapping the food. 'I'm not letting this go to waste.'

West laughed, then fell silent until they had passed through Abingdon's town centre. 'So, Judy Sarsgold... If she's involved, what's in it for her?'

'Apart from any monetary gain? I'm not sure.' Mark unclipped his seatbelt as West turned into the police station car park. 'So, let's go and ask her, shall we?'

————

Judy Sarsgold was wearing a white blouse over blue jeans, her brown hair tied back from her face and a petulant expression in her eyes as she watched Mark and West walk into the interview room and prepare the recording equipment.

While West read out the formal caution, he maintained eye contact with Judy, biting back the doubt that had set in, the niggle at the back of his mind that he had missed some vital clue, that maybe – despite Lucy's assurances – he might have saved a life.

A polite cough from his colleague brought him back to the task at hand, and he opened the folder under his elbow. He took his time extracting each of the photographs from it, laying them side by side on the table facing Judy, then stabbed his finger on the last one. 'Tell me where this clothing came from.'

She shrugged, barely giving the photographs a second look. 'I don't know. I don't work at the shop.'

'But you *do* manage them, don't you?'

'Yes.'

'So, where does the clothing come from?'

Judy sighed, and held up her hands. 'Anywhere. I mean, we

have donations dropped off at the shops at any time. That's why we have the locked cages at the back.'

'If they're for donations, why are they locked?'

'Because we had an issue with kids getting into them and throwing the clothing all over the car park last year. We had to do something.'

'Why haven't you got working CCTV cameras outside?' Mark said. 'That would've at least shown who was responsible.'

'We're a charity, detective.' Judy snorted. 'We can hardly afford the overheads on the shop, let alone pay out for extravagances such as security cameras.'

'How many employees do you have?'

'Three on part-time contracts, the rest are all volunteers.'

'We'll need names and addresses.'

'Of course.'

'Do you ever work in the shops?'

'Yes.'

'Do you ever work in the Ravenswood shop?'

'From time to time, yes.'

'When was the last time you were there?'

Judy glanced sideways, her jaw working. 'Tuesday. Just in the morning though. One of the volunteers had the morning off and no one else could cover her shift.'

'When you arrived on Tuesday morning, where did you park your car?'

'Behind the shop, where I always park.'

'Was this van parked nearby?' Mark pointed to the next photograph, showing the vet's liveried vehicle. 'Did you see this?'

'I'm not sure.'

'Not sure? Ms Sarsgold, it's a long wheel-based van with the vet's logo all over it. You could hardly miss it.'

'I realise that, detective,' she said, 'but you know what it's like – things you see every day become scenery, nothing more. I couldn't tell you whether it was there on Tuesday any more than I could tell you if it was there Monday.'

'Was it?'

'What?'

'Was the van there on Monday?'

'How would I know? I wasn't at the shop then.'

'Are you sure?'

'Absolutely.'

Mark slid the third photograph towards her. 'Do you know Tom Mildenhew?'

'The vet? I wouldn't say I knew him,' Judy said, her brow creasing. 'But I've seen him around, obviously.'

'When was the last time you saw him?'

She screwed up her nose. 'Last Wednesday, maybe... I can't recall.'

'Where?'

'Outside the vet's of course – where else would I see him?'

Mark pushed another photograph closer, one taken from the CCTV footage that showed Mildenhew's last victim as she arrived at Didcot railway station. 'Who's this woman?'

'No idea.'

'Have you seen her anywhere before?'

'I just told you, I don't know who she is.'

'How—' He turned at a sharp knock on the door and frowned

as Caroline stuck her head around it. 'Sorry, Sarge. Got a minute?'

Heart thumping, he reached out for the recording equipment as West gathered up her notebook and the photographs. 'Interview paused at eight thirty-two.'

Mark hurried from the room, waiting until West closed the door behind them before following Caroline a few paces along the corridor. 'What's going on?'

In reply, the detective constable handed him a photograph, the page still warm from the printer. 'While you've been prepping and doing the interview with her, I've been delving into her social media accounts. That's from an old post I found from a few years ago.'

West peered over his shoulder. 'Bugger me.'

'Shit.' Mark's hand trembled as he held the photograph closer. 'Is that who I think it is in the background?'

Caroline grinned. 'Yes. It's Tom Mildenhew.'

'When was this taken?'

'At his graduation ceremony. Which means—'

'Judy Sarsgold is lying,' Mark snarled, turning back to the interview room. 'She's his bloody mother.'

# CHAPTER FIFTY-FOUR

Mark swung open the door to the interview room so hard that it bounced off the protective spring fixed to the wall and rebounded. He caught it before it hit him in the face, held it open for West, then crossed to the table, reached out for the recording equipment and restarted it.

'Interview recommenced at eight thirty-five. Why didn't you tell us that Tom Mildenhew is your son?' he snarled, towering over Judy Sarsgold while he rested his hands on the table.

The woman paled. 'How did you—'

'Your social media has a photograph from a few years ago at a graduation ceremony. Tom's in the photo with you.' Mark saw the warning glance that West shot his way, then took a deep breath before pulling his chair towards him and sitting. 'Explain.'

Judy turned to her solicitor, bowing her head while they spoke in low murmurs, then twisted back to face Mark. 'I was just trying to protect him, like any mother would.'

'Protect him?'

'Yes.'

'From what?'

'I just wanted to stop him.' Her shoulders slumped. 'Really, I did. We tried everything, you've got to believe me.'

Mark frowned, bile tumbling in his stomach. 'How long?'

'What?'

'How long has your son been murdering people?'

Judy waved her hand in front of her face as if afraid to utter the words. She brought her fist to her mouth for a moment, and then let out a strangled gasp. 'Maybe since he was a teenager. We were never sure.'

'Jesus,' West muttered. Then, 'Sorry, Sarge.'

Mark said nothing for a moment, his own thoughts similar to his colleague's shocked outburst. After a while, he reopened the folder and extracted the images captured from the railway station CCTV footage. 'This is Tom here, isn't it? With this man, and then earlier this week with this woman.'

Judy looked at each photo, hugging her hands to her chest. 'Yes. That's Tom.'

'Do you know who this man is?'

'No.'

'Your son murdered him. His name is Patrick. After your son murdered him, you took Patrick's clothing and belongings and sold them through one of your five charity shops, didn't you?'

'I don't know.'

'Tom also arranged for the murder of a man called Barry Windlesham. Barry's clothing has also been found in your shop.'

Judy said nothing, her jaw set.

'This woman here,' Mark continued, 'was murdered by Tom earlier this week. Her clothing was found in the sorting cages outside your shop in Ravenswood. Her body had been thrown into the back of the van he uses for work. And her kidneys were found in a fridge in the vet's surgery.'

Judy swallowed. 'Kidneys?'

'Tell me about Tom's involvement in illegal organ harvesting.'

'What?' The woman's eyes widened. 'I don't know anything about illegal organs, or kidneys.'

'Then why were you hiding the victims' clothing?'

Judy wiped at her eyes. 'I just thought, I suppose, that if I did that it'd give us time to work something else out, to try and get him some help.'

'Help?' Mark said. 'It doesn't sound like that worked before. What happened at his school, before he went to university?'

Judy stuck out her chin. 'He was provoked.'

'I'm hearing no remorse here,' said Mark. 'None. Just excuses for your son's behaviour. And you willingly conspired to destroy evidence in at least two murders and an attempted murder that we know of. Did you do the same with the clothing for all the other victims that are buried at the airfield?'

She lowered her head and nodded.

'I'll need you to speak up for the purposes of the recording.'

'Yes,' she said, her tone petulant.

'What's Charmaine Abbott's involvement?'

'None,' said Judy, and leaned forward. 'Don't bring her into this. She had nothing to do with it.'

'Then why was she objecting to the redevelopment of the airfield site? She wanted to hide the bodies, didn't she?'

'No, I did. That's why I volunteered to act as her campaign manager.' Judy sniffed, slumping in her chair. 'She wanted to go ahead with it to start with, so we had to stop her. I persuaded her that the wildlife at the site was too important to lose, and she went along with it because she could see it was her best chance of being re-elected this year.'

'Who else is involved then?'

'You'll have to ask him. Tom, I mean. I don't know.'

'You said "it'd give *us* some time" just now when you were talking about the victims' clothing. Who were you referring to?'

Judy sighed. 'Look, after Tom was arrested when he was at school, we tried to get him assessed, tried to get some answers for what was going on, but we couldn't.'

'What did he get arrested for?'

'It wasn't his fault.'

'What happened?' said Mark.

'He and two other boys hurt another boy. That's all I'm going to tell you about it because it's ancient history.'

Mark glared at her. 'So, who's his father? I take it that's who you've been referring to regarding that incident?'

'I've got nothing to hide.' Judy shrugged. 'The bastard's just as responsible as Tom is for this mess.'

'Who's his father?' said Mark, leaning forward. 'Tell me.'

'Felix Darrow.'

# CHAPTER FIFTY-FIVE

Mark paced the carpet between Kennedy's desk and the door, alternating between checking his watch and glaring at the clock on the wall.

Beyond the DI's office, the incident room was thrumming with renewed energy as the team pored through witness statements and the growing amount of evidence being processed by Jasper's teams at the vet's surgery and airfield site.

West was nowhere to be seen, having rushed to a hastily arranged meeting with the Crown Prosecution Service to alert them to the likelihood of several arrests over the coming hours, and to seek advice about what charges should be laid against each suspect.

'If you don't sit down, I'm going to zip tie you to one of those bloody visitor chairs,' Kennedy grumbled.

'Sorry, guv.' Mark sat, but was unable to keep his heel

bouncing off the carpet, his heart rate thumping. 'What's taking them so long? That patrol should've picked up Felix by now.'

'They probably got stuck in traffic,' said the DI, his tone patient. 'And you can't start the interview until West gets back anyway.'

Mark exhaled, and twisted in his seat as Alex appeared at the doorway, excitement in his eyes.

'Got a minute, guv?' he said, directing his question at Kennedy. 'I've got something here about Tom Mildenhew's background that might help us.'

'Come on in,' said Kennedy, waving to the empty chair beside Mark. 'What is it?'

Alex was already opening the folder in his hand as he sat, and handed over copies of the contents to them both. 'I did some digging around on the national database about that incident at the school Judy Sarsgold mentioned. It happened at a secondary school in Northamptonshire – it took a while to find it because Tom's using her maiden name these days, rather than his father's. Judy remarried six years ago but got divorced at the beginning of last year. When Tom was at that school, he was still known as Tom Darrow.'

Mark skimmed the report. 'It says he stabbed another boy in the stomach. Why wasn't he convicted?'

'None of the other kids would give evidence in court,' said Alex. 'There weren't any teachers around when the stabbing took place, and back then there weren't cameras in the corridors.'

'What about the young lad who was stabbed?' said Kennedy, flicking through the pages. 'Did he survive?'

'Only just.' Alex delved into the folder and waved another page. 'He needed a blood transfusion and didn't return to school until the next year, but I've managed to track him down. He's a depot manager for a food distribution company near Milton. Hope you don't mind, guv, but I took the liberty of calling him before coming to see you.'

'What did he say?' said Mark.

'He reckons Tom Mildenhew is evil – those were his exact words,' said Alex. 'Apparently he was regularly turning up to school with bits of animals – claws, teeth, things like that. Their head teacher made Tom open his locker one day because they noticed a stink coming out of it, and when he did there were dead mice, a squirrel, even a small cat. He was suspended but his dad put up such an argument that they relented and allowed him back to school after two weeks. The stabbing happened four days later.'

'Jesus,' said Kennedy.

'After the arrest and court hearing, Tom Darrow disappears,' said Alex. 'His mum and dad changed his surname to Mildenhew and enrolled him in a private school here in Oxfordshire. From there, he went to university.'

'And the rest we know,' said Mark, handing back the paperwork. 'That's good work, Alex, thanks.'

'No worries.' The young detective constable rose and headed for the door. He paused, his hand on the frame. 'Do you think we'll be able to get a conviction this time, guv?'

'I bloody well hope so,' Kennedy growled.

————

Felix Darrow wore an expression of utter indignation when Mark followed West into the interview room half an hour later.

The man was sitting upright, his blue cotton shirt freshly pressed and his hair slicked away from his forehead. Beside him, his solicitor peered at the two detectives over half-moon glasses with a sour expression before returning to his note-taking.

'Interview commenced at eleven fifteen,' said Mark before reciting the formal caution and dealing with introductions. 'Tell me, Mr Darrow, whose idea was it to conceal your son's identity so he could continue his schooling as a teenager?'

'We didn't conceal it,' said Felix, his tone patient. 'We did what any parent would do in the circumstances to give their child a second chance in life.'

'Your child, Mr Darrow, is a killer.'

The other man's eyes narrowed. 'Prove it.'

'Your wife has already admitted to processing Tom's victims' clothing through her network of charity shops, particularly the one in Ravenswood, and we have these.' Mark laid out the CCTV images from the train station. 'This man, Patrick, and this woman were murdered by your son. He removed the woman's kidneys, Mr Darrow. We're yet to ascertain whether she was still alive when he did so.'

Felix remained silent, his gaze stony as he looked at the photographs.

'We have eleven bodies that were found interred at the airfield site,' said Mark. 'We also have the death of Barry Windlesham to consider, and the death of a man seen stealing Mr Windlesham's belongings from the John Radcliffe hospital the night he passed away. Tell me about your aggregates business.'

'What?' Felix's eyebrows shot up. 'What's that got to do with anything?'

'Because Tom didn't bury those bodies on his own, did he Mr Darrow?' Mark held the man's gaze. 'Your vehicles provide the perfect cover for burying those victims at the airfield. What did you do when Barry Windlesham bought the place, sidle up to him and suggest you carry out some test earthworks for him to see what the soil was like prior to the planning application going in?'

'No, of course not.'

'Really?' said Mark. 'Because it seems to me that you telling everyone you were in favour of the development going ahead was a bluff on your part to deflect your involvement in those graves. After all, you lead the planning committee – you would've known there would be enough objections without having to add your own and draw attention to yourself. Am I right?'

'No,' Felix said, his voice wavering.

'And your current wife, Alicia. What's her involvement? Does she help move the bodies too? Or does she help Tom kill them?'

'Keep her out of this, detective.' Felix glared at him. 'And I resent the accusation.'

'You can resent it all you like,' Mark snapped. 'We've got a forensics team over at your depot and your home this very minute, and all of your vehicles are going to be tested as well.'

The other man paled, then turned to his solicitor. 'They can't do that, can they?'

The solicitor gave a curt nod in return, but remained silent.

'You knew Barry's movements at the site, and you used that knowledge so you could give your son, Tom Mildenhew, the all-clear for moving the bodies, didn't you?'

Felix's mouth worked, but no words passed his lips. Instead, his eyes darted to the door, then back. 'If I tell you what I know, what happens to me?'

'Your assistance will be noted, but I can't promise anything,' said Mark. 'That's up to a jury.'

'I was scared of him,' Felix blurted. 'I didn't know what to do.'

'Eleven burials, Mr Darrow. You could've told us before you helped him with the first one.' Mark turned to another page in the folder. 'Tell me about this woman, Sofia Cartney-Bowler.'

'I don't know her.'

'Are you sure?'

'Yes. Who is she?'

'She was an anaesthetist who helped your son illegally harvest organs from his victims. She died last year, and we want to know who's taken her place. Who else is helping Tom, Mr Darrow?'

'I don't know. I didn't know what he was doing with them, just that...' Felix looked down at his hands, twisting his fingers together. 'I just didn't want him to get into trouble again. He's our only child, you see. His little brother died.'

'When?'

'When Tom was six. His brother was two years old.'

Mark swallowed, and cast a sideways glance at West before turning back to the other man. 'How did your youngest son die, Mr Darrow?'

'Tom said it was an accident.' Felix's voice was urgent. 'He told us it was an accident.'

A shiver ran across Mark's shoulders as the man's words sank in. 'Mr Darrow, where is Tom now?'

# CHAPTER FIFTY-SIX

'We've got him,' said Kennedy as Mark and West emerged from the interview. The DI punched him on the arm, smiling.

'Too damn right,' said Mark. He jerked his thumb over his shoulder. 'I'm not sure who's the worst out of these two, him or Judy Sarsgold.'

'I didn't mean Felix Darrow,' said the DI, his eyes gleaming. 'Tom Mildenhew's just been arrested at Portsmouth trying to board a ferry to France.'

'Really?' West's eyes widened. 'What happened?'

'He nicked a car from the pub car park in Ravenswood yesterday morning and the owner reported it missing. Hampshire Constabulary spotted it on ANPR at the docks after we raised the alert, and they arrested him half an hour ago.' Kennedy beckoned to them. 'They know how urgent this is, so they've arranged to bring him straight here under escort. He should be here within the hour. In the meantime, I want to make sure our case against him is watertight. I don't want him leaving this building unless it's because we're moving him to a custody cell.'

He led the way up to the incident room, where Alex and Caroline were standing at a table near the whiteboard collating copies of the evidence into folders for the team.

'We're nearly ready, guv,' said Caroline. 'All we need is Tom booked in downstairs, and we'll have the final piece of evidence we need.'

'Good,' said Kennedy. He picked up one of the folders and began sifting through it. 'This is really good work, you two. Mark, Jan – I think you'll find this will support your interview strategy if you're going to start with the basics.'

'I had Doug Holton work through the latest purchase orders and stock lists,' Caroline explained. 'We discovered a discrepancy in what he'd ordered and what should have been used if the drugs were only used on animals, but it's not as much as Gillian says would be needed to anaesthetise a human. He – or an accomplice – must be getting those from somewhere else, because what's here is probably being used to keep the organs in such a state that they can be transplanted.'

'Okay,' said West, updating her notebook. 'Have any complaints been made by pet owners over Tom's conduct at the surgery, given his juvenile record and history of animal torture?'

'None,' said Caroline. 'Which makes me think he was being careful to avoid suspicion. I mean, he might've still been torturing animals, but he wasn't doing it at Holton's surgery. According to Doug, he's been a model employee.'

'Onto interview tactics, then,' the DI said. 'Concentrate on our mystery woman and Patrick Westington for now in order to get those charges laid, and we can expand on the other bodies at the site afterwards. And if you need extra time to question him, let me know so I can get it signed off by a magistrate.'

'Will do.'

Kennedy's office phone rang, and he jogged over to answer it, the four detectives crossing the room to join him. The conversation was short, and when the DI put down the phone, he gave them a thumbs up. 'Tom Mildenhew is in custody downstairs. Give them an hour to process him and arrange for a local solicitor to turn up, and then he's all yours.'

'Good. That'll give us time to finalise our interview strategy,' said Mark. 'We'll do that in the observation suite downstairs so we can see when he's brought into the interview room.'

Caroline handed him and West the completed evidence packs. 'Go get him, Sarge.'

He nodded in reply, then turned and led the way to the door.

'Mark?'

He turned at the DI's voice. 'Yes, guv?'

Kennedy stood outside his office, his face grim. 'Be careful with this one, Mark. He's bloody clever, and he's managed to get away with this sort of thing before. He'll be ready for you.'

Mark shot him a wolfish smile. 'Don't worry, guv. I'm ready for him, too.'

# CHAPTER FIFTY-SEVEN

Mark watched the screen in the observation suite as Tom Mildenhew was led into interview room three by Grant Wickes. The constable was professional in his nature, showing Tom to his seat and asking if he wanted a cup of water, before leaving and closing the door.

Tom sat for a moment, taking in his surroundings while his hands remained clasped on the table. His gaze found the camera in the corner of the room, and he gave it a slight smile before twisting in his seat to look at the recording equipment. All the time, his posture remained ramrod-straight, despite his dishevelled appearance.

He was wearing faded black jeans and a dark blue hooded sweatshirt, and looked as if he hadn't shaved for a few days, and Mark was sure that when he entered the room he would see dark circles under the man's eyes.

'Good,' he murmured.

'Are you ready?' said West. She stood next to the door, both folders under her arm together with her notebook.

'Yes.' Pushing back the chair, he took one of the folders from her. 'You?'

'Let's do this, Sarge.'

They met Tom's solicitor in the corridor. He was a stalwart within the legal community and although Mark didn't envy the man's position as a defence solicitor, he respected his professionalism. He nodded by way of greeting, held open the door for the man, and followed him and West into the interview room.

Once the mandatory introductions were made, Mark eyed the man in front of him.

'Why did you kill Patrick Westington, Tom?'

'Who?'

Sliding out the well-thumbed photograph of the two men at Didcot railway station, Mark pushed it across the table. 'This man, here. Patrick. The man you murdered after removing his kidneys. Then, once that was done, you arranged for your mother, Judy Sarsgold, to dispose of his clothing and your father, Felix Darrow, helped you bury him at Ravenswood airfield, alongside the other ten people you've murdered.'

'You can't prove anything,' said Tom. 'These are spurious claims made by my parents. They're trying to cover up their own actions.'

'They allege their actions were to protect you,' said Mark. 'Because you've been carving up innocent people for their organs, which you've then arranged to sell illegally. And for the past fourteen months, we will allege that you've used Doug

Holton's veterinary surgery to carry out those illegal procedures.'

'Good luck with that, detective. It's a sterile environment, washed down after every procedure.'

Mark pulled out a single sheet of paper from the folder. 'Well, it's a good job our lead forensic technician likes a challenge. He and his team already found traces of that woman's blood when they tore apart the sink in the operating room. These swabs were taken from around the plughole.'

Tom's jaw clenched, his gaze never leaving Mark.

'And then,' Mark continued, pulling out a separate report, 'we found this. It's a partial fingerprint on the glass jar that was found in the refrigerator in the operating room, the one containing her kidneys. Now, I realise you probably think you're clever, and you probably wore gloves while you were removing her organs, but at some point before you left Holton's surgery, you touched that jar again. Maybe it wasn't in the right place in the fridge, or maybe you just wanted to take a look at your handiwork – I don't care. But what I *do* care about is that this partial fingerprint has been matched to yours that were taken when you were brought into custody this afternoon.'

Mark sat back as Tom's expression turned from indifference to rage. It was so sudden that West's hand dropped to the emergency button under the table. He reached out and placed a calming hand on her arm, all the time watching Tom.

'Why kill them, Tom? You could still have made good money from the sales, couldn't you?'

The man calmed a little then, as if accepting his fate. He gave a slight shrug. 'It made sense to. I was going to let them live, but when the first one died I realised it worked in our favour if they didn't live. I mean, if they're dead, they can't talk can they? They can't blackmail us by threatening to tell your lot what's going on.'

'Who else is working with you?' Mark said, biting back his disgust. 'Carrying out a kidney transplant is a complicated procedure. Was Sofia Cartney-Bowler your anaesthetist?'

'She was, yes.' Tom's gaze turned wistful. 'She was so good at it. The donors never had a clue they weren't going to wake up. It made it so much easier – and so less stressful for our recipients.'

'How did you find your… clients?'

'Word of mouth. Once we'd done two or three, people contacted us.'

'How?'

Tom shook his head, and smiled. 'Not yet, detective. Not yet.'

Mark slid another photograph from the folder. 'What about this man, Dale McArthur? He was the surgeon Sofia worked with when she was asked to leave the private hospital. Did you kill him?'

'No.'

'Who did?'

Tom's smile widened. 'Patience, detective. You'll have to do better than that.'

'Sofia died months ago,' said Mark. 'You've carried out at least two operations since then, so who's your anaesthetist now?'

'No one.'

'What?'

Tom held up his hands. 'What's the point? They're going to die anyway, so I might as well save money.'

This time, Mark felt bile at the back of his throat. He swallowed and turned his attention to the contents of the folder for a moment while he gathered his thoughts. Beside him, West gave a slight cough, and when he looked across at her, she had turned pale.

Exhaling, he raised his gaze to the man in front of him once more. 'So who helps with the operations, Tom? It's impossible to do that sort of procedure on your own.'

Tom shrugged. 'The recipients bring their own experts. After all, they have to look after them once the procedure's done.'

'Got any names?'

'Maybe.' The man contemplated a fingernail. 'It depends on what's on offer.'

'Not a lot at the moment, Tom. Not with the number of people you've murdered. You've got a history of killing, haven't you? Starting with your little brother.'

'What?'

Mark kept his gaze steady. 'Your dad told us about you killing Ben when he was only two years old. Two years old, Tom – an innocent little kid. And what—'

'Is that what Dad told you?' Tom said, wiping at tears of laughter. 'Is that what he said about Ben? Oh my God, that's too funny.'

Confused, Mark waited until the man's laughter abated. 'Are you telling me that Ben isn't dead?'

'He's dead all right,' Tom said, his gaze hardening. 'Thanks to your fucking lot turning up at the airfield site.'

Mark reared back in his seat as it dawned on him. 'The burned body we found in the industrial unit. That was your brother?'

'Yes,' snarled Tom. 'And he's the only one who ever understood.'

'Why store the bloke who stole Barry's clothing in the freezer at the industrial unit though? Why risk moving the body twice?'

'We didn't have a choice. We were going to find another burial site but when you lot started sniffing around we...' A flicker of fear flashed across Tom's face, and for the first time, he lowered his gaze. 'Ben panicked. I didn't know about the fire until I heard it on the news. I knew straight away he was one of the bodies they said was in the fire.'

'Was Ben the one who tried to shoot Barry Windlesham?'

'He couldn't even do that right. He bloody missed. I told him not to use one of Dad's antique pistols. They're fucking useless.'

Mark frowned. 'Felix never reported a gun being stolen. He isn't even on the firearms register.'

'Of course he isn't,' Tom said, rolling his eyes. 'He didn't want your lot poking around, did he? Last thing he'd want – put the customers off, that's what he said.'

'What?'

'Well, who do you think organises all of this?' Tom demanded. 'I'm too busy doing the operations – I can't be responsible for finding the clients as well, can I?'

Mark rose from his seat. 'Interview terminated at three forty-two.'

He rushed from the room, West gathering up all the

paperwork before running after him, the door slamming shut in her wake.

He didn't stop until he reached the custody suite, where Felix Darrow was standing at the desk while the custody sergeant processed all the paperwork and handed back the man's possessions.

'Hold on.' Mark recited the formal caution once more and turned to Felix. 'I'm arresting you, Mr Darrow, under suspicion of organising the illegal harvesting of organs that has led to the deaths of at least twelve people. You do not have to say anything. You—'

'Told you, did he?' Felix sneered.

'You told us you didn't know.'

'Of course I bloody well knew.'

'And you didn't think to report him?'

'Of course not. At least he's been earning some money out of it,' Felix spat. 'Which is more than can be said for when he was doing this as a teenager.'

Mark turned to the custody sergeant. 'Take him back to the cells please.'

'Sarge.'

West shook her head as Felix was led away. 'Now we know where Tom gets it from,' she murmured.

'The whole family's rotten to the core,' Mark said. 'All of them.'

# CHAPTER FIFTY-EIGHT

The following evening, Mark and Lucy set out from the narrowboat just after six o'clock and ambled along the tow path towards the bridge.

There was a warmth to the air now, the promise of an early spring, and house martins darted and swept over the meadow's long grass. The traffic leaving Abingdon's town centre had slowed from the earlier commuter rush, although a steady stream of cars was heading across the bridge towards the football club.

He reached out for Lucy's hand, and kissed it. 'I love you. Sorry I haven't been around much these past two weeks.'

'I love you, too,' she said, squeezing his hand. 'And you don't need to apologise. I'm just glad you got him before he could kill anyone else.'

'Me too.' He checked his watch. 'The match starts in twenty minutes, so we should probably get a move on.'

'Okay. So, are the boys playing as well tonight?'

'Yes. Jan said it's a dads versus lads game – something they do two or three times a year to get the whole family involved.' He let her go ahead of him through the gap between the gate and the hedgerow, and clipped Hamish's lead to the dog's collar before following her.

A little farther along the road, he spotted the telltale low roof of a cricket pavilion and made a mental note to investigate the match schedule when he was next online. He enjoyed the relaxed atmosphere of cricket, and the prospect of warmer weather and spending a Saturday afternoon reading the newspaper while watching a local game put a spring in his step.

The length of the cricket club's ground bordered that of the town football club and the two shared a common car park currently jam-packed with vehicles belonging to the players and spectators of the match about to start.

After checking for traffic, they hurried across the road with Hamish at Mark's heels. The little dog didn't pull on the lead for long and seemed happy to stick his nose in the grass verge that bordered the concrete apron abutting the clubhouse while Mark waited.

'Ready?'

The dog sneezed, then backed out of the hedge he was investigating and looked up, his tongue hanging out.

'Good boy. Don't embarrass me by trying to pick a fight with the other dogs that might be here, all right?'

Lucy laughed. 'You're more likely to embarrass him after a few beers.'

'Hey, not fair. Also, not true.' He grinned, then put his hand around her shoulder and hurried towards the football club's entrance.

A flimsy metal gate had been pegged open at the entrance to the football club's grounds beside a shed that housed an elderly man waving people through as they passed.

He nodded to Mark, who raised his hand in greeting.

'Okay to bring in the dog?'

'As long as you don't let him loose, that's fine.'

'Cheers.'

Mark glanced to his left to see the two teams already warming up on the field, and quickened his pace.

In front of him, a low brick building housed the office and changing rooms for the teams, a concrete path leading between that and the pitch. Beyond their position, he could see a row of dark green-coloured wooden terraces for spectators and wandered towards them, keeping up with the throng of fans and family members.

'Mark!'

He peered over the heads of the couple walking in front of him to see West holding her hand aloft to get his attention.

He weaved between two teenagers to where she stood next to the fence dividing the pitch from the crowd, a bag slung over her shoulder.

'Made it, then? That black eye of yours is starting to look better.' Her smile faltered a little when she saw Hamish. 'Is he going to cause trouble?'

'Best behaviour, promise.'

'Keep him on that lead, okay?'

'Yes, boss.'

She relaxed then, and gave Lucy a quick hug. 'Thanks for coming. I thought this might be a good way to wind down after the past two weeks.'

'It was an excellent idea,' said Mark. He turned as two eleven-year-olds ran up to them in football kit, and grinned. 'Hi, boys.'

'Hi, Mark,' they chorused, then one of them turned to West. 'Mum, can we get a hot dog?'

'After the match,' she said. 'We'll all be hungry then, including Hamish I'd imagine.'

The boy scowled for a moment, then brightened as his brother tugged at his sleeve.

'C'mon, Harry. We're going to be late otherwise and I don't want to start on the bench.'

They ran off, and Mark turned to West, smiling. 'I still can't tell the difference between them.'

'Easy,' she said with a chuckle. 'Harry's the gobby one. Luke tries to keep the peace. Come on. There are some spare seats over here. We can watch while we chat.'

'Sounds good. Lead the way.'

Moments later, they were shuffling onto a wooden bench halfway back from the field that was under a wide canopy designed to protect spectators from inclement weather but today was providing shade from the setting sun.

The floodlights around the pitch flashed to life, bathing the turf with bright white beams that illuminated the players as they ran onto the field.

Mark brushed off leaf litter that had been blown inwards, then made way for West and eased onto the seat beside Lucy, his heart skipping a beat as an ominous creak emanated from the bench.

'Don't worry, it always does that,' West said.

'Shouldn't they fix it?'

She pulled a Thermos flask from the tote bag now at her feet, then poured a generous amount of coffee into plastic cups and handed them to him before speaking. 'Probably, but there are so many other priorities, like insurance. It's only a small club.'

He shrugged to concede the point, and went to hand one of the cups to Lucy.

'Hang on.'

He glanced over as West extracted a hip flask from the bag, and held it up, her eyes amused.

'You might want a splash of this to keep you warm once that sun sets,' she said. 'Don't worry – Scott's the designated driver tonight. Thought we might head off to The Pelican after this. It's about three miles away. It's a nice pub, and doesn't get too crowded for a Friday night. The boys like the meals there, too, and it's dog-friendly.'

'Cheers.'

They tapped their aluminium mugs together, and then a short, sharp whistle drew Mark's attention back to the playing field.

'Where's Scott?'

She pointed. 'Number five.'

'Ah, yes. Got him.'

They watched for a few more minutes and then, after checking the spectators behind them were engrossed in the game, he leaned closer to West and lowered his voice. 'I spoke to Kennedy earlier. He's confirmed that the surgeon's car accident wasn't suspicious or linked to our investigation in any way.'

'Thank goodness. What about Tom's brother, Ben?'

'It's definitely him in the video the two teenagers provided, and that's been corroborated with the footage from Gregory Lesk's neighbour – his home security footage clearly shows Ben walking up to Lesk's front door after Barry put the envelope through it, but then he leaves, probably to catch up with him by the river. Judy Sarsgold verified his identity. And she's admitted to sending the threatening letters to Barry. She said she was trying to warn him off because she was worried what Tom and Felix might do.'

The first half of the game proved to be a close-run tie between the boys and their fathers, with both teams awarded penalties within the first ten minutes.

Mark laughed as one of the dad's efforts resulted in an own goal, but then their team pulled a goal back with a superb shot from an ageing midfielder fifteen minutes later.

West held up her hand as the referee's whistle blew to signal half-time, and Scott bounded off the field towards the stands. 'Better go down and have a chat. Coming?'

'Sure.'

Mark shook hands with her husband while Lucy spoke with Harry and Luke about their efforts, and then Scott put his hands on his hips and exhaled before jerking his chin at the retreating man in the black uniform.

'Did you see that? Bloody referee needs glasses. Best shot of the season, and he rules it as offside.'

West blinked, then nodded. 'Oh, yeah – definitely wasn't

offside. Hopefully level the score in the second half though, love?'

He beamed, and ran off to join his teammates.

West rolled her eyes as they retook their seats. 'He's all energy and enthusiasm. Wears me out living with him sometimes. It's like living with a Labrador.'

Mark waited until she'd taken another sip of her drink. 'Does he chew the furniture as well, then?'

'You bastard,' West choked, beating her chest with her fist. 'I told you to warn me before you make comments like that.'

## THE END

# ABOUT THE AUTHOR

Rachel Amphlett is a USA Today bestselling author of crime fiction and spy thrillers, many of which have been translated worldwide.

Her novels are available in eBook, print, and audiobook formats from libraries and retailers as well as her website shop.

A keen traveller, Rachel has both Australian and British citizenship.

Find out more about Rachel's books at: www.rachelamphlett.com.

AUD
POLL